A New Beginning, Book Two

The Cross of One Horse

STEVEN G. HIGHTOWER

THE CROSS OF ONE HORSE
Copyright © 2021 Steven G. Hightower

Paperback ISBN: 978-1-7358416-1-8

Hard cover ISBN: 978-7358416-3-2

This is a work of fiction. Any references to historical events, real people, or real places are used fictitiously. Other names, characters, places, and events are products of the author's imagination, and any resemblance to actual events, or places, or persons, living or dead, is entirely coincidental.

Library of Congress Control Number: TXu 2-272-528

For more information about Steven G. Hightower, visit www.stevenghightower.com or Facebook .com/anewbeginning2020.

Front cover art: © Bogdan Sonyachny | Dreamstime.com ID 90474397
Back cover art: © Randy Harris | Dreamstime.com ID 2337641
Cover design: Debra L. Butterfield

Printed in the United States.

OTHER BOOKS BY STEVEN G. HIGHTOWER

The Smoke of One Thousand Lodge Fires,
Book 1 of A New Beginning Series

This book is dedicated to the love of my life, my wife Ellie.
I am forever grateful for your unwavering support. Your kind spirit,
positive outlook, and permanent smile are contagious to all who know you.
Thank you for the years, sweetheart.

Prologue

The years we spent along the San Saba rolled by like a soft rainstorm drifting slowly across the prairie. For most of the seasons we spent in this special place, The NuMuNuu (*The People*) were happy, well fed, and we faced no immediate threat from our enemies. This time of goodness and plenty, however, was coming to an end.

I patrolled often. I would ride out two or three days from the camp on my reconnaissance missions. The signs after the fifteen seasons I had spent here were becoming more obvious, and I was encountering those signs with much regularity. The white man was coming. Even in our secure isolated location in the remote canyons along the San Saba, we were in danger. Our way of life, our culture, our survival as a people was uncertain.

The plan was good. I would travel a full season ahead of *The People* to prepare the way. I was a protector Warrior. I would do all within my power and abilities to ensure their survival. This day I observed the camp from the hilltop above the river. I spotted Prairie Song, my granddaughter, as she exited our lodge. She walked to the river, dancing with her doll, smiling as the younger girls from the camp joined her. She spoke to the little girls through her doll, acting out the little dance in her animated way. I could hear the laughter of the younger girls even from my location on the hilltop. Prairie Song had such a gentle, kind spirit that all the children were drawn to her. I was immensely proud of my granddaughter; in many ways she reminded me of my wife, Kwanita.

I breathed deeply. The sun shone brightly on the scene below me. I could hear the water as it flowed across the little rapids below the camp. The wind whispered lightly in the towering native pecans that grew along the riverbank. The smoke from the lodge fires rose in little whisps here and there throughout the Home Camp. One day this scene would come forth from my soul and be recreated within the mural of my life.

I had no idea in what year I would exit the *Dream Time*. I needed to remember exactly what I had been privileged to witness this last day: my Tribe, my family, and friends living in peace, natural and free. I whispered a silent prayer that my effort to protect and defend would be met with the blessing of our Creator.

I sat atop the ridge, observing for the entire day. My quiet time was filled with prayer and song, but for the most part silence, as I attempted to listen. The Voice of Truth came to me in a soft almost indiscernible whisper. I understood.

As the sun set, I descended the canyon and entered the cavern. The ceremony was simple and filled with faith. Tosahwi placed his hand upon my shoulder and blessed me as I drifted into another time far, far away from all that I loved and cared for.

The plan was good.

Chapter 1

Life on the reservation was, I don't know, difficult, or dark maybe. As I look back and remember, the correct word is hard to find. Life on the reservation felt hopeless in many ways. That might be a better term, hopeless. Most young people just wanted to find a way to leave the reservation. There were very few good jobs. Careers one considered successful or fulfilling did not exist. About the only option for a young person was working for the tribe. There were many service jobs available within the tribe. In accepting one of those menial positions, a person quickly became trapped within the confines of the "Rez." Trapped within the broken world we all lived in. A low paying job, substandard housing, no higher education opportunities, daily exposure to the depression and brokenness that seemed to lay just beneath the surface of every face. Living within those problems, within that mindset, and those living conditions, could actually be dangerous. Alcoholism, drug abuse, petty crime, even gang activity, we as a people were exposed to all of it, daily.

A few did escape. The gifted often escaped into the white man's world. Those gifted ones became doctors, lawyers, scientists, or a myriad of other exceptional professions. Once having escaped, most of the gifted never returned to the Rez.

But the majority never escaped. The Rez became their life. Their reality. For many, life on the Rez became their nightmare. It was quickly becoming mine.

Dak. That's what they called me, short for Daklugie. I don't think anyone knew my first name my grandfather had given me: Joshua.

Daklugie was the son of Juh (HO), the great Apache chief. Juh was the nephew of Geronimo. It was a good name. The name carried respect, at least from most of the older tribal members. The elders knew the genealogy of the name, the lineage of the warrior Daklugie. My great-great-grandfather Daklugie was a hero.

My grandfather William Daklugie was my hero. But he was gone now.

I thought of my grandfather every day. If I had a wish or an answered prayer that God might grant me, it would only be one thing: to have him back. To have more days with my grandfather. Days to fill with me, the student, by his side, him teaching me from his wealth of wisdom. My grandfather knew the old ways. He knew life. How good it could be. I closed my eyes and heard his voice.

"Dak, your life can and will be a blessing. No matter where you are, or what your circumstance…you, my grandson, are and will forever be a blessing. You, Dak, carry the blessing within you."

His words echoed in my mind as I sat in the office of the Tribal police. I was here to identify the remains of my mother.

Chapter 2

Most of my peers did not know the history of my name or my family. To my classmates, I was just a quiet loner. But my classmates knew something else about me; they knew I could run. I was also an expert at ball handling. I played forward on our high school basketball team. At five foot nine on a good day, it was not my height that gave me success on the round-ball court. Nor was it my ability to shoot. Just the raw speed and ball handling. I could make a lay-up left- or right-handed. We ran the fast break. The game plan was singular. Pass the ball to Dak, outrun the opponent, make a lay-up. If on the rare occasion I didn't break free, I passed the ball back to my friend Caleb. My best friend Caleb could shoot. Three pointers were his specialty. The game plan worked. Our team won the state championship last year. We were a heavy favorite to repeat.

However, my life was about to change. I had no idea how much so.

****

The room was dimly lit and smelled of some awful chemical. The gurney in the middle of the room held her body beneath a thin sheet. I wanted to be sick. Officer Victorio placed his hand on my shoulder.

"Are you okay, Dak?" he asked, a look of genuine concern on his face.

"No, I'm not," the tears beginning to rise, "let's just get it over with," I said.

He pulled the sheet back partially, revealing the beaten, bloody, and bruised face of my mother. The hand marks around her neck were clearly visible in the bruising pattern. I nodded. It was all I could do. I knew her spirit was no longer in this shell of the body that lay before me. An emptiness invaded my soul. It felt as if someone had punched me in the stomach. I didn't have to ask why. I knew why. The man was an animal, a cruel animal.

Officer Victorio covered her body gently with the thin sheet. I could tell from the look on his face he also had no questions as to why. Or who.

The man hunt was on. It would only be a matter of time. Victorio would see to it. The animal would be found.

We walked together through the offices, a heavy weight pressing down upon me. Officer Victorio offered a kind smile. He reached out to touch my shoulder in reassurance. I buried my face in his chest and arms. I tried to fight back the tears; he wouldn't let me.

"Dak, it's okay, go ahead let it out." Victorio knew about heartache. He held me like a child, comforted me by saying little, just holding, comforting, a wounded young man.

After a few moments, my tears began to empty. I took a few deep breaths. He let go of me as I took a step backwards; I saw the tears in his eyes also.

As a war veteran, Officer Victorio knew loss on a deeply personal level. I would be forever grateful. He showed me that day how a real man handles loss.

I would remember that moment for the rest of my life.

Chapter 3

Officer Victorio dropped me off at the house. It was a Saturday morning. The house was empty. The few worldly possessions my mother owned were scattered about the living room. I walked down the hall and entered her room. Looking back, I was amazed at how little we owned.

Backtracking through the small single-wide trailer to the kitchen, I opened the fridge. It contained two cans of beer and a leftover pizza. I wasn't hungry. I sat at the little kitchen table, my head in my hands, wondering what was next. I had no relatives, other than my grandma. She lived in a group home forty-five miles away. I had a couple of days to figure out my life.

The knock at the door was abrupt. Who could that be? We rarely had visitors. I opened the door and a woman with some form of badge or ID around her neck introduced herself.

"Dak, I'm Ms. Kuruk."

I didn't reply.

"I'm with child protective services. May I come in?"

I just stood there. Bear woman. I had learned enough Apache from my grandfather to know the translation. Her name seemed to fit her demeanor.

"What do you want?" I asked.

"I need to speak with you about, well, your future. Where you will live. Who might take care of you?"

I felt like I had been hit in the gut again. My mind began to take it all in. They were not going to allow me to stay here. I was a minor, at least for another ten months. She was here to take me. The scenarios began to play out in my mind. I would become a foster kid. The worst. I knew a few of those unfortunate souls from school. Their stories…were simply awful.

"No, you may not come in!" The intensity of my words shocked me as they echoed through the little trailer. I slowly closed the door. Bear Woman began to knock loudly.

"Dak, please, we need to talk."

"Go away, Bear Woman," was my reply as I bolted the door.

I hurried across the trailer to my room. I grabbed my backpack and a change of clothes and donned my winter jacket. A quick stop in the bathroom for a few toiletries and I was out the backdoor and climbing the hill behind the little trailer as Bear Woman continued knocking on the front door.

Once in the cover of the trees and up the small hills behind the house, I turned to observe my little world from above. I had spent ten years with my mother in the little single-wide trailer below me. I don't know why it struck me with such emotion. I was only seven when the housing authority granted us permission to move there.

At the time, it felt like a castle.

We were so excited, my mother and me. Finally, a place of our own. Something to be celebrated on the Rez, where housing was in short supply. From where I stood, I couldn't remember or see now, why we were so thrilled at the move. My grandmother's car, which she had given us, sat on blocks to the side of the trailer, its engine blown years ago. Some of my toys from younger days were scattered about. An old bicycle with twin flat tires rested against the little tin shed. A plastic jeep I had received for my eighth birthday sat turned on its side, a wheel missing. It had been a gift from my grandfather. Tears rolled down my cheeks as I spied the portable basketball goal in the weeds along the muddy driveway. I had practiced thousands of left-handed lay-ups there.

Something inside me knew this was goodbye.

"Goodbye, little house," I spoke aloud in a quiet voice. "Thank you for keeping us warm those many cold wintery nights. Thank you for the Christmas and the birthday parties. Thank you, little roof, for keeping us dry. Thank you, little house." I turned, setting out across the hills toward the highway.

"Goodbye, Mother," I said aloud. "Thank you for taking care of me, the absolute best way that you could. I am so sorry your life was such a struggle." My tears flowed freely. As I walked along the hidden forest path, I began to sing the song of mourning. The song my grandfather had taught me.

Chapter 4

The wind was bitter cold. Late November was the time winter finally took hold of the high mountains of central New Mexico. At least the wind was at my back as I made my way down the highway toward Alamo. I needed to see my grandmother. It was forty-five miles from here, but I wasn't concerned. *The People*, meaning Native Americans, were not shy of hitchhikers along the roads of the Reservation. It was a primary means of transportation for many of us who didn't own a car. Traffic was light. Even so, within ten minutes an old truck pulled over as it passed me. The truck slowed and came to a stop in front of me. I jogged forward a few yards and opened the door of the passenger side and hopped in.

Mr. Natchi greeted me with a nod. He revved the engine, and in a cloud of smoke, we were off.

Mr. Natchi was a Tribal Elder. Although the Tribe functioned much like any local government, with a Tribal Council and president elected by the voting members of our community, some of the old ways remained very much in place. There was not a vote or any formal appointment to the position of elder. It was more of a tradition. A time-honored tradition among the Apache. As an elder, Mr. Natchi was respected and honored. My grandfather William Daklugie had also been an elder. The two men had been friends from boyhood. Mr. Natchi knew what had happened…with my mother.

Many of the older ones were aware of many things. My grandfather had taught me their wisdom and knowledge and knowing of events, or happenings, was due solely to their time spent in prayer, or as my grandfather called it, his "Time of Quiet." Elders had a knowing. Mr. Natchi knew.

"I'm going all the way to the Base, Dak; I can drop you at your grandma's."

"Thank you, sir."

A light snow began to fall as we rode along in silence. I appreciated not having to explain.

I looked around the inside of Mr. Natchi's old Ford truck. Dog tags were hung from the rear-view mirror. His Vietnam veterans hat sat on the seat between us, the number of some vessel or ship across the front in large gold letters. The gun rack in the window behind us held two large caliber rifles and a lariat. My door panel was full of ammunition boxes. Nothing unusual for a man who lived and worked cattle on the Rez.

The drive was all downhill. As we descended out of the high mountains, the altitude changed rapidly. Within fifteen miles the topography and climate also shifted dramatically. The snow that was falling in the higher elevations to the east behind us, turned to rain here in the high desert. In the distance, I could occasionally see the massive deposit of gypsum known as White Sands. The light rain continued to fall, but the old worn wipers on Mr. Natchi's Ford mainly just smeared the raindrops into a blurred unfocused view. Much like what was in my mind, just a blur of unknowns, my future clouded and unclear. We rode along in silence for half an hour, both of us enjoying the company of being together, yet alone in our thoughts.

I felt I needed to clear my head. We were still ten miles or more from my grandma's. I became restless. Mr. Natchi looked my direction a moment and seemed to know my thoughts.

"Need some fresh air, Dak?" he asked just as I was about speak. I nodded. He pulled the old Ford over on the shoulder of the road.

"Dak, the blessing is within you. You, son, are, and will be, a blessing to all of our people."

His words awakened something deep within my soul. Those were Grandfather's words. I opened the truck door and stepped out into the bright sunshine as the rain ended abruptly.

"I know," was all I said. I began to run. I loved to run.

Chapter 5

At five foot nine and one hundred fifty-five pounds, I was built to run. I covered the first mile at a warm-up pace. Seven minutes elapsed between mile markers; while at this pace, my body moved effortlessly along the shoulder of the road. I decided to speed up. Working hard now, the next mile floated by in six minutes flat. I began to sweat under the winter coat. Stopping a moment to remove it, I tied the jacket around my waist, then continued.

Running transported me, not just physically as I moved along the highway, but rather mentally, or spiritually. I clipped along at the six-minute pace for another two miles. My mind shifted; the rhythm of my breathing settled me from within. The rhythm of my feet gently striding along the pavement added to the comfort—or was it peace—that I experienced when I ran.

I cannot explain, even to myself, what happens to a person who truly runs. Only those who have experienced it can know. This ancient motion, this way of moving…blessed me.

I covered ten miles that morning. My grandmother's house came into view. I didn't remember all the turns and stoplights and stop signs I had just navigated to arrive here. I recovered my wind quickly as I slowed to a walk. Approaching the home, I could hear the women singing. The song was familiar. It was the song of mourning. I lightly whispered the ancient tune, singing along with them.

They knew. I was relieved; again I would not have to explain.

I waited for the song to end. I knocked on the paint-chipped, dented front door.

Grandmother opened the door and greeted me with a frail hug. I looked into her eyes, holding her hands. A resolve showed itself in her blank stare.

"Dak, I am so glad you are here, come inside. We have been waiting for you."

The five Native American women were sitting in a circle on the living room floor. Incense sent up little puffs of smoke from a delicately carved bowl in the center of the circle. The atmosphere within the room was somber. This was a mourning ceremony. My grandmother, Mrs. Bina (Music) Daklugie, returned to her seated place in the circle, motioning for me to sit next to her.

I sat in the circle and joined in the songs. The songs were reverent, worshipful, and filled with sincerity. There was much Apache tradition in the ceremony, but now the prayers were directed to God the Father, in the name of his Son Jesus. These women represented the absolute best witness of who we as a people had become. Most of us were now Christians.

Grandmother opened her Bible and read in our beautiful native language. *"The Lord is my shepherd I shall not want…"*

****

I spent most of the afternoon with Grandmother and the elder women of the tribe. We talked and shared a meal together. The conversation seemed always to turn to me and stories of my childhood. Laughter occasionally erupted from the women at a story or detail they all remembered or recalled. It was a wonderful afternoon. The time and stories lifted my grandmother's spirits. She looked my way occasionally and smiled approvingly.

I knew she was proud of me. I decided I may have been more comforted by this time and in the company of my grandmother and her friends, than anyone else in the room.

Mr. Natchi knocked on the door late into the afternoon. A general fuss was made over Mr. Natchi by the elder widows. I heard more than one comment in our native tongue about his availability as an eligible bachelor. Mr. Natchi remained quiet, and a little redder faced than his normal Apache skin tone. He checked his pocket watch repeatedly, a sign to me that we really needed to head on up the hill to the Rez.

Grandmother finally rescued us both from the attention. "Dak, please come to my room for a moment."

Mr. Natchi was visibly relieved at the request. He bowed out politely and announced that he would wait for me in the truck.

We entered her room together.

"You will need these things of your grandfather's," she said.

I just stood watching her as she rummaged through the little closet in her room. She turned, holding the items. I was again stunned at the beauty, the history of what she held in her hands. My grandfather's hand-hewn wooden bow, an Apache war club, a deer skin quiver filled with a dozen or more hand-shaped arrows, and his hunting knife. I hadn't seen these items since the last hunt I had gone on with Grandfather. The quiver was decorated ornately with strikingly colorful bead work. The war club had brightly dyed deer sinew threads dangly from its handle. The plant-stained colorful arrow fletchings protruded from the end of the quiver.

A lump formed in my throat.

"Dak, you will need these for your journey." She said the words to me with a knowing in her eyes.

I took the items from her. All I could do was nod in agreement; of what I was agreeing with, I had no idea.

"The blessing is within you," she said to me, smiling.

I stood silent, only nodding. This was the third time today I had been reminded of Grandfather's words.

We walked to the door and said our goodbyes with a promise to see one another at the funeral in a few days. I had no way of knowing this would be our last meeting, our last time to see one another. If only we knew more of our futures.

Since that day I have often thought, if I had known that would be our last time together…I am sure I would have stayed and lingered just a while longer.

Chapter 6

The trip back into the mountains was again quiet. Mr. Natchi and me riding along in the old Ford. The rain changed to snow as the temperature dropped while we climbed in elevation along the highway toward the Rez. I observed as the heavy wet snow began to coat the sides of the road and the trees along the edges of the forest. My mind wandered as I thought of the upcoming Monday morning at school. Would they come for me tonight? Where should I stay? Should I even attempt to return to the house? Or would Bear Woman be there waiting for me?

So many questions.

I did not own a cell phone. I guess we were poor. It did make communication difficult. I really needed to go see Caleb. Or maybe even Nita. She would be concerned.

Butterflies floated around in my stomach at the thought. They always did that when I thought of Nita.

Mr. Natchi peered in my direction. "Where to, Dak?" he asked.

"Umm, could you just drop me at the high school?"

"No problem, Dak, you think she might be there?" Mr. Natchi asked, a sly look on his face.

The old ones always knew things. I turned away, feigning innocence to no avail. "Well, I can jog over to Caleb's...umm, if, well...yes sir...she might be there," I answered honestly.

"She will be there, Dak. Remember it is your greatest responsibility to care for all her needs. Emotional, spiritual, physical. It is a Warrior's greatest calling."

I became embarrassed at his words. I don't know why. It was the greatest advice an Elder might offer to a young man.

We came to a stop along the snow-covered road in front of the school. The flakes were now enormous, easily the size of silver dollars, and laden with moisture. I pulled the hood of my jacket over my head as Mr. Natchi drove away with a knowing look and a wave of his weathered hand.

I could hear the snowflakes as they landed heavily on the top of my hooded jacket. Looked like a real storm was gathering, I thought to myself. I started to jog toward the gym located at the rear of the high school. Turning off to the side of the building, I stashed my grandfather's hunting weapons in the thick brush. No one seemed to be around or aware of my activities. I hurried toward the gym.

The door opened suddenly as I was reaching for the handle. I looked up into the eyes of Coach Tower, my basketball coach.

"Dak, we were just talking about you." He looked into my eyes and opened his arms wide.

For the second or third time today—I was losing count—I let go of my tears.

What was it that these men knew about grief? Coach Tower was also a military veteran. He had served three tours of duty in Afghanistan. He, too, knew loss and how to minister to those it touched. The door closed behind him leaving the two of us standing in the snow, his arms around me. Again, something deep within my spirit was comforted, without words.

He released his embrace, but said nothing, a compassionate look on his face. He understood, and I knew that.

"Have you seen Caleb?" I asked.

"Yeah, he just left a few minutes ago, said he was heading home. But Nita is here."

Sheesh, I thought to myself, these guys, how did they know so much about me?

"Hey, can we talk?" he asked.

"Sure, Coach, how about tomorrow?" I asked.

"Okay, I'll be here at the gym after church, come by anytime. And, Dak, you might think about staying at Caleb's tonight. It would be a good idea to…you know, have a friend close by."

"Oh, okay sure, I was going to anyway," I said. But I caught an intentional look in his eyes.

"There was a Mrs. Kuruk here earlier, asking some questions. Just thought you should know."

I understood perfectly. In the same way I had understood so many instructions from my coach on the basketball court. Just a look from him and I knew what to do on any particular play.

Coach Tower was telling me not to go home.

I was inwardly incredibly grateful for Coach Tower. But he knew that also, with just a look from me.

Chapter 7

Several groups of students were practicing free throws, a few sat in the stands, while others sat in groups on the floor, their eyes focused on their cell phones. Amid this activity, she saw me the moment I entered the gymnasium.

I called her Nita, as did all her friends and family. Nita was short for her proper name, Kwanita, which meant *God is Gracious*. Nita was all of that and more to me. Our eyes locked onto one another's as I heard my name called from across the gym.

Mr. Duncan, our high school principal, called to me again from across the room.

"Dak! Dak, over here." He waved his arm, motioning me over. Standing next to him was Ms. Kuruk. Bear Woman.

I waved. "I'll be right there." Glancing at Nita again, a look of comfort in her eyes, I turned and headed to the boys' locker room.

I moved rapidly out the back exit of the gym and ran as fast as I could to the trees and brush along the side of the building. I located the bow, war club, knife, and quiver full of arrows. I slung the bow and quiver across opposite shoulders, just the way my grandfather had worn them. I ran to the rear of the school grounds toward the west. The fresh snow slowed my progress, as it was five or six inches deep, heavy, and wet. While running, I neatly tucked the knife and war club into my belt. Within another minute I was concealed in the heavy tree cover and brush. I stopped a moment behind a large tree. Glancing back, there was no one following. I breathed deeply, knowing I had again avoided the confrontation, or bad news that certainly awaited, and was carried along by the Bear Woman.

I stood in the trees a few moments, catching my breath. I so needed to speak with Nita. Maybe she understood. I was sure she knew about my mother. Would she attempt to follow? How could she even know where I might go?

As my breathing returned to normal, I thought a moment about where to go, what to do. Looking down at my equipment, I had all I needed.

I knew suddenly exactly where I would go.

I turned to take the ancient trail that led up into the high mountains. The trail I had walked many, many times with Grandfather. The way would be treacherous with the new wet snow. But I knew it well. We had hunted up there among the high peaks every season since I was just a small boy. I knew of shelter up there and where the water ran fresh. I knew the trails the game traveled. Most importantly, I knew how to move silently, stealthily. I knew much of the old ways. Yes, it was truly clear to me now what I would do.

I glanced back toward the school, and I saw her. She was standing in the upstairs window of our science classroom. She was holding her right hand high, motionless. Her palm open toward me.

Even from this distance I recognized the concern, the compassion on her face. I also saw hurt in her eyes, and longing. I had no way to explain.

I returned the gesture. I held my hand high, my palm open, motionless.

"I love you, too…my Nita." I turned away and started up the ancient trail.

Chapter 8

The trail was obscured by a blanket of white moisture laden snow and ice, yet I could still discern the vague outline of the long-traveled path. I climbed and slipped and struggled over the way. I needed my moccasins. My running shoes quickly became wet and soaked through. My feet would become very cold once I stopped. I wasn't going to stop until I reached the shelter. The Cave.

It was four miles to my hidden destination. The terrain caused very treacherous footing beneath the snow-covered trail. My feet continually hung on the many blowdown trees that crisscrossed the path in no particular fashion. Many of the small trees I could not detect until I stumbled over them. This made the journey very difficult. But I was determined.

I was also hungry. I thought of the few pizza slices I had left behind. My stomach growled as I worked my way along.

After two miles I came to the first of several ponds. These small lakes had formed after years of run-off and debris collection in the steep canyons. Little natural dams had formed all along the canyon I followed. They were pristine and picturesque. The water they held was cold and still pure enough to drink. I licked my dry lips, suddenly aware of my thirst.

I paused at the first lake and lay on the forest floor, drinking my fill. The water was cold and refreshing. I felt a new strength enter my body after drinking slowly, again and again.

I sat back against a large pine tree. These small lakes were also filled with native brown trout.

My stomach rumbled again.

I had no fishing gear at all. But I possessed the knowledge of Grandfather. I knew the old ways. I skirted around the high end of the small lake. Removing the hunting knife from my belt, I selected the perfect size green branch from a white fir and chopped it away from the tree. I went to work with the knife, removing the branches and skinning the tree branch of its bark. Carefully I then split the end of the branch into a fork. Then I sharpened the ends of the fork and carved a small notch, leaving a sliver of shaved wood. This created a strong barb at the tip of my new fish spear. The sharp barb would hold the trout once I speared it. Using the hunting knife, I sawed through the fat end of the spear at just the right length. The fish spear was now about six feet long. Perfect. But the skill to use the spear counted most.

I crept near the mouth of the small lake. There, a few feet away, I could see the trout swimming up and down the narrow entrance where the water fed into the pond. I knew from my teaching if I could see the trout, the trout could see me. If they detected my presence, I was certain they would disappear into the deep water.

I became one with the forest. I became a rock, then a tree trunk. Then nothing.

I prayed.

The trout continued their feeding movement, in and out of the small entrance. An hour passed.

I heard my grandfather's voice whisper to me. "Patience, Dak, and you will be full."

Eventually a fat brown swam into the entrance, and then up the little stream about ten feet. I was only the wind moving in the trees…just a branch falling. The spear penetrated the back of the magnificent brown in a perfect placement. The barb held firmly as I lifted the six-pound trout out of the water. The other fish quickly scattered into deep water. They would not be fooled by the moving tree again.

I opened the throat of the magnificent fish. She flopped around in the snow, her life ebbing away as she bled out.

I knelt to my knees, and in the tradition of my people gave thanks for the life of the fish.

Rising from the snow-covered ground, I tied the trout through its gills onto one of the sinews hanging from my grandfather's war club. I would eat well tonight.

Chapter 9

Just knowing the trout would feed me made the remainder of the trip into the high mountains much easier. The snowfall had tapered off to just a few flakes now and then; the late evening sky occasionally showed itself through a broken cloud layer. The temperature was dropping steadily now as the sun lowered in the late afternoon sky, and I was beginning to feel the effects. I arrived along the top of the ridge and stepped across the rocky ledge that faced southwest. The warmth of the rock outcroppings here, even though above ten thousand feet, had melted the falling snow. The energy the rock faces retained would continue do so for another storm or two. Then the snow would stay for the winter. I was relieved the snow had melted on the southerly facing outcroppings. They were rugged and extremely dangerous when covered in ice and snow.

Now I traveled slightly downhill. The going was easy. Working my way along the rock outcroppings, I spied the crevasse in the rock just a few hundred yards away. Unless one knew this country well, a person would never know the cave was there.

The entrance to the cave was tall and narrow. From any angle it appeared to be just a fracture in the granite face of the rock, with a deep shadow. I must have been six or seven years old when my grandfather had first taken me up here on the long trek. He had taught me then about the entrance and how cautious one should be. I carefully stepped into the darkness of the cave.

Once entering, I took only a few short steps, staying well to the right side of the entrance and making sure I could touch the smooth cave wall to my right. I paused, allowing my eyesight to adjust to the darkness. Slowly I began to make out the severe drop to my left. The two-foot-wide rock ledge I was standing on became visible. I waited.

It took about five minutes for my eyes to fully adjust. Now, with the dim light coming from the cave entrance, I could safely make my way along the shelf. The drop to my left was more than fifty feet straight down. I wondered how many, over the years, might have stumbled down and into the chasm.

I traveled another fifty yards or so on the level path that ran along the right side of the cave. I paused again. The light from the entrance I could still detect, but I needed light to continue. Feeling along the upper shelf, I located the two LED flashlights my grandfather always kept stored here. Switching on the flashlight, an unbelievable world appeared before me.

I descended the slope, the mineral beneath my feet a solid white calcite formation that resembled a frozen snowy river. The snowy river slope before me descended several hundred yards into an enormous room. Along the sides of the main room, little shallow rooms had somehow, over time, been shaped into small circular room-sized depressions. I made my way to the last little side room toward the back of the massive cave. Our survival gear was still here, exactly as we had left it. I was grateful and whispered a prayer of thanks. I was very cold; my feet seemed frozen inside the soaking wet running shoes. I was even beginning to shiver. I lit the little camp stove and the light, glow, and small amount of heat it created instantly warmed me.

****

After gorging myself on the delicious, flaky, tender white meat of the trout, I was simply exhausted. The tiny single burner cook stove worked perfectly. The smell of the fish cooking permeated my little room and added a slight amount of warmth. I removed my wet shoes and placed them near the little stove. The propane cannister would last for a few more meals. I would add to the supplies here the next time I ventured up among the high mountains.

I removed my jacket and used it as a small pillow. The floor of the room was covered in a deep layer of soft sand. The temperature in the cave was constant, and at around sixty degrees year-round, I was warm and full and safe for now. My eyes became heavy. There was so much to think about and many decisions to make. I drifted into a deep sleep.

Chapter 10

I awoke with a start. It was impossible to know how long I had slept, but I knew it had been a long full night of sleep. My body was rested; I felt strong somehow. I again gave thanks for the life and nutrition the magnificent fish had given me. I picked through the remains of the trout. The small meal was satisfying and full of nutrients.

Rising from my little sleeping room, I flicked the flashlight on and made my way to the spring.

The water was cool and refreshing; I drank deeply. The little spring formed a small pool of water about five feet across and ten feet long. I shined the light into the little pool and saw my reflection. My long dark hair and thin features stared back at me. I was taken aback somewhat at what I saw. I was seventeen years old, but I thought that I looked forty. Lines of worry and heartache reflected from the surface of the water and were etched on my face. For the first time in my life, I thought I looked like a man.

What would this day bring? I needed to return down the mountain. I had promised to meet with Coach Tower. I needed desperately to speak with Nita. More than anything, what occurred to me was that today I would start my new grown-up life as the man I had just seen in the pool.

All at once many decisions seemed clear. I would face Bear Woman; I would not become a foster child. I was able-bodied, intelligent, and could work as hard as any man. Thanks to my grandfather, I possessed skills that many of my peers had forgotten. I had also completed the training my grandfather had initiated. I had only one feat to complete, to gain the title he had desired to place upon me. That long honored tradition was within my reach. With a definitive victory over an enemy, I would sing the song. The song of victory over one's enemy.

On completion of whatever possible victory awaited me… I would become an Apache Warrior.

My grandfather had instructed me to be patient. I was not to pursue some invented victory. He said it would come to me when the time was right. The Great Spirit would show the way.

Rising from the pool, I made my way back to my little sleeping room. I gathered my things: the bow, quiver, war club, and the hunting knife. I stowed the little cook stove on the high rock shelf. As I placed the stove on the shelf my hand grazed something else. It was soft to the touch. I removed my hand and looked around the little room for something to stand on. There against the wall appeared a square stone about a foot high. I gathered the stone and moved it into position below the rock shelf. Standing on the stone I could now see what it was I had brushed against. Shining the flashlight up and down the little shelf my heart leapt at what I saw.

My grandfather's medicine bag! It was stunning, ornately decorated with the finest hand painted bead work. I lifted the medicine pouch and could detect immediately that it was filled with something. Gazing farther down the length of the shelf, I again was stunned. A book, or scroll was a better word, lay tucked in the back corner of the rock ledge. Stepping off the stone, I was in awe at this discovery. I moved the rock step over to my left. Stepping up again I could now reach the scroll. I carefully lifted the scroll from its resting place. With my right hand I gently lifted the medicine bag. Gingerly I stepped from the stone with the treasure I held in my hands.

As I beheld these ancient items, I knew in my heart they had been left for me.

I whispered a prayer of gratefulness and said aloud, "Thank you, Grandfather."

I sat in my little room and read by the light of the small flashlight…for hours.

Chapter 11

The old parchment papers were bound with leather loops and contained within a thick leather binding. The lettering appeared to be some type of heavy paint; the calligraphy on the pages was stunning. On opening the left side of each page, the information was printed in Apache along with sketches of each subject. On the opposite side of each page was a handwritten translation in English. It was evident the translations were transcribed in the easily recognizable hand of my grandfather.

I understood immediately, the knowledge within these pages had been gained over centuries. This written record of wisdom I knew was priceless. Not in a monetary way, but rather in the immeasurable value of the wisdom the pages contained.

I closed the scroll, knowing I needed to make the long walk down the mountain. I carefully placed the scroll-book back into its hidden resting place. Once again, I gathered the tools of my grandfather, the tools all Warriors carried.

In my mind a whirlwind of knowledge, wisdom, healing, medicine, water sources, enemies, rotated in a deluge of thought and consciousness. I had only scratched the surface of what the scroll contained. It would take me years of study to comprehend and put into practice what I had read over the last few hours.

The scroll-book was a complete manual of the old ways. It was like being filled with a delicious meal. Like a sampling of the finest fare.

This book had the ability to feed one's soul.

Using the flashlight, I made my way out of the large room, up the snowy river, and across the shallow ledge. I turned off the light and covered the last two hundred yards using the growing reflected light from the entrance. I paused just inside the cave and listened. For what I did not know. I sensed something amiss. I had heard the faintest of movement outside the cave. I waited…now just two steps from the entrance. I heard again the sound that was out of place. The scraping of a footstep. Heavy clumsy steps on rock. The sound was moving away from the cave.

Who could possibly have followed? Who might be up here among the high peaks after the heavy wet snow? I chanced a quick peak out of the entrance. Just a millisecond to peer in the direction of the sounds. I jerked back quickly. Had he seen me?

I held my breath. Then drew an arrow from my quiver. Skillfully I nocked the arrow in the bow string. The footsteps had stopped. No further sound came from outside the cave. I drew the bow and stepped out of the narrow entrance.

There below me just thirty yards away, staring directly at me…stood the cruel animal.

The man who had killed my mother. The man froze. Then began to laugh.

"You? The little suckling appears. Put your toys away."

He sneered at me like I was some kind of insect. Like he might squash me with his filthy boots on a whim. Those boots had tracked the same mud they now held into our little home. They had lowered my mother to the floor in agony. Those boots had destroyed the door to my room. I did not waver in my aim.

"You killed her." I spoke through gritted teeth.

"What can you do about it, little sprout? You are just a scared little boy. Put your toy down now!"

The cruel animal screamed at me with the voice I had heard before.

"You will die here today just like your grandfather did. He was a coward. You are nothing, his little mite. You have no courage, neither did your mother."

The words he spoke stung within my heart. How could this man say such things? I knew the truth. I knew the man was lying. But these untruths hurt. The words wounded something deep within me. The lies also awakened something deep within me that was fierce and unwavering.

As I look back, I find it odd where our minds go in times of deep distress. The words of my grandfather reverberated within my mind and heart. In a millisecond, in a flash of awareness, I remembered.

****

It had just been a normal Saturday morning. We were preparing our gear for the long walk into the mountains. The hunt would begin in just two days.

My grandfather had given me a great responsibility, at least it was for an eight-year-old boy. Sharpening the arrowheads was of the utmost importance. I knew what my grandfather had taught me. "A hunter can perform every skill required for success, but without a good edge on the hand-hewn stone arrowheads, he might indeed go hungry over the long winter." I would make certain the arrowheads were perfect.

As I looked back on that morning so long ago, I now recognize his way, this tool, my grandfather always had chosen to teach me. William Daklugie knew how to impart wisdom to a young man. It was always the same. Get me completely busy with any number of a myriad of different chores. Then amid casual conversation, he would speak truths. It was then in the busyness of a task, that he would so casually bring into our conversation some underlying life principle.

"You know, Dak, if you desire to see good days, you must keep your tongue from falsehoods." That's all he said. He turned and began loading a small pack, making himself busy.

I continued working feverishly with the sharpening stone, testing the edge repeatedly. Yes, they were getting there. I ran the sharpened flint arrowhead gently down the front of my lower leg. Examining the arrowhead, I found just what I was looking for, a few fine hairs. Perfect I thought. But I had heard exactly what he said.

****

My mind refocused, the animal reached behind his back and drew the long knife. I said nothing of the lies; I spoke not a word of the pain he had caused. I focused, my training rote.

"See the arrow hit its mark, Dak. In your mind see only the kill zone. Place the arrow perfectly in your mind first...then allow your body to obey what your mind has already seen."

The cruel animal started toward me with the knife. There was no doubt in my mind, he intended to kill me. I released the arrow. It met its target perfectly in the center of the kill zone. The cruel animal fell. I moved toward him, nocking another arrow as he dropped to his knees, writhing in pain, the arrow protruding from his chest. He reached inside his vest. Before he could remove his hand, the next arrow penetrated his throat. He fell to his side, dropping the revolver he had drawn from his vest. The gun tumbled over the rock face, falling hundreds of feet below into the steep rock canyon.

Now I was over him, my thoughts pure, clear, and intentional. He cowered in fear, unable to move. I removed my grandfather's long knife from its sheath. I knelt beside the man, took hold of his dirty hair with my left hand, and sliced quickly, efficiently with the razor-sharp knife.

From the depths of my being, from a place I had never known, my War Cry sounded across the mountains. The cry echoed into the depths of the deep canyons below me.

I held the scalp high as the cruel animal breathed his last. The echo returned to me from the mountains. I stood over him in victory.

I began to sing the song my grandfather had taught me. The song of Victory. The song reserved for a Warrior only upon the fulfillment of a great victory.

I, Joshua Daklugie, had just become an Apache Warrior.

Chapter 12

The trip down the mountain in the early afternoon sun was easy. The snow that had fallen would not last.

"Just a bit too early to stay," I said aloud. The same words my grandfather had spoken many times. Early snow often quickly melted along the Rocky Mountains this far south. In many places where the sun penetrated the forest, the ground was already clear. The temperature had already reached into the high fifties. I stopped by the small lake and cleaned my knife and my hands and arms. I watched the blood drift into the lake water and disappear. In my soul I felt a cleansing. I felt no remorse. I knew this was a thing that needed to be done.

It became warmer as I descended farther in altitude. By the time I reached the tree cover behind the school it was a pleasant autumn afternoon.

From the rear of the school there was no activity. Nothing unusual for a Sunday afternoon. I knew there would be a few students hanging out at the gym. I skirted around to the side of the building, hidden mostly in the trees. Coach Tower's truck was in the parking lot. I would meet with him later. For now, I needed to find Nita.

I began to run. The housing section where she lived was just a mile to the east, again downhill. I covered the mile in six minutes. However, there was no peace in my run this day. How would I explain all that had happened? "Just speak the truth," I said to myself. I knew deep in my spirit what I had been taught from childhood. "The truth sets all men free." I had read these same words in my grandfather's scroll just this morning.

I would hold nothing back from her. The same would be true for my next stop. I also needed to see Officer Victorio.

I slowed, catching my breath, walked up to Nita's front door, and knocked.

As the door opened, my heart seemed to rise and get hung high in my throat. I stood and stared into her longing eyes. Her arms were open wide. Her voice like that of an angel.

"Dak, come inside." She stepped forward and embraced me. I could become lost in her embrace. My tears again rose, spilling along my cheeks. They pooled along my jaw then dripped onto her shoulder. She kissed them. The moment was the most intimate contact that had ever occurred between us. My future love kissing my tears. My heart was full. Even with all that had happened in the last twenty-four hours, I felt hope. I had a vision of the future and a promise of good days ahead. She was everything a Warrior could ever want. And somehow, I knew she would be mine.

We just stood a moment. Caught in a revelation of destiny. I spoke the words I had heard spoken over me many times.

"You, Nita will be a blessing to our people. That blessing is within you."

She just smiled and said, "I know."

She took my hand, and we entered the room. Her entire family was seated at the table.

Her father spoke to me. "Welcome, Dak. Put your things there in the entry," indicating my weapons, "we were just about to eat. Please join us." I did as instructed. He motioned for me to sit next to him. Nita took a seat opposite me. "Let us pray." The leader of our tribe bowed his head and began to pray.

David Runningdeer was a natural born leader. He was one of the few who could have escaped the reservation. After graduating at the top of his class at West Point, he served his time in the military. He earned many awards, medals, and military honors during his time in the Army. In a few short years he rose to the rank of Lieutenant Colonel. Many thought his future was unlimited. Politicians especially. However, those in the circles of bureaucracy did not know the man's true servant heart. That heart was for his people. Mr. Runningdeer, against all sound advice (most of which emanated from the white man's world), returned to the Rez.

Mr. Runningdeer had been elected president of our tribe four consecutive terms now. There were no term limits for the position of president of our people. Most were confident he would remain in power for years to come. Most also knew "power" was not the proper term for his oversight of our people, myself included. Most knew he led our people as a servant. His servant spirit was clearly visible in the prayer he spoke over his family, over me, over his daughter

Nita, as we sat around this mighty Warrior's table. I was humbled.

He ended the prayer and looked directly into my eyes. I respectfully returned his gaze. Sympathy showed on his face. He placed his hand on my shoulder. "I'm sorry about your mother, Dak. Officer Victorio will make certain justice is done."

"Yes sir...I need to see him after our meal," I said. He simply nodded in understanding.

It was good to be with my people, with this family. I observed a mother, a father, and six brothers and sisters. Their ages ranged from a toddler of ten months to Nita, the oldest who was my age, seventeen. This family all tended to one another's needs, sharing in the feeding and caring of all. Laughter, food, love, and conversation permeated the scene. This is what I desired. This was a picture of what a full blessed life should be.

I stared across the table at Nita. She smiled. It was as if she knew my thoughts.

I wondered if I had destroyed any chance of living a life similar to what was being lived out before me.

Chapter 13

The Sunday afternoon waned as the family all pitched in doing the dishes, clearing the table, and tending the little ones. Nita returned from the baby's room after putting her down for a nap. The home was filled with love and the most normal serene circumstances of life.

I, on the other hand, was inwardly the opposite. The questions within my mind of my future and my immediate problem of where to live loomed in the forefront of my mind. I considered the meetings I needed to have with Coach Tower and Officer Victorio. But the most pressing issue in my mind was that I desperately wanted to talk with Nita privately.

Mr. Runningdeer observed me with an understanding look. "Dak, why don't you and Nita head to the front porch? I know you need to talk." With a look of relief I know he saw, I said a little too enthusiastically, "Great idea, yes sir, um sir." He just smiled at my awkwardness as Nita and I headed toward the front door.

We sat in the swing. She took my hand and simply looked at me, ready to listen.

"Nita, I have to, well, I need to leave. I'm going away. I'll be leaving school. They won't let me stay at the house. Child Protective Services is already after me. I'm not sure exactly what to do."

She just listened, a kindness in her eyes. "There's more, the man that killed my mother, he tried to kill me also." I felt her tense at my words. "Nita, I'm not a child; I'm a man. I am a Warrior."

None of what I was saying seemed to faze her. She just listened with an understanding look. I paused, after spilling what I had been holding in for the last two hours.

"Did you kill the cruel man, Dak?"

"Yes, I did, Nita," I said with resolve.

"I understand; you did what had to be done. You are indeed a Warrior." She began to sing the song of victory over one's enemy. I sang softly along with her.

"I am going with you, Dak. Come, let's go tell Father. He will drive us to the station. Officer Victorio will know what to do."

"But, Nita, this may cause trouble for you. I don't want anything to hurt you or your family. I can face this myself. I will tell Officer Victorio the truth. There will be an investigation. The FBI will become involved as they do with any murder on the Rez. I am not asking for help or your father's involvement. I just came to explain and tell you why I must leave. My life will not be the same, ever. I just wanted you to understand…"

She stopped my rambling talk by raising her finger to her mouth and a scarcely discernable quiet shush escaped her lips.

"Dak, I'm going with you."

"Ok, I get it, Nita, if you insist. You can go with me. Don't misunderstand me, I think your presence will help me as I explain all this to Officer Victorio." I paused a moment, then continued my rant. "Okay, let's go with your father. I suppose we should explain all this to him before we leave. Do you think he will understand? I really don't want to disappoint your father of all people."

Again, she raised her hand to her lips, making the slight shushing sound.

"Dak, that's not what I mean. Yes, we can go to the police. But what I am saying is, I am going with you. I have had a vision; I will go where you go."

I swallowed hard, her meaning becoming clear in my mind.

She gracefully rose from the little front porch swing and walked to the front door. Her father greeted her just inside the door. I heard him say, "Is it time to go see Victorio?"

"Yes, Father," she replied.

I sat in the front seat of Mr. Runningdeer's double cab truck. He seemed distant, which was not his normal demeanor. Nita sat in the rear seat of the truck, also riding along in silence. This would be a difficult meeting.

"Dak, is there anything I should know?" he asked.

As I thought about how to reply, Nita spoke up from the back seat.

"Father, the man who killed Dak's mother, and his grandfather, attempted to kill Dak this morning. His evil has ended. Dak has become a Warrior. Dak has removed a great evil from our land. He has defended all of us. Dak has killed the cruel man."

The leader of our people gazed toward me but said nothing. In his eyes I read something different. It was the look of a Warrior, a perceptive look. Within his eyes I observed a resolve, a fierceness. He was proud of me.

"Your grandfather has taught you well," he said.

****

This was the second day in a row I found myself in Officer Victorio's office. He listened intently as I recounted today's events up on the high mountains.

"And the gun went over the rock cliff?" Officer Victorio asked.

"Yes," I replied.

"What of the knife he pulled, would it still be there with the body, Dak?"

"Yes, I suppose, however all of the items went over the cliff. The gun, the knife, and the body."

Officer Victorio looked at me; his look also showed a kind of admiration or newfound respect.

"I'm not sure how to procced here." He looked toward Mr. Runningdeer. "The body will be difficult to recover. The animals will have their way with the remains tonight. There may not be much evidence left by the time we could get a team up there. The hike in, repelling down the rock cliffs, then how to get the body back up those cliffs, then of course the hike out carrying the remains. Then there is the FBI. They *will* want to make an arrest. Those guys are all about the show.

"Dak, as far as they are concerned, you will be considered guilty until proven innocent. Moving the body after you defended yourself is the real problem. It will be seen as an attempt to cover up what happened."

I sat with my head held high. None of this mattered to me.

"I did what had to be done, sir."

Everyone in the room knew what I said was true.

"This man is being hunted by every law enforcement agency in the state. The next elk hunt starts on Wednesday. The vultures will give the body away. The guides will find him. This complicates my decision here.

"Dak, my job is to enforce the law, to protect the innocent, and pursue the guilty. I believe your story, Dak. I know by looking in your eyes you are telling me the truth. I also know self-defense is not a crime. I know who the guilty party is…in this terrible chain of events. I see no further need to investigate. I want you to sign the statement you are making to me here today. My thought is, we wait. The four people in this room know the truth. I suggest for now that truth stays within this small circle of four people."

We all looked around the room and each knew this request would be honored.

"I will handle the situation if I hear from one of the guides. In the meantime, go see Mrs. Kuruk tomorrow. Explain to her that you are seeking to be an emancipated seventeen-year-old. That will help you and slow her down a bit."

He slid forward the written report, indicating for me to sign. I did so.

"Oh, and date it here." He looked at his watch. "What is the date anyway, the fourteenth, right? On second thought just leave that. I will fill it in myself."

Everyone in the room knew it was the eleventh. Officer Victorio was giving me three days.

Chapter 14

The drive back to the Runningdeer's home was quiet. Nita's father seemed lost in thought.

I sat in the back of the truck with Nita. She too seemed to be alone in her thoughts. She reached for my hand and held it tightly. I felt a level of relief and resolve. The words of my grandfather once again echoed in my mind.

Dak, there is nothing quite as good for the soul as releasing inner turmoil, or secrets, or even one's mistakes in life. These kinds of burdens are not meant to be held within. Bearing another's burdens frees the one who attempts to carry what they cannot carry alone.

The relief I felt that Sunday afternoon as I rode along the backroads of the reservation with Nita holding my hand was beyond compare. I was grateful again for the many days with my grandfather. I knew there was much trouble ahead and there were many problems to be solved. Something inside me knew with this amazing woman beside me, I could face any problem, overcome any obstacle, achieve any goal. A goal was beginning to form in my mind. A goal of not just solving the immediate issues before me. This purpose was much greater. I wanted what I had seen in her home. The picture of a man serving his people, his family, was burned into my heart. I had no idea how to accomplish the objective forming in my mind. That did not change the fact that it was there, planted in my very being.

The truck slowed as we neared the high school. Mr. Runningdeer looked at me in the rearview mirror.

"Dak, you need to stop here?"

"Yes, sir, I do," I answered, as I spotted Coach Tower's truck in the parking lot.

Mr. Runningdeer pulled the truck into the parking lot and stopped. "Nita, will you be staying?' he asked.

"Father, I need to speak with you and Mother," she replied.

She had burdens of her own, issues to resolve. I knew tonight she would speak to her parents about our journey. I suddenly recalled her words.

Dak, I have had a vision, where you go, I will go. I looked in her eyes and saw a deep understanding. We had much more to talk about.

"Okay. Dak, where will you stay tonight?" Mr. Runningdeer asked.

"I'll stay with Caleb, sir. Thank you for your help today. I know you are busy, but could we talk again soon?" I asked.

"Plan on dinner with my family again tomorrow. I will see you then."

"Thank you, sir."

I gathered my grandfather's weapons and opened the door and stepped out of the truck. Nita, to my surprise did the same. Then she embraced me. It was not an embrace of a friend or family member. I felt a deep comfort in her arms. I returned the intimate embrace, and I felt one with her. She kissed me on the cheek for the second time today. I opened the truck door for her, she gracefully stepped in, and the two drove away.

I saw her hand rise in the side window of the truck. She held it high, her palm open to me.

****

The sun was just beginning to rest on the high mountains to the west out behind the school. The sky appeared a light blue with streaks of pink and turquoise glowing in the high clouds. The wind seemed to whisper to me as it stirred in the trees of the forest that sloped into the mountains before me. My long dark hair, which I wore in the tradition of my people, fanned out from my forehead and flowed off my shoulders in the breeze. I lifted my head slightly into the setting sun. I closed my eyes a moment. I knew. I saw what my grandfather had spoken over me so many times. What my grandmother and Mr. Natchi had reminded me of just yesterday.

The blessing was indeed within me. I would soon carry that blessing to my people.

I was an Apache Warrior.

I walked to Coach Tower's truck and opened the door. I quickly found what I was looking for, a pen and an unopened envelope. I wrote a note on the back of the envelope that could not possibly contain all I needed to communicate to him.

"Coach, I will not be returning for my senior year. Life is calling. Thank you for what you have taught me. Dak." I left the note on the driver's seat. It wasn't much, but he would understand. We had learned a way to communicate that did not require many words.

I turned and closed the truck door. I put on the bow and quiver, placed the knife and war club in my belt, and headed for the ancient trail. The scroll was waiting for me in my little cavern up on the high mountains.

Chapter 15

Nita Runningdeer sat with her parents at the dinner table in the Runningdeer home. The younger children had been fed, bathed, the stories read, and the prayers recited. The little ones now slept soundly in the safety and comfort of the home.

Nita had always been open and honest with her parents. This conversation would be different and difficult. How might she explain what had been revealed to her in the vision?

She knew what Dak would do in this situation. She had seen him do this very thing today, in Officer Victorio's office. He simply told the truth. She would do the same.

"Father, I have had a vision." Her father looked intently at her with a questioning look. She paused; her mother seemed to freeze at her statement.

Nita's mother was Comanche. They had met while both were working in Washington, DC. Mr. Runningdeer, an Army officer, the future Mrs. Runningdeer working with the BIA as a Native language translator. Their introduction by a mutual friend and the following whirlwind romance, quick engagement, wedding, and the beginning of their family was, as her mother had said to her many times, a blessing. "Our love was orchestrated by the Spirit. It is the only explanation I have to describe what I knew in my heart from the moment we met. I knew your father was and would forever be my man."

Her mother gently placed her hand on Mr. Runningdeer's arm.

"Go on, child, tell us what you have seen," her mother said.

Nita thought a moment of her mother's gifting. Mrs. Runningdeer was gifted by the Spirit in many ways. One of those special giftings was that of prophecy. Nita knew her mother would understand. She did not, however, know how her father would react to what Nita knew in her heart she must do.

Nita continued. "Father, I closed my eyes a few days ago and clearly saw my life path. Within that path I saw the history of our people, Father. We were in great danger of extermination. A vast army had come against our people. Many were killed, many others taken prisoner. There were only a few of us left. The enemy desired to wipe the remaining survivors of our people from the earth. The plan was set in motion. The leaders of this army were poised to proceed with their plan of...genocide. But then I saw a scale, a balance of some kind. Within the balance of the scales there lay a way for us to survive. One man held the weights for this great scale. In his hands, he held the weights of wisdom that would assure our survival and tip the scales in our favor."

Nita paused a moment and observed her parents clinging to one another.

"Go on, child," her mother said.

"The man who held the weights of wisdom was Dak. Joshua Daklugie."

Nita's parents sat wide eyed; they both nodded, indicating for her to continue.

"In my vision, standing by his side was a woman, clearly the woman was Dak's wife," Nita said.

"And you were that woman, Nita? His wife?" her father asked.

"Yes, Father...and...I must go where he goes."

Chapter 16

made my way into the forest. I traveled quickly as dusk rapidly descended into the deep canyons I moved within. The trail was much easier to follow as most of the early snow had melted during the warm autumn afternoon. The forest smelled of fallen pine needles and the scent of autumn flowers. The damp forest floor allowed me to move swiftly, silently. I covered the four miles in a little over an hour. It was near dark with just a dim light still illuminating the western horizon as I arrived at my new home. The stars were beginning to show. I paused outside the cave and listened. I heard the coyotes calling to one another and the howl of a wolf from deep in the canyon in front of me. The animals would indeed have their way with the remains of the cruel man this night.

I turned and entered the cave. Carefully I made my way along the rock shelf to the right side of the cave. The darkness quickly enveloped me with such a small amount of light reflecting from the entrance. I felt my way along the descending slope, counting my steps. Two hundred yards, I would remember to leave the flashlights closer to the entrance on my next journey out of the cave. I thought I must be close to the two-hundred-yard rock shelf. I felt my way along in complete darkness. No rock ledge. No shelf. I continued along bending down now to feel the surface below my feet. Smooth calcite? I was already on the snowy river. I had missed the shelf. I turned around and began to count my steps out. How foolish of me, I thought. Leaving the flashlight so far in was fine on a bright sunshiny day. However, now darkness had fallen outside my shelter. Locating the flashlights was suddenly a serious problem. I felt something brush by the side of my face. Just a slight wind, was it? Then I felt it again, and again. I held the rock wall now on my left and moved another ten paces. I heard the movement this time. A wing, a slight barely discernable movement of air against my neck. I stopped, frozen in place, fear creeping into my mind, and then I heard his voice. *Dak, it would be best not to enter the cave right at sundown for the bat flight takes place at dusk each day. They will not harm you, but it would be best not to disturb their movement.* The words of my grandfather echoed in my mind.

I took a deep breath, relieved at knowing what the slight sound and motion was. I sat on the stone floor for a few minutes waiting. I could hear the faint sound of a thousand wings flitting past me in the darkness. Once the soft sounds ended, I rose again in the pitch black. The bat flight was over.

Feeling my way, I took five steps. The rock shelf revealed itself in my left hand. A few inches more…Yes! There they are. Taking the LED flashlights, I pressed the switch on the smaller of the two. The light was blinding at first. Most humans have never experienced complete darkness. My eyes had attempted for twenty minutes or so to adjust to the total darkness. It took a few moments for my eyesight to adjust to the light. Ahead just a few steps was the beginning of the snowy river. I took another deep breath, relieved to gain my bearings. I understood this could have quickly become a dangerous predicament. I would be much more cautious in the future. The deep drop in the front of the cavern awaited such foolish decisions.

Making my way deeper into the cave I reached the large room without further incident.

I drank deeply from the pool of spring water, then moved into my little cozy sleeping room. I stood on the stone and removed the scroll and my grandfather's medicine bag. Using my jacket again for a pillow, I settled in for the night. Switching my flashlight to low, I opened the scroll, eager to continue reading the fascinating truths contained in this treasure before me. I opened the first page…I felt the soft worn leather binding in my hands and within a few seconds…fell fast asleep.

****

Monday morning, I awakened in the deep recesses of my cave in the high mountains. I thought of Nita, wondering would her morning be routine? Getting ready for school, preparing breakfast for her siblings, having her mother drop her at the high school. Something within me knew our routine days were ending. I whispered a prayer for her and her family.

Rising, I walked to the spring and drank my fill. Hunger again. It was something I was beginning to adjust to. I was grateful for the late afternoon meal I had shared with Nita and her family. I thought of my plan for today. I needed to retrieve a few things from our home. My moccasins, some supplies, batteries, a bottle of propane. I also needed to deal with Bear Woman. However, I saw no reason to hurry down the mountain this day. Returning to my little room I settled into the soft sand floor and opened the scroll.

I became lost in the words of wisdom. I recalled my thoughts of healing plants, meat preservation, edible plants, the locations of hidden water sources, and hot springs. The knowledge for surviving was exact and incredible. Although I knew from my grandfather of tanning skins using brain matter, the process was described in detail. Even my location in the cave was drawn on an intricate map. I was in awe; this cave did not end here. The detail of passages throughout the mountain and down onto the plain was clearly drawn on several pages. Other exits shown on the map as triangles. Even an exit near the old soldier fort where the snowy river ended was shown. That was incredibly twenty-five miles from where I now sat. The location of tar pits within the cave were shown, along with instructions for making torch lights.

I read every page. Toward the end of the scroll, the book contained the ancient ceremonies of our people. Included were weddings, death songs, victory songs, even depictions of the many dances and their meanings. Again, some of these I knew from my grandfather's teachings. I read on. There was much about the Old Ways I did not know.

The last few pages contained an incredible great mystery. Something I had never thought possible. I read in utter amazement.

The instructions were clear and succinct. The ingredients for the "medicine" precise. The explanation given in my grandfather's hand leapt from the page into my heart and mind. The words before me in writing, I could somehow hear him speaking.

"Dak, this medicine requires faith to succeed. It is not a mountain of faith. It is not a great river of faith, nor a mighty ocean of faith. To succeed in this ceremony, you must have a tiny seed of faith. Once the seed is planted, and you truly believe, this thing can be done."

I knew then. As soon as the words were read, I knew. I would travel into the past.

The medicine of the *Dream Time* would take me there.

I also understood Nita's words she had spoken to me. She would go back with me.

I arose from my position and gently placed the scroll and medicine bag back on the rock shelf. I wondered a moment if I should take them with me. Perhaps keep them in a safe place? I quickly decided there was no safer place for them than where they now rested.

I readied my weapons for the day, securing my bow and quiver. Placing the war club and knife in my belt, I headed out in the direction of the cave entrance.

On reaching the entrance, I placed the flashlights on the rock ledge near the opening. I cautiously listened for a moment before exiting. Hearing no sound, I exited the cave and moved a few yards silently. I was beginning to move like a Warrior. Walking down and across the rock outcroppings, I made my way toward the ancient trail.

I paused again momentarily and peered over and into the deep canyons below. I heard something. The sound of men's voices from far below. My heart seemed to stop a moment.

I gazed across the sky and saw exactly what I was looking for, the vultures circling high overhead. They had given away the location of the body. The guides had already or would very soon discover the remains.

I no longer had three days.

Chapter 17

It was after noon by the time I arrived at the rear of the high school. From the cafeteria, the smell of flame grilled hamburgers drifted in the air. I was becoming very hungry. I would return here closer to the end of the school day. For now, I decided to head to our little house for supplies. I began to run along the shoulder of the road. Almost immediately the hunger went away. I was losing weight, but the lightness of my body made the running even easier. Five minutes elapsed between the first mile marker as I could scarcely feel the road. I quickened my pace.

The old Ford truck passed me and pulled over a hundred yards ahead. I walked the last few yards, recovering my breath quickly. Mr. Natchi sat at the wheel with a knowing look on his face.

"Dak, I am glad I saw you. I'm heading to the Tribal store for a few items. Where can I take you?" he said.

"Well, I have several stops today, are you in a hurry?" I asked.

"At my age, I'm never in a hurry. I am here mainly to help you today," Mr. Natchi replied. Again, the intentional look shone in his eyes.

"In my quiet time today, I could think only of you and how I might help," he said.

I was not surprised at his words. I had spent enough time with my grandfather to know the Elders had much insight into the needs of others.

"Thank you, Mr. Natchi. I am very grateful," I said. Looking around the old Ford, I spied the large gallon sized bag of elk jerky on the seat. My mouth began to water.

"I brought this for you. I know you must be hungry." He slid the bag in my direction.

I opened it and the aroma of delicate pepper-spice, garlic, and onion met my nose. I removed two large pieces. The succulent taste filled my mouth as I chewed. Pure elk meat had a way of strengthening one instantly. As I consumed the second delectable piece, I felt the strength of the elk enter my body. I offered some to Mr. Natchi. With a wave of his hand, he declined. I removed another piece and chewed slower this time, savoring the delicious meat. My body instantly felt stronger.

"Where to first, Dak?" he asked.

"I need to stop by the house. I think I have a few things I may need."

"Ok. Brace yourself; she still has some get-up left in her." In a cloud of blue smoke, we slowly accelerated to about forty miles per hour. I caught the sly smile from Mr. Natchi as we rolled along the highway. I laughed aloud as a mini van driven by a mom and loaded with small children passed us.

It was the first time I had laughed in days.

****

We arrived at the little single-wide trailer that I had called home for ten years and pulled into the muddy drive. "I'll only be a minute."

Mr. Natchi replied, "I'll keep her running."

I really didn't want to return here. I entered the front door, which had an order to vacate sticker plastered across its front. Moving through the little trailer, I entered my room. My moccasins were in the closet. I scoured through a few drawers and located two AA size batteries. I located my meager stash of money that I had saved over the summer. I counted it quickly. Forty-four dollars that I neatly tucked into my front pocket. Moving to the hall closet, I gathered my pack frame. I then filled it with a few canned goods that remained in the pantry, and a small propane bottle. I could think of nothing else I needed.

Once again, I whispered a goodbye, and a thank you to our little house. This time I knew it was a final goodbye. I would never return here.

I hustled out the door and hopped in the truck. Mr. Natchi backed down the drive and turned onto the highway in the direction of the Tribal Store. Something in me wanted to look back. Just a quick glance, maybe a glimpse of my basketball goal.

"Best not to look back, Dak," Mr. Natchi said. "The future you will live is in front of you. It is not back there."

I understood. I stared straight ahead and thought of Nita.

****

The Tribal Store had always been one of my favorite places to visit. My grandfather used to bring me here on Saturday mornings. As we pulled to the front of the store and parked, I saw the smoke from the chimney rising into the afternoon sky. We entered together, the Elder and his young protégé.

The store always smelled of coffee, meat smoking, and tobacco. Most tribal members who stopped here had a short grocery list or needed a quick fill-up of gasoline. But to those like my grandfather and Mr. Natchi the store was a meeting place. In the past I would wander for hours through the aisles, discovering so many fascinating items while the Elders drank their coffee and smoked their pipes or cigars. I breathed in the intoxicating blend of the tobacco, coffee, and meat smoking. I closed my eyes as the smells took my mind to a place of goodness, safety, comfort. For a moment I forgot about the troubles that lay ahead.

Mr. Natchi moved to the rear of the store where a few tables were set near the woodburning stove. His friends, the other Elders of the tribe, greeted him. The words always seemed to be few. In our culture a person who spoke too many words might be considered foolish. Much communication still took place in the form of gestures or even slight glances and body language. Today was no different. Mr. Natchi introduced me to the group; however, most of them recognized me from the days I had spent here with my grandfather.

"Men, this is Joshua Daklugie." The small gathering of men simply nodded in my direction. It was a greeting. I acknowledged it with a slight nod of my own. The men were impressed at my response. Mr. Natchi walked to the coffee counter and poured himself a piping hot cup of coffee. He ordered hamburgers and fries, for two, from the counter. My stomach began to grumble. The very elderly grandmother behind the counter looked my way with a nod and said, "About ten minutes, Dak." Mr. Natchi took a seat at one of the tables and looked at his watch. I was free to roam.

I departed to explore the aisles. Camping gear, knives, a gun display, ammunition, fishing poles, and fishing equipment lined the shelves. Overseeing all the wonders contained here was some of the finest taxidermy work performed by our Native taxidermist. Elk mounts, mountain lions, bears, antelope, deer, even a few monster trout hung along the walls of the store. For a moment, I was a young boy again. Although now my thoughts were no longer of great adventures hunting with my grandfather. Now I wandered the aisles wondering what I might need most. Where I was going I would have none of what lined the store shelves in front of me. I eyed a sharp steel hatchet. It was twenty dollars, half of my funds…I placed it in my small shopping basket. Moving in and out of aisles, I thought again, what will I most need?

My grandfather's words echoed again within my mind. "Dak, if a man has fire, he can survive most anything."

I had read in the scroll about where to find the hard quartz that would create a spark. Yes, fire should be a priority. I located the flint and steel sets behind the gun counter. Five dollars each. They were sure to last many years. It would give me time to learn. I loaded two of them into my basket. Thinking back, I remembered my grandfather starting campfires with a small magnifying glass. I located a small two-inch magnifying glass and placed it into my basket. I had a few dollars remaining. What would I need most? I spied the knives under a glass case. I had my grandfathers' long knife, but I knew from experience, another sharp knife would be invaluable. I spent my remaining dollars on the best knife I could buy for twelve dollars. It came with a belt loop carrying sheath and sharpening stone.

"Fire, shelter, clothing, water, and a food source. A man can live well if he has these essentials, Dak," the words of my grandfather whispered within my mind. I had the ability to make fire. I had a shelter that contained fresh water. I knew how to hunt and process what game I might take for food. I spied the blankets along the wall. A blanket would make life survivable, whether in a cave or on the open prairie. These blankets were of an exceptionally fine quality. Hand woven by some of our Tribe. They were one hundred dollars each. I felt the thickness of the weave, imagining the warmth these could provide. I closed my eyes, and I could see the cold of the winter that was coming. Mr. Natchi's voice startled me. He spoke quietly. "Take two of those for your basket, Dak." His meaning clear. He would take care of the two hundred dollars. I did not object. It was the most respectful thing to do. I simply nodded in gratefulness. Mr. Natchi understood. He then dropped two LED flashlights along with a ten pack of AA batteries into my basket.

"Our lunch is ready, come join us," he said.

The food was delicious. Elk burgers grilled over an open flame. A slice of sharp cheddar melted into a grilled bun. Crisp produce, mayonnaise, and mustard, Hatch green chili, hand cut french fries slathered and drowning in ketchup. I tried eating slowly, but it just wouldn't do. For lack of a better term, I wolfed it down within five minutes. The Elders smiled at me. The old grandmother behind the counter also smiled as she placed a plate of warm apple pie on the table in front of me, the ice cream slowly melting along the sides of the plate.

"Coffee with your pie, Dak? she questioned.

"Yes, ma'am," I replied. She poured the coffee then added warm cream and about four teaspoons of sugar. She remembered how my grandfather had prepared coffee for me over the years.

After our meal, Mr. Natchi stood, and we said our respectful goodbyes to the Elders. The two of us stopped at the register to pay out. The total was presented as I reached for my forty-four dollars. "Dak, you keep that. The men wanted to assist you. They are paying for everything you need today. They were honored to do so," Mr. Natchi said.

I just stood there and said nothing. I looked toward the rear of the store, opened my hand and raised it high to the men seated there.

Several hands returned the gesture.

I felt like crying. Gratefulness welled up within my soul at the kindness of my people.

Chapter 18

You need to see Officer Victorio now?" Mr. Natchi asked, as the old Ford fired up in its normal cloud of blue smoke.

"Yes, sir," I replied. We drove away from the Tribal Store; this time I did look back. I wanted to remember the good days I had spent here, including this one. Mr. Natchi smiled at me.

We drove across the four lane and wound our way through the most populated area of the Rez. Here the houses were laid out along winding streets. This was the only place on the Rez that resembled most of what American neighborhoods might look like. The brick homes had all been built in the 1960s. For about three blocks, the houses were all the same floor plan, just flipped about every third home. Old trucks and cars lined the streets, most of them abandoned. The little yards, comprised mostly of dirt in front of the houses, contained an assortment of toys and bicycles. The little brick homes in rows ended abruptly as the terrain beyond the development quickly changed into thick brush and forest. The road turned to dirt and we left a cloud of dust trailing behind us. Turning back toward the four lane Mr. Natchi slowed as we neared the offices of the Tribal Police. The building was swarming with activity. Several rescue vehicles lined the street along the front of the building. A firetruck with its crew busy loading equipment was parked along the side of the building. A group of men were meeting in a circle in the front of the office. I spotted Officer Victorio at about the same instant he looked toward Mr. Natchi's truck. We slowed but did not stop.

Officer Victorio nodded at me with an understanding look. I slunk down in the seat. I had very little time.

The body had been found.

"How 'bout we drop by the school instead, Dak?" Mr. Natchi asked.

"I think that's a good idea, sir."

"Is there a place you can stash your gear?"

"Yes, sir, I know of a place."

We pulled up to the west side of the high school where the forest was thickest. I neatly stashed my weapons and survival gear, concealing them completely in the underbrush. Mr. Natchi opened his truck door and stepped out. He then opened his arms and hugged me. While in the embrace he began to pray. I remember everything he prayed for and about that day. Safety, strength, wisdom for my journey, the blessings of the Spirit on my days. Those words all easily come to my mind. The moment for me was one of those that get tucked away into a special place in your mind. That place is where the memory never leaves you. Where a person can recall every detail, the time of day 3:15 p.m., the sounds that were present, the wind in the pines, the ringing of the school bell as classes were dismissed. I still recall the smell of the old Ford as it idled roughly. The look in my Elder's eyes. The hope that look held.

"You will be forever a blessing to our people, Dak." He began the song.

We sang together for a moment...the song of victory. When the song ended, he turned and climbed into his truck. He reached behind the seat and removed an ornately decorated set of traditional skins. Leggings, a loin cloth, an ornate breastplate, along with a deerskin jacket. I was in awe at their beauty.

"I have kept these for you. They were made for me by my mother when I was seventeen. I had become a Warrior at roughly the same age as you are now. I think they will fit perfectly."

I had no words. I guess the look on my face spoke what my lips could not.

"You're welcome," Mr. Natchi said with an understanding smile on his face.

"I... can't...these are much to valuable, I—"

"Dak, you will need these for your journey." He handed the clothing to me through the window, his eyes locked on mine. He nodded to me and smiled. I understood. Too many words were not needed in this moment.

I knew this was yet another goodbye.

As he drove away, he did not look back.

I walked toward the rear of the school and neatly tucked the skins into my pack frame, again hiding my possessions away in the heavy brush. I then quickly returned to the front of the school just as most students were gathering around their respective busses for the long rides across the reservation to their homes. I frantically searched the crowd for Nita. She was nowhere to be found.

Spying a group of her friends, I walked toward them. Her close friend Raina waved me over.

"Nita did not come to school, Dak," she said with a look of concern on her face.

"Why, what's going on, Raina?"

"I'm not sure exactly. She texted me last night." Raina looked uncertain whether she should share with me all that she knew. Hesitating, she continued.

"Okay, well, I guess she and her parents had some kind of disagreement. You better go see her; it sounded serious. She was terribly upset."

My mind raced as I turned and started to run toward the little housing development. Nita and her parents never argued. She was a perfect daughter, smart, compliant, responsible. This had to be about me. I covered the mile in less than five minutes.

As I neared the home, I immediately noticed both her parent's vehicles. I approached the front door and knocked gently.

"Dak, I'm glad you're here," her mother said through a veil of tears. "Please come in."

Mr. Runningdeer paced across the living room in front of the fireplace.

Evidently, he had been waiting for me.

"Where is she, Dak?"

I was shocked at the question. He instantly noticed the confused look on my face.

"What do you mean? Nita isn't here?" I asked.

"She left last night, Dak. I was sure she was with you…and to be honest I wasn't that worried knowing that," Mr. Runningdeer said. Picking up his cell phone he began to dial. "However, now I think we should call Victorio." He placed the phone to his ear. I shook my head and motioned for him to hang up. He did so, slowly lowering the phone.

"I know where she is, or I think I know where she is. I haven't seen her but I'm sure of it."

Her mother moved toward me with a graceful step. "She will not return, Dak. Will you take us to her?" she asked. "We just want to say goodbye in love…not under the circumstances in which she left last night." She peered toward her husband. He lowered his head.

"I'm not sure what's going on, Dak. She is the apple of my eye and my life. This is too soon. I wanted to see so many things in her life. My reaction was to protect, defend. It is a difficult thing for a father. You will one day know how I'm feeling. I am not gifted with the visions, as my wife and my daughter are. I can only see today. But I understand now. Our future is in the balance, our people. Will you take us to her, please? We just desire a proper goodbye."

"It is a difficult trail, sir. Let me go and meet with her. I promise we will return here tonight."

"I don't think you have the time for that, Dak," he said matter of factly.

I understood.

"It will be dark soon, so let's take my truck. Auntie will stay here and watch the other children. Let's go now," Mr. Runningdeer said. I nodded my head in agreement. We all turned to leave as Mrs. Runningdeer took up a set of neatly folded traditional animal skins decorated in the traditional way. Brightly colored beads and incredibly detailed needle work adorned the clothing. I recognized the dress Nita and her mother had made for her "Coming of Age Ceremony." With an understanding look, her mother loaded the clothing and a small bag of personal items into the back seat of the truck. We drove along the road as the sun rested along the back of the high mountains. I knew Nita was up there. Waiting, waiting to begin the journey back.

Chapter 19

Mr. Runningdeer pulled into the parking lot in the rear of the high school. I quickly located my supplies and loaded everything into my pack frame. I again strapped my quiver, long knife, war club, and bow across my shoulders. I shouldered the pack frame and supplies, all the while Nita's parents watched me, in wonder I was certain. Leaving the parking lot, I located the beginning of the ancient trail and we began the long walk up into the high mountains.

We moved in silence for a mile or more. Breaking the quiet, Nita's mother asked, "When will you enter the *Dream Time,* Dak?" I was taken aback at the question and what it revealed. She knew? I did not know how to answer the question.

"Soon," I replied.

I could tell that regardless of his good physical condition Mr. Runningdeer was struggling with the steepness of the trail. I paused, allowing a moment for him to gain some breath. I began again at a little slower pace. We were nearing the first lake when I caught the flash of movement. I froze. But I knew what it was, or who it was that had moved.

Motioning for Nita's parents to stay put for a moment, I moved ahead about twenty yards. There by the calm waters of the shimmering little lake stood my future wife. The scene I would never forget, again the memory taking its place, permanently within my mind.

Perhaps it was her longing, vulnerable look. The obvious fear melting into relief as she recognized me. As I think back now on the scene, this must have been the same look many loves have recognized throughout time. That moment when a loved one has arrived to rescue, protect, or bring a blanket of security that would envelope and surround them. That knowing and relief, that the loved…can simply melt into.

Nita melted into my strong arms. I softly kissed the tears that gently rolled down her cheeks. "You are safe now, Nita," I whispered into her ear.

Looking back down the trail, I motioned to her parents who had been observing to come to us.

Her parents with tears in their eyes embraced their daughter. No words were spoken, but a healing took place that late afternoon near the beautiful lake along the ancient trail that led into the high mountains.

"So, is this goodbye, daughter?" her father asked.

"No, Father, not yet. I would like to return home. I need to say goodbye to my brothers and sisters. I need to hug them and touch them one last time."

I took the lead as we all turned and started down the trail.

****

It was dark when we pulled into the driveway of the Runningdeer home. Supper was on the table and the little children all bolted from their seats, greeting their mother and father and Nita with hugs and excitement. The little ones bounced and tugged at Nita. I noticed her hands touching each child on their heads and faces in the excitement of the greeting…She was blessing each of them.

We gathered around the table. Mr. Runningdeer prayed special blessings on all his family. He gave thanks for many things…but he mostly prayed over his daughter. Laughter and smiles filled the home. The family again all pitched in with feeding, clean up, baths, and bedtime stories. The knock on the door came just as Nita and I and her parents were settling in for what I was sure would be a long talk.

Her mother rose from the sofa and opened the door to Pastor Eknath. The pastor entered the room with warm greetings for all. Mr. Runningdeer motioned for me to help with coffee making in the kitchen. I knew something else was on his mind. He spoke softly to me as we prepared the coffee.

Reaching into his pocket he drew out a small golden ring. "Dak, I know this is a time of most unusual circumstances. However, consider the honor of my daughter, and our people. This ring belonged to my grandmother. It is yours to do with as you see fit."

I was stunned but understood perfectly.

We returned and served the coffee amidst polite chat. I caught Nita's eye and motioned for her to join me in the kitchen.

"I know we haven't had a chance to talk, Nita." She looked deep into my eyes. "Our life journey together will begin tonight. I'm not sure of all that is ahead, but may we, or we can start…I don't have the right words. I love you, Nita." I took the little gold ring from my pocket. She raised her left hand in response as I placed the ring on her finger.

"This is an honorable thing we are doing here tonight, Dak. Thank you for honoring me, my family, especially my father."

I was amazed at her strength and resolve. She seemed to be much more aware than I about the path we would walk together.

The ceremony in the living room of her family home was sweet, sincere, and deeply spiritual. Pastor Eknath spoke the words in English and Apache. Mr. Runningdeer gave his daughter, Kwanita Runningdeer, to me as my wife, in faith and honor and tradition. We visited long into the night. It was an evening filled with goodness and blessings.

That night I slept on the couch, making sure everyone knew this was where I would sleep. Nita slept in her room with her little sisters. Mrs. Runningdeer was the last to retire for the night. She brought me a blanket and thanked me for "honoring her daughter." I would attempt to do that very thing all of my days.

Chapter 20

At six the following morning as the entire house lay sleeping, Nita and I silently exited the Runningdeer home and made our way to the ancient trail. Mr. and Mrs. Joshua Daklugie climbed the trail we would walk many times over the next few years.

Many thoughts floated within both our minds as we walked together along the way. I wondered what she was thinking. I glanced back occasionally just to check on her. She always returned my glance with an enchanting smile. I'm sure there was also much wonderment in her mind concerning the days ahead. I just kept thinking, wow, I'm married. I had become a Warrior and a husband within the last forty-eight hours. Thinking of Nita and who she was as a woman, central in my thoughts and stronger than any other emotion or thought within me…I was proud to be her husband.

We made good time up the ancient trail. Both Nita and I were in excellent physical condition. We paused a moment outside the hidden opening to the cave. We stood holding hands, looking toward the south and west. On the desert floor below us we could easily see the few small towns dotting the surface and the little dark highway lines that connected them. Whites Sands gleamed in the distance and beyond; even the mountains of northern Mexico could be seen.

"At one time this was the land of our people, all you can see and more," I said.

Nita squeezed my hand.

"Dak, we must make certain that even the small piece we now inhabit, our Homeland, is not taken from *The People.*"

I looked into her eyes and understood a little more of what she had already seen in her visions.

The sound of movement deep in the canyon below us reached our ears. Occasionally a faint voice echoed up the canyon walls. The men were coming to recover the body. I led Nita to the shadow in the rock. We entered the cavern. I stopped and located the flashlights on the rock shelf. Turning mine on, I quickly explained the necessity of touching the rock face on our right before proceeding. Nita turned her light on and shined its beam toward the deep drop to our left.

"I see," she replied. "Have you ever been down there?"

"No, I'm not sure what we would find. I don't think it would be very pleasant."

"Maybe…or maybe it is a good place to hide something of great value," she said matter of factly. I was beginning to see for the first time how differently a woman thinks or considers things. This was my first lesson in being a husband. A man should always seek a woman's advice and perspective, I thought to myself.

"Interesting thought," I said.

I led the way along the rock shelf; we descended along the snowy river, and into the large room. Standing a flashlight upright, we began to unload our meager supplies.

Nita busied herself with tending to and setting up a makeshift kitchen. She located the canteens my grandfather had stored here and filled them from the spring water just below our room. She then prepared our little sleeping room. She spread a blanket over the sand floor. She carefully folded back the second blanket atop the first to use as a cover.

While she was at work settling in, I unloaded my weapons and the exquisite skins Mr. Natchi had given me. I neatly stored the hatchet and extra flashlights and batteries on the shelf in our sleeping room. I removed the scroll and placed it near the bed Nita had fashioned for us. All at once I realized this bed was for us. I swallowed hard and turned to Nita.

"Looks like we are all set, husband." A twinkle shone in her eyes as she spoke the words.

"Nita, I know this was not as either of us would have planned. I don't expect, I…well, we can take things slowly." She moved toward me and embraced me. We melted into one another's arms. We kissed intimately. She took my hand and led me onto our little bed.

****

Afterwards, as I lay in thought attempting to gain some perspective, I was amazed. Mr. and Mrs. Daklugie lay on the warm blanket in our little room within a cave upon the high mountains. There was no place on Earth I would rather be. My wife began to cry. I was suddenly terrified. I thought I had done something wrong.

"Nita, are you alright?"

She turned to me smiling, the tears still flowing down her face. I did not understand.

"I am fine, husband. I cannot explain my heart. I know this is the first time for both of us...today I am no longer a girl, just as you are no longer a boy. Dak, you are now a Warrior and a husband. I am now an Apache woman. My tears... are tears of joy."

I did not know how to respond. I had no words. In the dim light of a flashlight within our little world, I reached for her, desire rising again.

Ecstasy was a new sensation, emotion, and feeling for both of us. We loved away the day unashamed, blessed by our Creator. Then we both fell into a deep satisfying sleep.

Chapter 21

I arose at what I thought must now be the following morning. While Nita slept, I moved up the cavern and out. The sky was beginning to lighten in the east. An east wind blew fierce and cold; the temperature must have been in the teens or lower. There was no sound from the canyons below. I knew we could not return to our old life; the ticking clock had expired. I gathered a few sticks and branches for a fire. Turning away from the only world we had ever known, I quickly descended back into the cave.

I was surprised that Nita was awake. She lay in our snug little room reading from the scroll. We greeted one another with a gentle kiss.

"How are you this morning, wife?" I asked, smiling brightly.

"I am blessed, my husband," she replied. "Dak, when should we depart?"

"I see you have read the ceremony."

"Yes, and your grandfather has everything that is needed in his medicine bag."

I looked into her eyes and knew we would leave today. She read me easily. "We should eat and drink throughout the day, all that we can hold. We don't have much food. We should save the elk jerky and a few canned goods for our recovery time."

"I understand. I will prepare us a feast. My mother sent along two containers of food in my pack. I'll prepare what we have; it will feed us throughout the day."

I was amazed her mother was aware of what lay ahead for us and had even provided what we would most need to be prepared for our journey. I studied the scroll while Nita heated the meal in the small tin over the little single burner camp stove. Within minutes the smells of pot roast filled our new home.

We had one fork. We sat and dined together sharing bites of delicious roast beef, carrots cooked tender and juicy, potatoes, tender celery, and onions. Nita warmed the fresh baked bread over the little flame. I ate until I felt I could not have another bite…until Nita opened the chocolate bars her mother had sent along.

It was a meal fit for royalty, and I felt that was exactly what I was, a king. King of my little world, my beautiful queen by my side.

We spent the remainder of the day studying the scroll. The *Dream Time* ceremony was simple and straight forward. Faith was the primary ingredient. And we were filled with that faith. We were young, strong, pure, and prepared for the walk that lay before us.

I arranged and neatly stored all our supplies. We decided to dress in our native skins. Mr. Natchi's deerskins fit me perfectly, and Nita's ceremonial skins added to her already striking appearance.

We agreed to wait for one another, in the event we awakened at separate times.

I started a small fire with the wood I had gathered early that morning. To my surprise the smoke gently flowed away from us and down the cavern's snowy river. We began the songs. We sang together softly. Nita served us the sacred drink prepared from my grandfather's medicine bag. We moved into our little sleeping room, Nita pulling the cover blanket over us. We continued to sing the song of New Beginnings. I took her hand.

The songs faded from our ears; our bodies felt light as if we were floating. My awareness faded into what most of us experience that single instant before deep sleep comes over us after a long hard day of labor.

Then Mr. and Mrs. Joshua Daklugie entered the *Dream Time.*

Chapter 22

I awakened slowly to a pitch-black world. Where was I? I clumsily rose from my sleeping position. My hand touched the warmth of a body lying next to me. The grogginess of deep sleep confused me for a moment. Where was the light switch? How could it be so dark? I felt the soft sand under the blanket I was now seated on. I heard the sound of water dripping…my senses gradually came to me…the cave!

I stood and reached for the flashlight. Locating it on the small shelf within our little sleeping room, I flipped it on. Nita lay on her side, her body turned away from me. I lowered myself to one knee and touched her shoulder. She was breathing deeply and completely unaware.

Nita was still in the *Dream Time*.

How long had I slept? As I became fully awake now, I felt as though I had slept a good long night. I was thirsty and hungry. I followed the sound of the dripping water to the little spring. Drinking deeply, I now became fully aware. I recalled the ceremony; I remembered the last day Nita and I had spent together. The *Dream Time* was powerful medicine. I paused a moment wondering… how far into the past had we traveled?

Returning to the little room, I again watched Nita sleeping. I had no way of knowing how long she would sleep. Looking around our little home in the cavern, I quickly became aware of my hunger and located the food stores. I would prepare a full meal for us later. For now, I slowly chewed a piece of the elk jerky Mr. Natchi had given us.

As I ate, I felt like praying. I was thankful. Thankful for the food, our health, the gift of my wonderful wife. I prayed for our future that seemed so uncertain right at this moment.

I knew, however, our steps were being directed. The Spirit was strong within both of us. I prayed that I might hear from the Spirit. As I prayed, I paused again, the words of my grandfather drifting through my mind. *Dak, when you pray you must listen. Learning to be still is the most important part of quiet time. Make certain you spend more time listening when you pray than you spend speaking. In doing so you will develop ears to hear and a mind to know.*

I stopped my endless requests, and perhaps for the first time in my prayer life…I just listened.

The voice was not audible. The communication did not come from my own inner dialogue. The instruction was clear and simple. It was more like a knowing, a truth was spoken over me. In the center of that truth was one wonderful, overriding, all-encompassing thought or emotion.

I was loved.

As a young man, I had sat through many Sunday services. I had heard of the love of God the Father. I had read the words many times. I thought I had understood the message of good news "that shall be for all people." However, until this moment I had not heard nor understood the truth that was whispered deep into my soul. I was indeed loved. That small light of love was kindled, a glow of light deep within that would burn forever.

I also knew or had heard that my life was set apart. My life had purpose. That purpose came to me in the quiet of my mind. I would forever be a protector of my people. I arose from my knees and moved toward the cavern exit. Just exactly how, and where, and in what way I would live out this role of protector wasn't clear. That did not matter for now. The principle my grandfather had taught me I knew well. I would never attempt to create some contrived or manufactured victory. Just as in the victory I had won over the cruel man… I knew the battles would come to me. It was a certainty. What mattered most, what I had heard communicated to me this awaking day was I was a Protector Warrior.

I began my walk out of the cave. I needed to see and discover exactly where we had exited the *Dream Time*.

I detected the light from the cavern entrance while still some two hundred yards from the exit. I turned off my flashlight and allowed a few moments for my eyesight to adjust. I made my way along, staying within arm's length of the cave wall to my left. I paused a moment at the deep drop, recalling Nita's thoughts. I would descend into the deep hole soon. I now believed she might be correct. It was in fact a perfect place to hide something of great value.

I smelled the smells of winter as I neared the exit. I recalled the cold I had felt the day we entered the *Dream Time*. Peering out I saw the ground was covered in ice and snow. I observed the pale blue sky from within the cave. I listened. I knew it would be important to keep our presence unknown to any who might be living in the area. Who was an enemy, or who was a friend, might be difficult to discern for a time. As I stood and listened for any sounds outside the cave, I heard nothing.

I stepped slowly, cautiously into the bright sunlight.

The trees were flocked in a layer of snow and ice. The air was very cold, probably near zero. The atmosphere was clear and had the feel of freshly washed air. I could taste the fresh clean air in the same way a person can taste and smell the clean air after a heavy rain. Everything seemed so polished and pure. I noticed the White Sands on the desert floor in the distance.

Then I notice the first of many telling signs.

There were no little towns on the desert floor, as Nita and I had observed the last time we had stood here together. There were no little dark lines representing the highways that connected those little towns.

There were no little dark spots that would represent farms or orchards. There appeared no evidence whatsoever of man inhabiting the high desert floor before me. The land in every direction I looked seemed open, pristine, and unoccupied.

We had evidently traveled far into the past.

I moved silently along the rock outcroppings. The layer of snow and ice made the walk nearly impossible. If I slipped or lost my footing, there would be nothing to stop the inevitable slide into the deep canyons. I knew instantly it would not be possible to navigate the ice-covered rocks or to descend the ancient trail. We were, in effect, snowed in.

I gathered as much firewood as I could carry. My mind considered what our plans for survival would be. We would need food soon. The jerky and canned goods would last only a few days. I spoke aloud my thoughts, "How am I supposed to hunt in these conditions?" My words swept into the silence of the wilderness and drifted away into the canyons below. The sound of my voice disturbed something. I heard movement below me on the rocky cliffs. Someone, or more likely something, had heard me. I decided to investigate further. I stacked the firewood near the entrance to the cave. Then I worked my way to the west, away from where I had spoken and heard the movement.

Cautiously I settled among the large boulders, finding a little nook where I was safe from slipping yet was afforded a view in the direction of the sounds I had heard. I was well trained by my grandfather in scanning terrain. I wasn't looking for anything in particular. Just movement. I saw a branch move. I noticed a piece of ice fall silently from a tree. I waited.

Patience was the greatest tool any hunter possessed. I knew this. I became a boulder on the side of the high mountains.

An hour passed. I was freezing.

I saw them coming all at once. I had been staring at an unusual group of rocks just over the cliff and slightly across the hill from the cave. When the first one moved, that motion gave way my vision to the rest of them. I could see them each individually now. There were dozens of them. Too many to count. All moving as one…in my direction. I dared not make a move. Why would I venture out of the cave without my weapons? It was a mistake that I hoped to never repeat.

None of them had seen me. I simply froze, with dozens of eyes scanning the mountainside in my direction I knew I would soon be spotted. I could not believe the speed at which they moved across the ice-covered cliffs and boulders.

Chapter 23

Nita awakened slowly. Her awareness dawning, her mind focused within a few moments of her eyes opening. She knew exactly where she was.

"Dak," she called out. There was no answer. Rising from the soft sand, she felt her way along the wall and located a flashlight. Switching it on she realized quickly...she was alone.

Observing her little room, she noticed Dak's hunting gear neatly stacked in one corner. Nita was puzzled. Maybe he is at the little spring. Moving down the cave a few yards toward the spring, she called to him.

"Dak, are you there?" There was no reply. She shined the beam in the direction of the little pool, nothing. Why would he venture out without his weapons? Then fear slowly sank into her heart and mind. She was alone.

Moving quickly, she gathered the weapons. She placed the bow and quiver across her shoulder as she had seen Dak do. She tucked the knife and war club into her belt. She moved cautiously toward the exit. She became aware, something in her spirit whispered to her. Dak needed her.

Nita knew she needed to move quietly. She did so. Nearing the exit, she could clearly see the light from outside. She turned off her light and silently covered the few yards toward the entrance. Pausing just one foot from the exit, she heard the sounds of movement below the cave exit. This was not the sound one person would make. She thought.

She removed the bow from her shoulders, nocked an arrow, and chanced a quick peek out of the entrance. She quickly drew back into hiding. She had never imagined there could be so many in one place. Thinking through what must be done, resolve settled within her heart and mind. Nita took a few deep breaths, drew the bow, and stepped into the open air outside the cavern.

When she was very young, her father had instructed her well with the bow and how to use it properly. She knew the most important thing was to choose a target, rather than just shooting wildly at the group. She focused, saw the kill zone. They were moving quickly; the shot would have to be timed. Just before she released the arrow, she caught the movement to her right. A hand waved. The strategy worked. The target froze, unsure. The arrow pierced deeply into the kill zone.

****

She saw me stand from the hidden position I had been in.

The entire hillside came alive with escaping mountain sheep.

The animal fell. Pawed at the ground for a moment, then breathed its last.

I stood in jubilation, raising my hands high. I let out a war cry that reverberated throughout the canyons below us. My wife, my woman, had just taken one of the most elusive animals that roamed the Rockies, a magnificent mountain sheep. The animal would feed us for weeks.

I moved to her; she was frozen in disbelief.

"Dak, I…I…what are you doing out here? It's freezing."

I just smiled and gave her a hug. "You are an amazing woman, Nita." I reached for the long knife in her belt. I felt her trembling as I touched her waist. She shouldered the bow and looked at me in anger.

"You will never leave me alone again without some explanation!"

She turned and walked toward the cave entrance. She gathered an armload of firewood and looked my direction with a fierceness in her eyes I had never seen and hoped to never see again. Nita then turned and entered the cavern, leaving me dumbfounded.

I knelt over the beautiful animal and whispered a prayer of gratefulness for its life. I knew its energy, its strength, its spirit would feed us for many days. I opened the animal's neck. The warm blood coated my hands and arms, warming me. As I opened the sheep's belly, the steam rose into the atmosphere, and I became aware of how cold I was. I worked quickly, skillfully removing the gut sack. I left it on the ground close to the cave entrance. It was a risk to do so…but we needed more meat.

As I worked, I thought of Nita. Her words were true. I had made several mistakes this morning. I must begin to think differently. It was no longer 2020.

I could not just go for a casual stroll down the mountains. Every move and decision I made must be centered around protection and survival.

From my view of the desert below and what I knew of history, we had traveled back in time at least one hundred and fifty years. Possibly farther than that even. The high desert below me would be revealing settlements by the mid-1850s or so. Nothing within my view indicated any development.

I lifted the body of the sheep. I would finish the process within the comfort of the cave. I would make sure we used every resource the animal could provide us. The meat for food, the skin would make the warmest possible cover. The bones could be sharpened into tools and utensils. The liver would make a delicious breakfast. I had much work to do, and I needed to apologize. I needed to reassure my wife that I would never put her in jeopardy again.

An hour later we sat together by the warm fire and ate our fill of sheep liver. The smell of meat roasting floated along the snowy river cave. We were warm and safe and full.

****

Late into the night, well past midnight, I awakened. Nita stirred and whispered, "Be careful."

"I will," I said softly. I gathered my weapons.

The walk out of the cave brought my senses alive. I heard every little sound as I made my way along: the squeaking of a bat, the rustling of a little mouse, the water dripping as it tumbled along its course. I knew each of the sounds and what they were. I covered the light with my hand, making it as dim as possible. The way along the snowy river and ledge trail was becoming familiar. I had the thought I should learn to make this walk in the dark without light. I counted my steps out. It would take some time to learn the exact steps, but it could be done.

Reaching the cave exit, I saw the half-moon shining on the snow and ice. I waited just a step inside the cave. The frozen world outside the cave looked like a post card or a brochure cover for a high mountain adventure. The trees had a coating of ice along the east side, the dark bark a picturesque contrast in the shining moonlight. The boulders were the same. The north and east facing surfaces were covered in snow and ice while the pale grey of the rock surface where the snow had melted shone in the bright moonlight. Moving to my left, I saw the desert floor to the west and south. White Sands gleamed in the distance. I waited.

It was amazing to me how the warmth of the cave kept me comfortable when just outside the entrance the air temperature had to be near zero. I smelled the putrid scent of the gut pile from the sheep; I had intentionally punctured it earlier that day. If I could smell it, the bears could also, from miles away. They would come for it soon. The bears always took care of this clean-up duty of creation.

I stood listening. After half an hour my eyes became heavy. I settled in a squatting position against the warmth of the cave wall. I drifted off to sleep.

****

The sound awakened me, then the smell. This was not the smell from the gut pile, but the smell of the bear. Without a doubt whenever a distinct and rancid smell was encountered in the mountains, the bears were near. I had learned of this from hunting with Grandfather. I heard the warning grunt from the bear. There was evidently more than one bear out there.

I moved to my right. I could see the creature sitting with its back toward me. The sound of the bear devouring the gut pile was…gruesome. I nocked an arrow.

The kill zone was hidden from me. I would wait. Another larger bear appeared, approaching from below. Growling, teeth bared, this new fierce one a challenge to the bear nearest me. The animal with its back to me rose onto its hind legs, standing like a man. It was taller than I, over six feet. I knew a fight was about to break out, which would help me. They would be distracted.

Without warning, the bear from below attacked. I saw a cloud of teeth, claws, and blood as the two erupted in the brutal confrontation. I stood a few feet away, trembling at the ferocity of the fight for dominance. One of these male bears would live. One would surely die. Either from the battle or my arrow. I waited to see which it would be.

The fight moved to and fro across the ice-covered rocks. The snow outside the cave turned crimson in the moonlight. The sounds, the grunts and growls the male bears made caused the hairs on my neck to stand. I thought perhaps I should back away. Would they detect my movement if I did so?

After several minutes, the smaller animal began to lose strength. The larger bear bit the shoulder of the slightly smaller bear, tearing open fur and flesh, then the swipe of claws, more powerful bites. The smaller male attempted to run. The larger male held onto a hind quarter. There was no escape. Pinned to the ground by the larger bear, the battle was ending. The larger bear covered the other male in its weight. There was little resistance now. I heard the air pushed out of the smaller bear's lungs. The larger bear hammered its weight on his adversary repeatedly. Then there was no movement.

The large bear limped back to the meal. The victorious bear was also injured, yet it devoured the remains of the gut pile in seconds. It then turned toward the cavern entrance. It tested the air with its great nose. Had the bear winded me? My heart began to beat through my chest as the bear growled and moved toward me, then the enormous bear stood on its hind legs.

The arrow pierced perfectly into its chest, traveling deeply into the animal's heart. It fell within three feet of the cave entrance.

Tears ran down my face. I had no words for what I had just witnessed. I could scarcely breath. I was grateful, and in awe of the Creator, and His Creation.

Later that night we dined on the delicacy of roasted bear meat. The taste was unusual, but delicious. The aroma of the sizzling meat wafted throughout the cave from our little make-do kitchen. The nutritious meat was filled with much needed fat. Again, during the meal, I fought back tears as I thought of the battle, the raw power, the brutal fight of the bears. Deep in my soul I felt the strength and spirit of the bear enter my body as I consumed the nutritious meat. I saw that strength in Nita's eyes also. We were becoming wild, natural, and filled with confidence and resolve.

Nita and I would be warmed by the hides of these magnificent animals for years to come.

Chapter 24

We moved silently down the ancient trail. After seven days, the ice and snow had finally given way to a warm west wind. I had discovered a way to measure the sun's height above the horizon thereby determining the season of the year. The scroll contained the simple method. I had positioned the arrow vertically on a flat rock. Over the last seven days I had daily marked the length of the shadow when the sun was in the same alignment over a great tree. Clearly, the shadow the arrow cast was shortening. The sun's angle was rising higher overhead each day. The spring equinox, March 21, had already occurred. We were moving toward summer. Although, winter had held its grip in the high mountains for days.

The warm weather was a delight. However, we moved with caution. It was such a relief to be out in the sunshine after seven days in the cave. We had made ourselves busy with the processing of the bear meat and the tanning of the hides. We had set aside an enormous amount of sun-dried meat. Along the trail we followed there was plentiful game, including deer, elk, and turkey. Also, on the small lakes we saw ducks, and even mountain grouse in the brush, while the small ponds were teaming with trout. Food would not be a survival issue for now.

We both wondered when and where and who we might encounter. We had used our time wisely, practicing our native language. While not exactly proficient, we could both communicate basics and identify many common items from the scroll vocabulary.

Would our people be in the area? The Apache tended to wander and cover an immense geographical area. Although these high mountains were our home in the time that we had entered our *Dream Time*, this was not a place the

Apache would linger for long. The Reservation had been established here in the south-central Rocky Mountains in the late 1800s, well before New Mexico had attained statehood. We, the Mescalero, were located here however, not because this was the exact place of our homeland, but rather due to the fact that this was an isolated place, far away from the land in which the white man showed interest.

Nita and I had discussed at length what year we might have awakened. From what we could recall of the settling of the high desert that we observed each morning, we both were guessing the early 1800s to possibly 1850. We really had no way of knowing without exploring our surroundings further.

It had taken us over two hours to reach what was formerly the beginning of the ancient trail. We arrived at what we thought was the site of our high school building, or where it would be constructed in the future. There was nothing there, a small opening in the forest with a somewhat level field, in the center of which was a large shallow pond. The trail itself became difficult to pick out within the unspoiled landscape we were moving through. I was confident this was where we had attended classes, played basketball, and lived in a different time.

I turned to Nita. "This is it, isn't it?" I asked.

"Yes, Dak. The school was right here, or maybe more in the center of the lake."

We stared at one another, lost in wonder. Nothing of the life we lived just one week ago remained. It was sobering. The reality of being so isolated, so alone struck us both.

"Let's go a little farther," I said questioningly to Nita. She nodded. We traveled now, hand in hand. It was one mile to the site of her former home. The way previously was a two-lane paved highway. I knew the correct direction and started us out on the proper line. I counted my paces and knew when we were probably within one-hundred yards of where her former home was located. Again, there was nothing, just pristine forest.

We stopped in a small glade, the birds sang sweetly, the wind whispered in the treetops. A large herd of deer casually grazed along the edge of the glade. They were unafraid. I knew this meant they had not been hunted in a very long time.

Nita began to cry. I located a fallen tree, and we sat on the edge of the glade hand in hand.

"*Are you alright, my wife?*" I spoke in our native tongue. I looked deeply into her eyes, inquiring.

"*Yes, Dak.*" A resolve showed in her look. "*I know I will see them again.*"

I wasn't sure if she meant in a few years, or in a few days, or in eternity? I thought it best not to ask for now.

It was evident to us both the land we walked upon, this land we lived upon in our previous life, was totally and completely void of any other human beings. We were alone.

Part 2

Chapter 25

Five Years Later

We moved silently as one, gliding along the bank of the shining river. The buffalo herd to our south moved also, a massive dark shadow of life, ever in motion. The sky was a light blue; the wind moved in gentle puffs across the water. Nita was glowing, the swell of her belly growing daily. I landed the hand-carved canoe on the east bank of the river and tied it among the reeds.

We had spied the camp from a distance the day before. Tepees, hundreds of them, were set up in rows below the caprock. These were the first human beings we had seen in five seasons. We waited. I knew we had been seen. We would wait for them to come to us. Hopefully, a friendly delegation would greet us. We desperately needed their help.

We moved up the bank of the little river and seated ourselves under the shade of a large oak tree. There was an apparent commotion within the camp. Seven riders departed the center of the camp and started in our direction.

As the group approached, I noticed the ponies had no war paint, nor did the rider's faces. I let out the deep breath I had been holding. Finally, we had found our friends, our people.

The leader dismounted and walked toward us. He was a handsome man. His breastplate and skins were ornately decorated. His hair was long and flowing. He carried a medicine bag across his chest. There was something about the man that was imposing, or beautiful. I still do not have the words to describe our first meeting with Tosahwi (White Knife). The kindness in his eyes as he peered into mine relieved all my fearful thoughts.

"*Welcome,*" he said in Apache. But I reasoned from his dress and his mount that he was not from our tribe.

We bowed our heads in respect. "*Thank you, my friend. I am Joshua Daklugie; this is my wife, Kwanita.*" I spoke again in my native tongue. From the looks on the faces of the remainder of the greeting party, they had not understood a word I had spoken.

"*Come, Joshua, come, Kwanita, you will be a guest in my lodge this day.*" His intense eye contact was sincere and heartfelt yet questioning as he observed Nita struggling.

"*I know you have traveled far, let us celebrate together your homecoming.*"

We looked at one another, not understanding. Perhaps it was the fact that he was not speaking in his native tongue? How could he know of our story? What might he mean by using this word *homecoming*?

We had both learned much in the five years we had spent living on the high mountains. The most significant for me was undoubtedly how to remain calm in the face of danger or unexpected circumstances, or maybe patience is what I had learned.

I settled myself inwardly, understanding that the circumstances we were about to encounter would soon reveal the truth of our situation. With a calm look toward Nita, we began the short walk to the camp. I saw in her eyes what I had seen many times. Reassurance shone on her face in the silent communication that had taken place between us.

Tosahwi led us through the camp directly to his lodge. Many people had gathered and had formed a greeting line of sorts. As we entered the camp, *The People* greeted us with friendly smiles. We both felt like royal guests as we moved along the column of greeters.

I cannot explain how our hearts swelled at the impromptu welcoming we received. After having no encounter with other human beings for such a long time, we simply felt loved. Many reached out and touched us or patted us on the back. Many blessed us in the Apache tongue, and another native language we did not understand. Even so, I saw the tears in my woman's eyes as we entered the center of the camp. Somehow it seemed they had been awaiting our arrival.

Tosahwi motioned for us to enter his lodge. We did so. A warm fire in the center of the lodge greeted us. Seated around the fire were notably the Elders of the tribe and their wives.

Tosahwi motioned for us to sit. We did so, taking our place within the circle. Introductions were in order. Tosahwi introduced his wife first, Kele

(Sparrow). She patted the buffalo robe next to her, motioning for Nita to come and sit.

I introduced Nita and myself to the group. I spoke nothing further than our names. The introduction was met with polite nods all around the circle.

Next, Palanquito was introduced along with his wife. I remembered the name from my history class. He was a Chief of our people. I still could not determine the year in which we were living. One thing was obvious, this was an unusual setting. Chief Palanquito stood and spoke directly to us in Apache.

"*Welcome. It is good that you are here this day. Our people have joined forces; it is an uncommon thing. However, former enemies many times have become friends when there is another stronger enemy that threatens them both. Daklugie, this is happening. War is coming, and we cannot face the numbers of this enemy alone. The Apache and the Comanche will rise as one people. Our lives and the lives of our wives and children are in the balance.*"

He sat again after his short summation of the present situation.

"*Let us smoke the pipe and await the words of Daklugie,*" Tosahwi said.

I looked across the circle to Nita. This time it was she who revealed the reassuring look. I was glad for the pause as the pipe was passed around the circle. I gathered my thoughts. The minutes floated by. There was no rush for my response. The tobacco was strong and pungent. I took in a small puff from the pipe and instantly began to cough. The sound of laughter filled the lodge at my inability to smoke. I laughed along with them, acting out a dizzying motion with my head. The laughter faded. I hoped my Apache would be sufficient to ask my questions.

"*I have only two questions before I reply,*" I said. "*The first is, what year is it now in which the whites say we are we walking? The second is, who is this enemy that is to come?*"

There was a stunned silence within the lodge at my inquiry. At least from the reaction, I knew they had understood.

Tosahwi replied, "*The whites say this year that we are walking is 1808. The enemy comes from the south; some say they come from across the great water. They attempt to hold lands that do not belong to them. It is those who wear the shiny helmets and have the big gun. These are a ruthless people. They have captured and tortured our people in the past. We must not allow this to happen again.*"

I knew he was speaking of the Spaniards.

Chapter 26

When is the child due?" Kele, the wife of Tosahwi, asked. With a look of wisdom, she smiled at Nita.

"*In only two moons the baby will surely arrive,*" Nita replied.

"*And you have had much trouble I can see.*"

Nita nodded and held her abdomen.

"*Come with me now, Nita. We will meet with the women. There is medicine for you. I can see you need food and rest.*" Rising, the two departed for what I hoped was sound motherly advise. Her pregnancy was the primary reason we had approached the camp. Nita was not well. The pregnancy had been difficult. Just last night she had begun to bleed again. I was terrified for her and the baby more than I was concerned about the coming enemy.

The men continued to pass the pipe around the circle. There was no rush to our conversation. I was reminded again of my grandfather's words.

Dak, even a fool seems wise, if he holds his tongue. He is considered discerning in his silence.

I searched my mind for an event in history. I did not know of any battles in this time frame. I did know of the torture and mistreatment the Spaniards had dispensed upon the entire Native American population as they conquered and held what had been ours for centuries. Perhaps this was the time in which Spain was losing its grip on the plan of the Conquistadors.

That plan had been simple, to conquer the world.

I knew this much, the world was a big place, and this part of it belonged to Native Americans, not the army from across the sea.

The lodge became quiet. Eyes and ears were focused on me and what information I might have.

"*Surely,* The People *will have the advantage over this enemy,*" I said. "*Fighting together, as one people, fighting for our homes and family we will indeed have an advantage. From what I know of wars, those who fight for their homeland and those they love, even when outnumbered, often are victorious. Our enemy does not have this fight in their hearts. Their homes and families are far from here, across the ocean. They will not be willing to do what we will be willing to do.*"

A silence fell within the lodge as what I had said was considered.

"*The words Daklugie has spoken are true,*" Tosahwi replied.

Those gathered around the fire nodded and grunted in approval. For now, my words were an encouragement. There was much I did not know; however, I would learn quickly. An idea was already beginning to form in my mind. Perhaps if I were to meet with the leaders of the Spaniards…

****

That night we dined on buffalo hump and buffalo tongue. These delicacies were reserved for the most important celebrations. The meat was roasted and flavored with wild onion, garlic, and watercress. I loved the taste of the meal. Our guests had no way of knowing how hungry we were, at least that is what I thought at the time.

In hindsight, I am certain Tosahwi knew we were starving. The winter had been brutal, the game scarce. We had wandered far from the warmth of the cave on the high mountains.

There was no doubt in my mind that finally locating this large group of our people was at the direction and blessing of the Spirit. We would have become very weak within a few more days. I was consumed with gratefulness; my wife and unborn child might now survive.

I made sure after the feast they were both warm and safe within Tosahwi's lodge. When Nita was sleeping soundly, I quietly exited the lodge and made my way across the open prairie. Sounds of the night came alive. The night birds called to one another in the distance. I heard the frogs along the riverbank. Little light bugs illuminated the buffalo grass within each of my footsteps. I arrived, standing along the edge of the waters that had carried us to this place. Awareness enveloped my mind. Along the banks of the Pecos River, in the year 1808, I knelt and prayed.

The songs came from a place in my heart I had never known. I sang the song of gratefulness. I sang the song of healing over my beautiful wife. I sang the song of celebration, thinking of my child. I cried out to my God, with all that was within me.

A vision appeared within my mind and heart. I saw the future. Perhaps what I had seen in my vision would not come to be. Or perhaps God the Father might possibly be persuaded.

I wept and sang and pleaded.

Then as instructed by my grandfather, I waited in silence.

His voice came to me as a gentle whisper.

Chapter 27

Nita improved rapidly with the care of Kele and the other women of the tribes. Those experienced in these matters made certain she rested and ate the correct food. She instantly put on a few pounds, yet I saw in the eyes of the women tending her, there was great concern. I was told the bleeding had stopped, the best thing we could hope for, they said.

Nita took to the companionship, their concern, and attention in graceful fashion. I observed a fullness in her eyes I had not seen in many years.

She was no longer lonely.

I was included in the council meeting that occurred daily. Tosahwi had welcomed us into his family from the moment we arrived. I trusted him completely. On the third day after our arrival there was to be no council. Tosahwi had asked if we could ride out from the camp together. He chose a sturdy mare for my mount. We rode away from the camp in a slow gallop. The high mountains gleamed in the distance over one hundred miles away. Even from this distance, I thought I could make out the ridge that held our secret home.

We slowed our mounts to a walk. Tosahwi wanted to talk.

"What can you tell me of the Dream Time, *Dak?"*

****

I spent the entire day with Tosahwi. I explained all I could concerning the *Dream Time* although I did not reveal the existence of the scroll that day. A mutual trust and friendship was forming but I intentionally held back, and I am convinced, he knew it.

I needed to understand further.

I suppose I had more questions than he did. Our language skills prevented a complete understanding of one another. He was fluent in Apache and Comanche; I was fluent in English and struggled with Apache. Although using the language daily helped immensely.

We stopped on the edge of the river and dismounted. Allowing our horses a long drink, we hobbled them in the deep green grass along the riverbank.

"*You know and can speak the words of the white man?*" he asked.

I answered in English. "Yes, I know the words completely. It is the language we were taught from childhood. We grew up in the white man's world." Then I nodded.

He looked at me in wonder.

"*This is the greatest tool for our people to possess. Dak, many of the struggles we have faced have been due to misunderstanding. It has been many times impossible for* The People *to communicate simple terms to the whites. These misunderstandings have led to many deaths.*"

I did not reply. I was learning, considering, thinking back on our history. I was also thinking about the future and how to possibly prevent those miscommunications.

"*Dak, in what year did you and Kwanita enter your* Dream Time?"

"*The year was 2020.*"

We sat in silence for a moment. The questions were many, but we both seemed to take the time to sort out those that were most important.

"So, The People *survived this war that is coming? The people are surviving and living in 2020?*"

How to answer this simple, sincere question?

Although it was not a simple question. Tosahwi was asking if his people, our people would survive. What he must have known deep in his soul would be the relentless attempt of the whites to remove our people completely from the earth.

I saw the sincerity in his eyes and the longing to understand. This man was a servant leader also.

I knew much of the history of the Native American people of North America. The struggles that lay ahead for each person, every father and mother, every child within our camp. The difficulties that lay ahead for my people, the Apache, and the Comanche would be a grueling journey filled with heartache and loss. I thought of the trail filled with tears. I thought of Wounded Knee. Of the treaties that would be made and broken, of the poverty, and brokenness within my own reservation and many others across the United States. I thought of the many, many broken promises. But I also considered the strong will within our people, the spirit of our people.

Tosahwi's question resonated within my mind. I intentionally sat in silence for a few more moments.

"*Yes, Tosahwi, we survived. The People are overcomers. The People have a spirit within them to not only survive, but to live, and live well. Our people are blessed and healthy and thriving in the year 2020.*"

Just speaking those words that day as I sat with my new friend along the banks of the river, awakened something within my own heart. I had spent so much of the last five years just trying to survive. I had forgotten my gifting and purpose.

I was an Apache Warrior. I was set apart as a protector and defender. With all that was within me, I determined again that day I would live up to my calling.

Tosahwi took in a deep breath. A calm that was always present about him seemed to deepen at my words.

"*Come, let us see now about Kwanita,*" he said.

As we rode along in silence, I considered our immediate problem, this threat that was surely coming. I thought about what it was the Spaniards valued most.

I had something with which I could negotiate, and I had enough to turn back an army from across the sea.

Chapter 28

Four years Earlier

After a year of living in the cave, we had learned and discovered much. Game had been plentiful; our food stores were full; we had more clothing than needed. We had no encounters with other Native Americans. After a full year upon the high mountains, we were still alone.

We had begun exploring the cavern system using the drawings in the scroll. One of the greatest pleasures was the hot spring we had found just another few hundred yards into the cave from our sleeping room. I had fashioned a little dam and shallowed out a basin beneath the spring. The water was now about four feet deep and the pool almost twenty feet in length. The temperature of the water was near one hundred degrees or more. We ventured to the hot spring at the end of each day. What a treasure it was, especially in winter, to just soak in the mineral rich warm water. This hot spring and pool were more valuable in many ways than the other treasure I had found.

I started early on a summer morning. The pit at the entrance to our cavern, I had discovered, was impossible to climb or descend into. Shear rock walls surrounded the deep hole. I had attempted several times to start down from several angles; there was simply no way to descend.

Studying the scroll, it indicated several caverns that split off in different directions from the main cavern. Each was marked with a dead end. After days of exploring, I had identified each split on the map and correlated the map with what I found within the actual cave. One of the most incredible discoveries, beyond where the scroll map ended, was the secret exit. As the crow flies it had to be twenty miles or more to the newly discovered exit. It had taken us two days to navigate our way. Though once backtracked the way was simple. We discovered if we followed the snowy river from our entrance on the high mountains, the river of calcite ended only one hundred yards from an exit. Climbing steeply up a short path we crawled out after two days in the immense cavern into the bright sunshine along the banks of what had to be the Bonita River. This was near where the fort would be built in the future. The existence of the secret escape route would allow us to move a great distance undetected if that ever became a necessity.

I was amazed as we rested in the shade of the cottonwoods along the bank of the Bonita River. I could make out the ridge along the high mountains where our entrance was located, over twenty miles away.

The scroll was incredibly accurate, but for this detail and one other error, there was a tunnel we discovered that was not on the scroll. It was well into the cave about a mile from the entrance. It was small, only two or three feet wide, and only four feet or so in height. This is where I stood this summer morning, at the entrance to the unmarked tunnel.

I had my flashlight, a canteen of water, and extra batteries.

"Dak, please be careful," Nita said.

"I will. Wait thirty minutes, then move to the deep pit near the entrance. If I am correct, you might hear me or even be able to see me with my light shining up from the bottom. If I'm wrong, I should be back within the hour.

I realize now Nita would never have allowed me to explore this tunnel but for her very first observation of the deep pit and her casual comment about it being a good hiding place. We were both just too curious to leave this possibility unexplored.

I moved along cautiously; the way was difficult at first. I could tell I was descending. But after several tight turns and course reversals, it became impossible for me to know which direction I was moving. Within fifteen minutes or so the cavern suddenly opened before me. Vast ceilings hung thick with stalactites. Live water flowed from several different sources. The bats were suspended in thick groups, hanging from the ceiling. I followed what was a distinct trail. It was evident this path had been traveled many times.

I covered another few hundred yards continually descending, then abruptly the trail came to a dead end. I scanned the steep wall before me with the flashlight. It was smooth and tall; my light could not penetrate the distance above me. I could see nothing of the cavern ceiling above. Then I heard Nita's voice.

"Dak, I can see your light!"

"Wow! I am at the bottom, Nita. I'll turn my light off now. Shine your light toward my voice."

As I extinguished my flashlight, I clearly saw her flashlight beam from above. It had to be two hundred feet or more to the floor where I was standing.

"I can see your light, Nita!" I yelled from the bottom of the dark pit.

"You don't have to yell, I can here you perfectly."

It sounded as if she were right next to me.

"What did you find, Dak?"

"Nothing yet. I'm just starting to look around. Give me a few minutes."

I had not scanned the bottom of this room in any direction. I had focused only on the shear dead end wall in front of me. I switched my flashlight on and scanned in a circle three hundred and sixty degrees. My stomach emptied instantly.

Skeletons surrounded me. The bones lay scattered about the bedrock floor of the cavern.

Each set of bones had their hands tied behind their backs. Chains shackled the skeletons' ankles. The chains were fitted into stakes that had been driven into the bedrock.

On closer examination, it was obvious to me these people had been imprisoned, placed in chains, and intentionally left here to die.

My original thoughts about this dark hole that I had imagined from my first visit to the cave when I was a small boy, were true. Deep in my soul I had always known there was something awful at the bottom of the deep pit.

Chapter 29

Dak, are you alright?" Nita's voice came to me from two hundred feet above. Again, it sounded as if she were right next to me.

"Not exactly," I whispered as I backed away from the circle of death. "Nita, there are…skeletons…everywhere.

"Come back up; you don't need to see that. I'm going back to the unmarked tunnel. I'll meet you there."

"Wait, Nita," I replied, gathering myself. I took a few deep breaths. "I'm going to take a look around. I'm okay now." I stepped farther away from the bones of the unfortunate souls whose lives had ended in this dark dungeon.

Turning to my right, I saw nothing but shear rock cliffs rising vertically into the darkness. I directed my flashlight slowly in a complete circle, turning a full three hundred and sixty degrees. The opening and trail that had led me to this place appeared at the one hundred eighty-degree mark in my slow turn. I became a little more oriented, at least I knew how to get out.

Why? Why had they been left here? Who would do such a thing? The questions floated through my mind as I tried to comprehend what was before me. I knew the answer was contained within this terrible place.

I began a slow walk around the bottom of the deep pit. Using my flashlight, I carefully examined the surface of the smooth walls. There was nothing.

Was this just a place of torment?

Again, I started around the perimeter of the rock face, moving even slower this time around. It was, at first glance, just a small hand-sized stone protruding slightly from the surface of the wall.

But it was out of place.

"Dak, are you okay?" Nita asked from above.

"Yes," I answered. "I think I found something."

"Dak, talk to me; this is nerve racking. Just talk while you look."

"Okay. I've circled the room two times now. A kind of small stone is sticking out of the smooth rock. It's just out of place. I'm going to push on it or pull it out, or something. It fits in my hand like a handle. I'm pushing it in. Nita, it disappeared into the wall!"

I felt the floor under me move, I heard a loud scraping sound as the wall to my right opened about a foot.

"Dak!" Nita called to me from above. "Dak!"

I couldn't hear her voice as I had stepped inside the entry as the rock wall promptly closed behind me. I panicked as the wall closed and called out, "Nita!" Had she heard me? Pitch black enveloped me as the batteries in my flashlight died.

I was trapped.

Surely, she would come for me. Had she heard my call? Had she heard my description about the protruding handle-shaped rock?

****

I felt for the spare batteries at the bottom of my day pack. Locating them, I removed them from the pack. The pitch black that enveloped me made the simple task of changing batteries extremely difficult. Carefully I opened the front of the flashlight and removed the batteries. I slid the new batteries into what I thought was the correct position. Gently, I placed the used batteries back into my pack. I started to screw the cover back on the front of the flashlight. Gingerly holding the lens, reflector backing, the cap, and the little bulb in place, I twisted the cover onto the body of the flashlight. I couldn't get the threads to start in alignment. I took a deep breath and tried again. Holding all the little pieces with my left hand, I rotated the base of the flashlight with my right hand. It was just so dark. My eyes were wide open. I strained to see to no avail. I tried desperately to start the threads evenly. It all slipped. I felt the glass lens fall from my hands. In slow motion horror, the little bulb bounced across my hand as I grasped wildly for it. I heard the lens and the bulb bounce across the rock floor at my feet.

I lowered my body slowly to my knees. I moved my hands across the rock floor. How far could they have bounced? I could not locate any of the pieces. I was in trouble again. I began to pray.

****

Time is impossible to comprehend in complete darkness. I know most human beings have never experienced complete darkness. A dark room maybe, or a dark theater. But total utter darkness confuses the mind, distorts time, sets a person's thoughts awry. It could have been two days or ten minutes. I don't know how long I stood in the darkness. I felt for the poor souls just beyond the closed door. I waited…for hours.

Then I heard the scrapping sound again. The rock door opened behind me. The cool air rushed in. Nita called to me.

"Dak?"

"I'm here, Nita. Don't come in! I'm not sure how the rock wall opens from the inside."

"Thank God you're okay," she said.

"I'm coming out."

I moved into the bottom of the deep pit. We embraced. I don't know if I ever experienced relief on the level I felt that day. The skeletons were nothing to me now.

"How long was I in there?"

"Maybe thirty minutes at most. The trail through the unmarked tunnel was easy to follow. I ran most of the way."

I just stood there in wonder. If she had said twenty-four hours, or three days, I would not have questioned her.

"What is this place, Dak?" Nita asked.

"I don't know. My light went out. I couldn't replace the batteries. I dropped the entire mess in the other room. I never saw anything of what is in there."

"Let's go, my love. It doesn't matter. Let's just go home," Nita said.

I paused. "This is our home, Nita." The words left my mouth in stark realization: we live in a cave, I thought to myself.

"You're not going back in there," Nita said rather firmly.

"Nita, you can open the door for me. We need the flashlight. The pieces have to be right there on the floor."

"You look from out here. Let's open the door. I'll shine my light in. If you can see the parts and reach them from here, then okay."

Nita pushed the little rock handle and held it in. I shined the light onto the rock floor just inside the door. There in a little crack were all the pieces of my flashlight. The lens, reflector, bulb, and cover within a few inches of one another. I reached for them, easily lifting each precious piece from the rocks. I was relieved none were broken. I quickly assembled the flashlight and tested it. It came on in an instant. I took a deep breath, relieved we had not lost the valuable tool. Then we both simultaneously directed our flashlight beams into the little hidden room.

Against the rear wall of the hidden room were neatly stacked rows of some kind of bricks or blocks. The bricks were dark in color. "Nita, hold the rock in for a moment." She answered me with a cautious look and a nod. I took a few steps toward the rows of bricks, reached out my hand, and lifted one of them. It was extremely heavy, maybe forty pounds or so. The brick was covered in soot and sand. I quickly returned to where Nita was standing in the open doorway.

"What is it, Dak?" she asked.

"I'm not sure." Nita held her light on the brick as I removed my long knife from its sheath. Using the knife, I scraped gently along the surface of the brick, and then wiped the surface clean using the sleeve of my skins. The sight before us literally took our breath away. The shiny reflection of the pure gold surface reflected in the beam of Nita's flashlight.

It took a moment for the realization to sink in, of what I was holding in my hands. Again, we both directed our flashlight beams onto the neatly stacked rows of what we now knew were solid gold bars. We stood in awe and wonder at the number of them. Hundreds of gold bars were stacked neatly in rows along the wall of the hidden room.

Chapter 30

loaded the bar into my day pack. I guessed again that it weighed around forty pounds, possibly more. It was all I could carry. The little book interested me more than the gold. I found it along the back of a row of bars that had been stacked to a height of about four feet.

The writing in the book was in a graceful hand, elegantly written in what appeared to be formal Spanish. The language was nothing like the Spanish slang we had grown up hearing in the southwestern United States. Rather, this language appeared to be quite proper and formal—the dialect that would have been spoken by Spaniards, more specifically, early Spanish explorers. The book was bound in leather and similar to my grandfather's scroll. Written on the thin leather pages were exact details, recorded in neat columns. The total amount of gold stored here and the dates of delivery had been inventoried precisely. The years I recognized easily. This gold had been moved here in the early seventeenth century. Entries ended in the dates 1608, 1609, 1610.

In the rear of the book was a map. The map described in complete detail the precise directions to and location of another hidden cave. The location evidently was the former hiding place of the treasure and gold. I knew of the story of this hidden treasure. My grandfather had mentioned the existence of the legend many times. The Apache Tribal Council was also aware of this treasure and had placed a legal claim on it in the late 1900s.

Victorio Peak was clearly marked on the map. Detailed drawings of the mine and tunnels within Victorio Peak appeared on the pages before me.

This treasure had evidently been moved from there to here. Probably by the poor souls in the bottom of the pit. Whoever had moved the gold here wanted no survivors, no witnesses who might whisper the information of this hidden location.

Nita held the door as I explored for a few minutes the small room. There was more, heavy crates filled with coins and jewels. It was an unbelievable find.

"This is amazing, Nita! We were both correct about the deep pit. I sensed a place of death and disaster. Your thought of this being an excellent place to hide a treasure…we were both correct."

"We have no use for this, Dak."

"I know. It's just a bunch of shiny metal. Perhaps in the future it may prove to be useful to us. For now, being the wealthiest couple in New Mexico or possibly the entire United States means nothing. That gold won't feed us today, or keep us warm, or help us find our people."

"Let's go, Dak. Are you sure you want to take that with you?" she asked, indicating the one bar I had in my pack.

"It's just a story without some evidence."

"I understand," Nita said.

I took the lead as we turned and followed the trail. As we walked along, I thought of the men in the bottom of the deep pit. They had labored and struggled under slave conditions; I was certain they were Native Americans who had been taken captive. Then they had been left to die, their remains overseeing what many valued above all else in this life.

"Dak, stop," Nita said.

"What is it?" I asked.

"Just listen."

I stood in the silence, straining to hear. The cave was completely silent. We stood a moment hand in hand in the quiet.

My voice echoed as it broke the silence. "Nita, this treasure means nothing to me."

"I understand, Dak, I feel the same. But it has been revealed to us for a reason. One day it may become useful to us. For now, this secret you and I will keep forever."

She would not share with me until years later the voices she had heard that day. They sang the songs of death. Whispering through the centuries their death song to any who might have ears to hear.

Chapter 31

Tosahwi and I rode along in silence, making our way back to the Camp at an unhurried pace.

"*We will send more scouts toward the south tomorrow,*" he said.

"*What is the report from the men sent previously?*" I asked.

"*The men have not determined the location of the army from across the sea. However, the Mexicans tell us they have arrived, and are moving north. They say they will make war on the Mexican capital soon. Dak, these men are many. They move like locusts. They are brutal in their dealings with all people...as you know, they devour all that are in their path.*"

Concern filled Tosahwi's eyes. This man was a true leader and concerned with the safety and survival of his people above all. He reminded me very much of Nita's father.

We paused along the western bank of the river, the Camp visible to us in the distance, the spring sun warming us. I knew I must share with this great man, what I understood of my purpose, my reason for entering the *Dream Time*.

"*Tosahwi, Nita has had a vision.*" His eyes brightened at my words. "*This is the reason we have come to this time. I do not understand all that is to unfold. I know her gifting is true. Kwanita is from the Comanche people.*" Realization and understanding showed on his face.

"*Her mother was born within the Comanche Nation. In the future, The People are from a place called Oklahoma. She is half Comanche and half Apache. Her father is leader of our People in the future.*

"*Kwanita's mother was gifted with visions. It is why we were allowed to come to this time. Her mother understood,"* I said.

Tosahwi listened intently. His own understanding becoming evident.

"I understand, Dak. It has been spoken of for many, many seasons. The tale of the young man and his woman bringing life-saving wisdom to our people. I think you are this man, Dak. You will be a blessing to all The People."

This was becoming a heavy weight to carry. So many people prophesying about my life. Sometimes I felt like I was just a boy. Why would I be chosen for anything, let alone this great deliverer that so many had put their hope in? What could I possibly accomplish in the face of the certain struggle that was to come?

Tosahwi sensed the doubt in my spirit. *"Daklugie, you must never doubt the power of the Great Spirit working within your life."*

I looked directly into his eyes and saw the wisdom I had seen on so many occasions…in a different time. I saw the wisdom of my grandfather; I was learning, remembering. That day, I forever put doubt behind me. I would never again listen to the voices of weakness and doubt that many choose to focus on. Those voices spoke lies.

The great men who had surrounded me and taught me and believed in me, including this man, Tosahwi, those were the voices I would listen to and believe. I knew to believe the voice that had whispered to me just a few days ago along the banks of this river in my quiet time, even though I wanted very much to change what I had heard.

What I had heard was truth…

Chapter 32

The scouts departed the following morning. They moved steadily for a full hour before disappearing over the horizon toward the south. They would not return for at least two full moons. News and information traveled slowly in the year 1808...but it did travel. The value of knowing your enemy's whereabouts was immeasurable. The council would meet today. Many decisions faced the group. Today, the questions before the leaders: should the people stay in this location? Should we disperse? Where would we rendezvous if we did separate?

These questions were at the forefront of every discussion for days. I listened quietly to those holding the places of honor. However, I was learning, learning the customs and culture of both tribes. Showing respect in my silence, I gained even greater status by saying nothing. There was no consensus. After seven days of deliberations, the council determined to stay in our location below the caprock. The truth was, we needed more information; it was also true that life was easy here. Fresh water filled the river to overflowing from the springtime snow melt. The buffalo herd was never far away. Antelope, deer, rabbit, even grouse and quail were plentiful in this place. Feeding one thousand Warriors, along with the women and children, might be difficult in another place. We would await the return of the scouts here below the caprock.

I had never made friends easily. In school I was quiet and withdrawn. I considered Tosahwi my friend, although he was more a teacher or even a father figure to me. Friendship was much the same here as in my high school experience...with one exception.

Sumu Puku (One Horse) was my friend. Sometimes in life it seemed to me on very rare circumstances, when two people meet, there is a special connection. A bonding that cannot be forced or concocted. I had experienced this in my life only once…with Kwanita. My friendship with One Horse was the same. We were like brothers from the first day we met.

I was attempting to hunt antelope, a first for me as the animals did not live in the high mountains. However, here on the prairie they were plentiful. I noticed the meat was Kwanita's favorite. Indeed, the food from the animal's body was pure, tender, and delicious. Nita needed the nourishment. It was my duty to provide for her even while she was in the care of the women. She had asked. I would provide. I was a Warrior.

The hunt was not so easy. The animals moved at an incredible speed when spooked. I so far had only achieved the skill of spooking them and watching them run over the low hills and out of sight. For three days I had returned to the camp empty-handed. Tosahwi remained silent, although I detected a wry smile on his face each evening as he observed my empty-handed return from the prairie. The morning of the fourth day I set out on foot again, determined. In truth, I loved the solitude of the hunt on the prairie. I could still run. I loved to run.

Once over the first rise and out of sight of the camp, I began to run. I traveled south this day. The sun was just beginning to peek over the caprock to my left. The snow-covered high mountains, over one hundred miles away to my right, gleamed in the morning sun. I felt the light wind softly on my face and arms that my movement generated. That wind contained the smell of sage in bloom and occasionally the scent of cool moisture from the river. Quail scattered at the light sound of my footsteps, as did many cottontail rabbits. I spotted the red tail hawk and more than one eagle as I moved along swiftly. Gaining momentum, I became one with the prairie. A man, a Warrior, natural, unafraid…the peace of running indwelt my soul.

I ran for a full hour. I was at least ten miles or more from the camp. I spotted the antelope while slowing to an easy jog. Stopping, I quickly recovered my wind. The animals were moving away from the river after their morning watering. I would not fail this day. I became one with the prairie. I moved away from the herd toward the east. The light wind now coming from the west would not give me away. My plan was to move well to the east to intercept the herd. I would allow them to move toward me rather than following them.

I quickly covered two miles. Finding a low rise of land, I concealed myself in the sparse brush. I could move only a few inches and peer over the little mound. The antelope herd continued to slowly move my direction. Today this plan would work; I was convinced. I had a perfect shooting lane; the wind was right. The voice of my grandfather whispered in my mind again, "Patience, Dak, and you will be full tonight." I waited for hours.

The animals seemed to freeze about a mile from my position. They would simply come no closer. I would occasionally rise from my seated position only moving a few inches. As I peered over the little mound concealed by the brush, it seemed as if the entire herd was staring at me.

I lowered myself back onto the ground, completely concealed. I waited another hour before I made the slight move again. Slowly, indiscernibly, I rose again. I was just a leaf or the wing of a flitting bird. I peered across the prairie. The herd had not moved. This time I knew they were all staring in my direction. I could even feel their eyes on me. They knew I was here. How? I wondered? I sank back to my seated position out of site in total frustration.

That is when I heard the laugh.

"Ha, ha, the antelope saw you before you saw them."

He moved from my left, a scarce fifteen feet away. He stood smiling. *"They can see like the eagle."* He laughed again.

That was the day I met One Horse.

"Who are you, and what are you doing here?" I questioned in anger or was it embarrassment?

He laughed again as I turned to face him. However, his cheerful smile melted my anger quickly. He was tall for an Indian, at least six feet. His body was thin, even drawn looking. His skins were old and worn. The moccasins he wore had holes in the tops, the sides, and, I was certain, even the soles. His hair was jet black, long, and flowing. He laughed again, smiling broadly and extended his hand to me.

"I'm One Horse. I followed you from the camp. You are a good runner, I think. But sometimes you should look behind you to see who is following." He grinned his toothy grin again. I extended my hand to One Horse. Our eyes met...our souls somehow, supernaturally bonded.

"You kept up with me on the run?" I asked.

"Sure, I did, it was easy. I am a good runner also I think."

"I'm sure you must be." Looking him directly in the eyes I could not help smiling back at One Horse. Even his eyes seemed to smile at me.

One Horse seemed to think outwardly and furrowed his brow. *"Even a good runner can't catch an antelope."* Then quickly the smile returned. *"You are not a good antelope hunter I think."* It was hard to disagree with his observation.

"*I suppose you are?*"

"*Sure, I am...they are easy to hunt,*" One Horse said. "*Let me show you. Follow me.*" At his words he bolted like a rabbit. I quickly threw my bow across my shoulder and ran as fast as I could, attempting to catch him. I was amazed. One Horse ran upright with a smooth cadence and posture. It looked a bit awkward. However, he was gobbling up ground with his giant stride. He bounded over small brush like a hurdler, rounded the little hills like a professional running back. It took all my effort to keep up with him. After a mile we were out of site of the antelope. He stopped below a small hill; his breathing seemed near normal. I held myself bent over, a pain in my side, with my hands on my knees, blowing air profusely.

"*You okay, Dak?*" he asked, grinning his toothy grin. I held up my hand and nodded. I watched as he cut a long branch from a mesquite bush. He trimmed the sharp needles off quickly with his long knife. Taking a colorfully dyed skin from his daypack, he tied the small skin onto the end of the ten footlong branch. One Horse then noisily climbed the little hill we stood behind and planted the fat end of the branch into the ground at the top of the little rise.

"*That's it, a flagpole?*" I gave him the goofiest grin I could come up with.

He looked at me quite seriously in a confused look. "*What's so funny?*" After an awkward pause, the smile slowly spread across his face. "*Just kidding, Dak. Hurry, let's move.*" Again, he seemed to sail across the terrain, running about one hundred yards perpendicular to his flagpole. In a moment he was hidden in the sparse brush. He pointed to a small cluster of cedars indicating for me to hide there and ready my bow.

I could not believe my eyes. Within fifteen minutes the lead antelope buck appeared. The animal was staring directly at the flagpole and its little flag fluttering in the slight wind. A few seconds later, thirty or more antelope followed the buck up the little hill and stood staring at the brightly colored flag. I looked toward One Horse. His bow was drawn. I quickly nocked an arrow and took aim at a fat doe. The arrows released simultaneously. The herd scattered as the two antelope fell to the ground. He stood looking my direction with his big toothy smile, waving at me with the excitement of a five-year-old on Christmas morning.

"*I told you, Daklugie. I am a good antelope hunter!*"

Chapter 33

From that day forward the two of us were inseparable. I think we made quite the pair. One Horse was tall and lanky; I was short, and even though I had filled out some, I was still very slight in build.

We hunted together and prepared meat together for our immediate families. Our hunting trips were much different than the other Warriors of the group; while most of them moved across the prairie on horseback, we always chose to hunt on foot. Many days we would run five or ten or even twenty miles. We often slept on the open prairie, returning the following morning to the camp with our bounty. One Horse was from the Comanche Tribe. Our time together helped me immeasurably in learning their language. This learning enabled Tosahwi and me to communicate on a much more precise level. One Horse was my brother, our hearts knit together by some unseen hand. He was a special blessing to me.

Nita seemed to improve daily in the care of Kele and the other women. Her friendships also were forming. She, too, under the instruction of Kele, was quickly learning the Comanche language. Together in a very short time, we became the only two people in the camp who could understand and translate Apache, Comanche, and English. We were an asset and treated as such by Tosahwi and the other leaders.

The few months we spent on the open prairie below the caprock were like a wonder-filled dream. The days seemed to glow under the dome of the springtime sun. The rains came, transforming the prairie into a wonderland of knee-deep buffalo grass and in places flowers as far as the eye could see. *The People* were happy, content, and well fed. The trouble of an unseen, distant army seemed to vanish within the blessed existence in which we were living.

I was continually amazed at the warmth and love *The People* showed us. I also would never forget the desperation and near starvation we had survived before finding our People here. I was a grateful man.

It was in this time our beautiful daughter came into the world. Nita whispered to me in the night within the shelter of our lodge, "*Today is the day, Dak.*" I cannot explain the calm that overcame me. I seemed to know in my spirit that all would be well. Nita carried the same confidence. We arose and went about our morning as usual. I exited the lodge to retrieve Kele and the other women. They were all there, standing outside our lodge. They also knew today, this morning in fact, was the day. The women gathered their birthing equipment, along with my wife, Kwanita, and began a purposeful walk across a prairie filled with flowers. As I stood and watched them depart, Tosahwi and One Horse approached my lodge. Tosahwi took my arm, indicating for me to follow.

We followed at a distance, pausing a few hundred yards from the camp. The women had disappeared into a low valley filled with the fragrance of the flora of a springtime prairie.

Tosahwi motioned for us to sit. He began his songs.

I joined in singing softly. The songs were sincere prayers. This part of our culture was deeply spiritual. The expressions of the human soul…the acknowledgment of our Creator…the thankfulness of His blessings. The songs contained the remembrance of all we had been given, along with the recalling of the Great Spirit's wisdom, guidance, deliverance…and love.

I was moved that day, moved in a way I do not have words for. No words were needed. We sat together, three friends, in what I would forever refer to as, "The silence of song."

Tosahwi finally spoke. His words were prophetic.

"*Dak, the child within Kwanita's womb will be a great leader. It has been revealed to me that she will deliver to* The People *a Homeland. It will be in a time and a place far away from here. Dak, I do not understand all that is to come. However, this day we will set the child apart. Her training and education will be vital.*"

I simply nodded.

As if on cue, the women appeared over the little rise of land. They motioned us to come to them. We moved quickly, effortlessly, over the prairie of flowers. Kwanita was resting on the buffalo robe. Upon her breast was my beautiful daughter.

Tears of joy spilled across my face. Those same joyful tears broke forth from Kwanita's heart as our eyes met. Again, I had no words…and none were needed. This time it was the women who began the songs. Songs of celebration, songs of joy. We joined the worship, celebrating the hope and promise that only new life can bring.

"Do you have a name for the child?" Tosahwi asked.

I gazed through the mist of my tears and observed the incredible scene before me. The pearl blue sky, the high mountains in the distance to the west, the buffalo moving as one to the north, the prairie filled with flowers surrounding us.

Her name will be Topusana (Prairie Flower).

Chapter 34

The time we spent on the open plains floated along like a slow-moving cloud over the prairie. Several moons passed. Looking back, I would say those few months spent on the prairie, in the company of my friends and little family, were the best of my life.

In a day it seemed, the prairie changed. The west wind blew, the flowers wilted, and the buffalo simply vanished. Then the heat arrived, a stifling unbearable heat. It became impossible to sleep within the lodges, and then the bugs arrived. Life became a great struggle. It was clearly time to move. Swarms of grasshoppers devoured everything green and growing. Kwanita shared with me her vision.

"They are like the enemy that is surely coming, Dak." I was deeply troubled by her vision.

"Could there possibly be this many?" I questioned. She answered me with a knowing look.

The council meeting was brief. No word had come from the scouts sent far to the south. The Apaches, under the leadership of Chief Palanquito, would move to the west, up into the high mountains. I longed to go with them. Something within me understood this was not our path, although for now in the council meeting, I would not speak of this fact. The Comanche bands would move to the east and south. Tosahwi spoke of a land filled with water, game, and few enemies. I knew Kwanita, along with our new daughter, Topusana, desired to travel with the Comanche. One Horse looked toward me with an understanding look in his eyes and nodded in my direction.

The plans were settled. We would leave signs for the scouts, indicating where and when we had moved. They would easily locate us on any news of the great army.

I was amazed at the ability of *The People* to simply pack up and vanish. The following day the camp was broken. By midday, the bands were on the move. We, along with the Comanche led by Tosahwi, traveled a mile to the east and south along the uplifted ridge of the caprock. I stopped a moment and observed the location of our former home camp. The Apache had disappeared on the opposite side of the river. They would travel along the rolling buttes and canyons leading into the high mountains. They had already vanished from sight. The camp from this distance was indiscernible. We had left nothing behind to indicate our presence nor the time spent here.

In my heart I would never forget the days of healing, friendship, laughter, acceptance, and love we had encountered along what would later become known as the Pecos River.

I turned away, looking ahead, choosing to remember the birthplace of my daughter in a different setting, green, flowering, and filled with game. Now the prairie was scorched and brown. It was filled with the bloated bodies of the grasshoppers that had consumed its bounty. I thought of the enemy so far away. Would they consume and destroy all that was within their path? My purpose welled up within my soul. Somehow, I would protect my family and my people from the grasshopper hordes from across the ocean.

"*Dak, we should reach the San Saba within one moon,*" Tosahwi said, redirecting my mind and my mount as he pointed toward the south and east.

The travel across the plains was incredibly difficult. The heat seemed to grow each day. As we moved along at a slow walking pace, *The People* and the animals alike suffered. The water sources were our only hope. I consulted the scroll daily. Although, Tosahwi knew each secret place upon the earth where the water seemed to appear from nowhere. Without this knowledge, I was certain the entire tribe might perish. Our bands had separated daily as we moved along, each under the direction of their own chief. Some moved north, others south; still another group had left us just two days ago, moving south and west. Those who chose to remain with us numbered around one-hundred souls. Warriors, grandfathers, women, maidens, and children, all under the care and leadership of the great chief…my friend Tosahwi.

One Horse and I often ran ahead of the camp in the early morning hours. At times we would be accompanied by several Warriors. These jaunts were reconnaissance missions as well as necessary for finding the best path to follow. We had scouts miles or days ahead of the main group. Security of our bands and tribe was the primary objective of these advance explorations. The Comanche had many enemies; they might appear anywhere and at any time. During this movement, I learned much about survival, evasion, and even military tactics. All this learning centered around one purpose, protecting our people. In my heart I knew I was born for this very purpose.

We had traveled five days now, since departing from the riverside camp. Water stores were exhausted. The ponies struggled the most. Their heads hung low, and the pace slowed even further. The older tribal members drifted to the rear of the procession. Young mothers who carried their small children also began to drift to the rear of our group. Kwanita joined them, carrying Topusana in her arms. The heat penetrated everything. Tosahwi called a halt in a slight depression within a thicket of mesquite brush. The people quickly took shelter under any piece of shade the small bushes created. A council was immediately called. The scroll showed this as a place of year-round water. However, there was none. The obvious location of the spring revealed nothing but a small pool of dry dust.

The Warriors and Elders gathered and seated themselves in a small circle. The concern on the face of Tosahwi showed through his furrowed brow.

Pahkah (He who draws the bow) spoke first. "The People *may not survive this journey. The water has vanished.*" Many nodded in agreement, as they themselves breathed in the dust and heat of the day.

Tosahwi spoke next. He would be responsible for a plan. The scroll showed a place with an immense spring of water flowing from the desert. Pools of deep cold water filled with fish and surrounded by game. The location was three days travel from our current location. Studying the map, I estimated its distance at fifty miles. One Horse and I climbed a small embankment and gazed in the direction of the massive spring. I knew we could probably see at least half the distance of twenty-five miles or more. There was no indication from what we saw that there would be water out there on the scorching prairie. But I knew the scroll would be accurate. Tosahwi also was aware that water lay ahead. How would we survive for three days of travel…with no water?

"We will pray now. What you say, Pahkah, is true; however, this is no vision to proclaim, only bad news. All the people understand and can see our present trouble. Knowing the solution to our problem…that is what would be a great revelation and gift to The People," Tosahwi said. Pahkah sat in silence at Tosahwi's rebuke. We indeed all knew the dire situation we faced.

One Horse and I moved off the little hill and seated ourselves within the circle. Tosahwi began his prayers and songs. *The People* joined in the songs from across the camp.

The sound of the worship songs moved me deeply in my spirit. Here under the hot spring sun, the scorching wind did not bring any relief, only a bone drying heat. Yet, *The People* rejoiced in song through lips that were cracked and dried. Sunburned faces lifted upwards. Arms that were tired and scorched were raised. Voices, dull and cracked with dryness, echoed weakly within our circle as the wind swept the praise away and into the heavens. Tosahwi ended his song. The silence of the prairie engulfed us. There we sat, a people struggling to survive. Calling out to the Great Spirit…in desperation for help. We sat in silence a full hour. Only the wind as it gusted in little puffs could be heard occasionally as it moved through the small cover of brush we sat within.

One Horse rose from his seated position.

"I will run to the large water spring. I will return tomorrow with as much water as I can carry. Have the people move along slowly. Even if only a few miles are covered, it will help."

I stood beside my best friend. *"I will also run with One Horse. With two of us we can carry a small drink of water for each person upon our return to The People."*

The offer, or maybe sacrifice, was met with silence. Not a single person spoke. Several minutes passed. Tosahwi rose from his seated position, raised his arms, and began again his prayers. Prayers for a helping hand to deliver us to the large spring. Prayers of protection for the runners. Prayers for us to survive the journey. *The People* joined in this song, as one.

We would depart as the sun set. Two friends would run through the night. The quarter moon would guide us. The prayers of *The People* would strengthen us. I had never run fifty miles, let alone attempted the following day to run another fifty miles. Deep within my soul I knew…we must succeed. My daughter, my wife, our people's lives hung in the balance.

The People settled again into the sparse shade of the scant cover of mesquite brush. We would attempt to rest the remainder of the day. I joined Kwanita and Topusana. I dug a small bed into the earth. The ground was cooler just a few inches below the surface. We placed Topusana in the little depression and covered most of her body with the cool sand. Then I stood over them both, casting a small shadow in which the two could lie and escape the scorching sun. They fell into a deep sleep as I stood in the searing heat, shadowing over my little family.

Chapter 35

I was awakened by the touch of Kwanita. One Horse and Tosahwi stood at a distance. I had no idea when I had crumpled to the ground and fallen asleep. However, the rest was exactly what my body needed. Kwanita stood beside me as I arose from the sand. She placed her arms around me and blessed me. I felt a strength from her simple touch that I could never explain to this day. It was as if she had given me some supernatural blessing of power.

"Just breath in, Dak, and accept my strength," she whispered in my ear. I did as she instructed. With a look of understanding our eyes met. I never felt so strong.

One Horse moved my direction, lifting the animal stomachs. We shared the load. The stomachs would be filled with water and tied off for our return trip. I thought a good horse would help; however, none of our ponies would ever survive the trip. I knew they were being spared for another purpose. Food. In the event the worst happened. None of this was spoken of as this day was ending. It was simply known.

The western sky was ablaze with a fiery red and orange hew. The wind was settling; dust hung in the sky and could be seen in the fading light. The temperature had dropped a few degrees; the smell of a few fires drifted our direction as the people prepared to break camp. The entire camp would move slowly throughout the night.

Tosahwi handed me a pouch of dried meat. Without words One Horse turned to face the exact direction of the huge spring that lay fifty miles ahead and began to run. I followed his lead. We did not look back.

The first few miles were wonderful. It was just like many days the two of us had spent running, hunting, exploring together. We did not speak for ten miles.

We fell into the rhythm of simply moving, two men with a distinct purpose, a mission. The ground the first ten miles was smooth and easy to negotiate. The quarter moon high overhead gave just enough light for us to avoid minor obstacles and brush. An hour passed and then the terrain changed. The smooth sand surface became rocky and filled with small crevasses only a few inches deep. The uneven surface and occasional unseen rocks hindered our progress. After what we estimated to be three hours, we slowed to a walk.

"How far have we traveled, Dak?" One Horse asked.

"It's hard to tell, the pace has been good, maybe fifteen miles," I replied.

"We have been moving very fast, Dak. I think you are wrong. Look to the south." Peering to the south, I could clearly see the outline of mountains along the horizon.

I had studied the scroll for days. I knew the only mountains were those to the south and west of the great springs. *"Could it be?"* I asked.

"Yes, Dak, we have traveled at least twenty-five miles. We must be halfway there in what I think from observing the moon. We crossed the twenty-five miles in just over three hours." We drank the few ounces of water we had carried as we walked along briskly. I felt the tiredness in my feet and legs. But I would not speak of that.

"The next twenty-five miles will not be so easy," he said.

As I observed the position of the moon now hanging slightly to the west, I knew we had another four hours or so before the moon set. Then soon after, the scorching sun would rise. We absolutely had to cover the next twenty-five miles before sunrise. I was already struggling. One Horse seemed strong. He picked up the pace again; I knew it was around a six or seven mile per hour pace. My legs felt heavy for the next mile. I struggled to keep pace with One Horse. He turned and observed me a moment. Then gave me his trademark toothy grin.

"Dak, let your mind go to another place. Do not think of the run. Think of the happiest place and time in your life, go there." He grinned his handsome toothy smile and accelerated further.

I thought of Kwanita…in another time. A time where we simply turned a faucet handle if we were thirsty. A time where we played basketball and walked hand in hand on snowy evenings. I thought of the times with my grandfather, eating apple pie in the tribal store. I lost all sense of time and space as I ran through the night across a moonlit prairie. I could no longer hear. I floated; I flew as I became one within my soul with my woman and my people. To run was to live in this place of oneness. I became a spirit runner. I felt a peace; I felt no pain, as we sailed along under the hanging moon. I lost all sense of time. I just ran and ran, with purpose...for hours.

In my mind, I saw the great trees surrounding the spring. Many miles had passed. In the distant recesses of my mind, I heard a voice calling. It was familiar, growing louder, disturbing this place of peace I had found. I tried to dismiss the voice. It grew louder, calling to me. The voice somehow troubled me. I did not want to listen. *"Dak...Dak...stop."* My vision focused; I was running beyond the great spring!

One Horse! It was his voice calling to me. *"Dak...Dak...STOP!"* I slowed to a walk; my mind slowly returned to reality. I had just passed the great spring. One Horse placed a hand on my shoulder as I became fully aware. He pointed in the direction of the spring behind us now.

A small crystal-clear lake appeared in my vision. I stopped. I could now hear the springs of Mescalero flowing through the little channels they had shaped into the earth. We walked back to the edge of the beautiful lake, the pain in my feet, legs, and body coming alive. I saw for the first-time this place that had been used by my people for centuries.

I became fully aware. The sun was rising. One Horse lay on the edge of the pristine lake and drank deeply. I knew from my history classes this place would soon become known as Balmorhea.

Chapter 36

I limped to the edge of the small lake. The pain in my feet and legs now coming alive with my awareness. I kneeled, I prayed, and I drank as much cold water as I could hold.

Neither of us spoke for several minutes. We recovered our breath, both amazed at the sight before us. The deep pool we drank from was crystal clear. We could see the bottom of the lake clearly, even though the pool had to be at least fifty feet deep. Thousands of fish swam freely in the water of the small lake. Bass, catfish, bluegill moved in enormous floating clouds of life. The water seemed to have an upwell of current flowing from the bottom toward the top. The fish rode along the unseen wave of moving water. Rising, then descending, an unbelievable bounty of nourishment that we needed desperately.

One Horse reached into a small recess below the waterline in the side of the embankment below him. Wrestled his arm a moment, then withdrew his arm from the pool with a huge catfish engulfing his fisted hand.

"How did you do that?" I asked.

He smiled. "Dak, I think sometimes you don't know much for a Warrior. These fish are always in the holes along the sides of rivers or lakes. You can run good, but you are not a very good fisherman, I think."

I sat up, admiring the struggling fish. One Horse gave thanks for the bounty while smashing its head with a sharp rock.

"And I think you might not be a very good chef!"

"I don't know what that is," he replied with a questioning look on his long face. "But we need to eat and fill the water carriers. Enough of taking it easy, Dak."

I had to laugh out loud at his confused expression.

My legs and arms ached deep within, making it difficult to stand. I knew they would continue to ache until we started to run again. One Horse started a fire and ran a green branch through the body of the fish, rotating it slowly over the fire. I began filling the animal stomachs with as much water as I could carry and tying off the top ends. I could not believe how difficult the skins were to lift. I placed two of them across my shoulders…I could barely stand. Concern must have shown on my face. One Horse spoke. *"Dak, we can do this. Put them down for now, let's eat."*

The fish was delicious, and filled with protein, and even much needed fat and oil. The portions were huge and we both ate our fill. The load of water that sat at our feet seemed to challenge us both. We sat in silence, pondering how we might carry such a massive weight over so many miles in the scorching sun that was gaining intensity as it rose higher in the eastern sky.

Then we heard the sound of a horse nickering.

****

Tosahwi motioned for his band to stop for a few moments of rest. They had moved steadily through the night. The sky had lightened in the east; the west wind had settled only an hour ago. Dust hung in the sky a glowing orange-red tint that seemed to set the eastern sky ablaze. *The People* and the animals suffered terribly. He knew they could not stop for long. Each step they took moved them closer to the water. Every mile, every hour counted now.

In all his years on this earth, he had never experienced this kind of heat, this kind of hot miserable wind. He had never seen the drying of the ancient springs. His prayers were changing. Yes, he was praying his people would survive…but he was also seeking. What was being revealed, here in the suffering? The Great Spirit had purpose in all things. Was this a sign of some kind? He was deeply troubled about the days ahead.

Kwanita moved toward the front of the procession. She opened the little blanket that held Topusana. Tosahwi placed his hand on the child. She was hot, her skin dry. He knew this meant the child had no water left in her system to produce the perspiration that might cool her little body. Tosahwi drew his long knife. He then ran his thumb along the sharpened edge, slicing deeply into his own skin and flesh. He offered the open wound to the little child, Topusana. She suckled the blood from the wound eagerly, her little eyes instantly brightening. The blood flow stopped after a few moments.

Tosahwi offered the knife to Kwanita. *"Wait until the sun is high."* She nodded in understanding. He turned and motioned for the people to begin to move. Perhaps a few more miles were possible.

He heard the commotion from the rear of the movement. One of the ponies had failed to rise from the sand. He nodded toward his Warriors. They took action quickly. Each person would have a small drink...of the animal's life blood. The butchered meat would dry quickly in the heat of the day. Each would now also have dried meat as they moved across the searing plain.

Although losing the pony obviously indicated how much *The People* were suffering, it was overall a good thing, Tosahwi thought. He knelt and gave thanks for the provision.

Tosahwi motioned for the movement to begin. The hot wind began to stir as the sun made its way higher into the sky.

****

We froze at the nickering of the horse. Hope leapt within my chest at the sound. One Horse rose casually and moved toward the edge of the lake. I wondered what his plan might be. He simply motioned for me to stay put as he walked directly toward the beautiful mare. She was a buckskin. A long flowing black mane draped across her neck and shoulders. She lifted her head in the direction of One Horse, showing a mouthful of deep green grass. One Horse spoke softly to her. I was amazed at what I was seeing and hearing.

"*Come to me, gift horse. You are a fine-looking creature; you will save my people...The Great Spirit has sent you to us. You are strong, I can see. Swift, I am certain, and as wild as a north wind. Today I will become your friend for life.*"

The mare nickered, her skin shuddering slightly in uncertainty. One Horse held his open hand out in her direction. I thought she would likely bolt and run. However, she simply lowered her head and walked calmly toward One Horse. When within arm's length, he reached for her. He rubbed her face, stroked her graceful neck gently, moved her mane from the front of her face. "*It is a pleasure to meet you, Gift Horse. You are a treasure.*" The mare nickered softly as One Horse continued to speak to her gently while touching her body, legs, withers, and hind quarters. The mare seemed to allow or welcome his touch. She nuzzled his arms as he spoke to her. I observed in awe as One Horse threw a leg over her back and the two galloped away. I heard the mare nickering as One Horse raised his voice in jubilation, "*Yes. Let me see how swift you can run, Gift!*"

114

I know it has been said and taught that the Comanche have a special gifting with horses. Today that gifting was remarkably showing forth through my friend One Horse. A communication had taken place beside the clear waters of Mescalero Springs. A bonding had been forged between a man and an animal. These two souls would become inseparable for many days to come. As unlikely as it may seem this day, I had witnessed a man and a horse...become friends.

Chapter 37

The two returned within a few minutes. One Horse dismounted and the two drank together along the edge of the lake. I had filled the animal skins with much water. I was sure the horse could carry at least two hundred pounds of water. I had worked on the math problem as I rested in the shade of the trees along the small lake. One hundred people: Two hundred pounds of water, thirty-two ounces of water per person. So much more than the handful we had hoped to carry on our backs. Enough even for some of the ponies. This horse was evidently a gift from above. I began to sing. From a distance, One Horse joined in the song of gratefulness. He continued to keep his hands upon Gift as he sang. As we ended the song together, I heard him say, "*It is time for you to meet my friend, Gift.*"

The two moved toward me as I lifted the first of the animal skins. "Gift," as we would all come to call her, seemed to rise and accept the load as One Horse placed the animal stomachs filled with water across her back. I tried to listen. Looking into the eyes of this exquisite creature…she seemed to communicate to me…an understanding.

We all drank deeply again and started out toward the north and west. Our families were out there, suffering.

As the morning sun made its way higher into the eastern sky, the heat began to build. The first mile was gruesome. My legs were heavy and sore, my shoulders ached, my mind wandered. There was no talk among the three of us. Gift seemed to know or sense the importance of the task that lay before us. Her eagerness to press on amazed me. She seemed to lead us and even press us with the pace. Thankfully after a few miles of walking, the pain in my body began to dissipate. I switched shoulders with my load of water. I had decided to carry a small skin of water for one purpose. Gift would need it. My friend One Horse had decided to do the same. We each carried about twenty pounds of water in separate animal stomachs. We would have plenty for the trip across what we hoped was now forty miles of sun scorched prairie. We walked on and on, one step at a time. Each step bringing us closer to our friends, our family.

****

Kwanita struggled with the simple weight of her daughter, Topusana. The mothers had all fallen to the rear of the procession; they seemed to struggle more than the others. It was not just the weight of the children's bodies that the mothers carried. Carrying the weight of a child, born or unborn, knowing the little children were hurting, seeing their thirst, their little bodies becoming weak, their minds becoming listless, was a tremendous burden. The mothers were carrying little souls.

They had walked through the night. Kwanita hoped they had covered ten or maybe even twelve miles. It was impossible to tell in the darkness of the night. She thought it amazing, the silence of the suffering. At least one hundred people, moving through the night across the open prairie…making no sound whatsoever as they traveled. Each bearing their own pain individually and bearing the burdens collectively as a *People*. This is how *The People* had survived many difficult times and events throughout their history by bearing one another's burdens. Doing so fulfilled a deep purpose of our Creator.

The morning brought a slight relief. As the sky had brightened, Kwanita and her friends could now see where to step. They had stopped to rest an hour or so in the relative cool of the morning, even though it had to be near ninety degrees. Kwanita knew Dak and One Horse had found the spring; she even knew of the gift horse. She had seen it in her vision. The vision had strengthened her inwardly, to know Dak and One Horse were moving toward them at this moment. This truth continued to offer a small glimmer of hope in her tired and thirsty body. She had shared the vision with Tosahwi as he allowed Topusana to drink from his hand. She realized he also was openly encouraged by the vision. One more day, perhaps even this evening, *The People* might share a small drink of water. Would it be enough? This was not revealed in her vision.

Tosahwi arose. *The People* feebly arose as one with him. He began to pray for rain as *The People* trudged along in the dust and growing heat.

****

Observing the position of the sun, I knew it was noon. We stopped along a small dry creek bottom. Gift drank sparingly from the water I carried and with this, the weight was reduced substantially. One Horse sat beside me as we drank our fill from his skin; we even poured a small amount on top of one another's heads. The cool water, as it instantly evaporated, dissipated the heat from our bodies and washed over us like a wave of relief, reviving something within me. I rose as Gift nickered her eagerness. We pressed on, climbing the embankment of the little arroyo. *"This will soon run full with water,"* One Horse said, as the dust arose from each step we traveled. I wondered when that water he spoke of might find its way to this place of suffering.

As we climbed the small embankment and a shallow hill above the creek bottom, I spotted a cloud of dust trailing away behind something on the distant horizon. That something was not visible. One Horse paused a moment, peering in the direction of the cloud of dust.

"There they are, Dak. It is our People."

"How far are we seeing, One Horse?" I questioned.

"Not more than twenty miles," he said as he turned to me and smiled his toothy grin.

"Enough of this resting, Dak; it will be easy, let's get moving. I think you don't know much about measuring distances."

I started to run, taking the lead. My mind again transported me to a different place and time. I was among the high peaks; it was snowing, and the wind was fierce. My grandfather was leading the way along the ancient trail. I became cold as I ran across the scorching prairie.

****

The People rested and drank in the shade of the small mesquite thicket. I was amazed at how quickly Nita seemed to recover after just a few ounces of water. Topusana also became active and aware after a small drink. Tosahwi instructed *The People* to drink only small amounts of water, then wait a few minutes before drinking again. Tosahwi's wisdom brought about refreshing recovery within an hour. The sun was setting; the dust settled. Relief was unspoken, yet somehow permeated the entire camp.

As One Horse assisted in the distribution of the lifesaving water, I could not

118

help but notice the special attention he was receiving from a beautiful young maiden.

Nadua (One who keeps us warm) stayed near One Horse continually. She would reach out and touch him on his arm or back, expressing her gratefulness. Kwanita noticed also. She nodded toward the two and winked at me. *"What's happening here, Nita?"* I asked.

"This has been happening for many moons now, Dak," she stated matter of factly.

"Is this a good fit?" I said my thoughts aloud, and instantly regretted the words.

"I know Nadua is the most lovely maiden in our camp, or any camp for hundreds of miles, I am sure. But I think you do not understand women. A woman needs a man that will take care of her in all ways. One Horse, along with your assistance, has saved our entire band, Dak."

I thought of the words Mr. Natchi had spoken to me such a long time ago. "It is your greatest responsibility to take care of all of her needs spiritual, emotional, physical." I was embarrassed at my initial thoughts. The men all thought the beauty of Nadua made her unapproachable, beyond a courtship. I was amazed that my friend One Horse could even gain a glance from the most beautiful maiden of all. But there he was grinning his toothy grin, his hair a tangled mess, his tall awkward body bent and aching from the ordeal we had both experienced. As he distributed the lifesaving water among our people it was plainly obvious…Nadua was in love with One Horse.

Chapter 38

We still had many miles to travel. The water we had carried was rationed equally among *The People* who managed to save enough for another small drink, just a few ounces for each person, for later in the heat of the day. The Warriors tended the ponies by rinsing out their mouths with a small amount of water. This small act of kindness would be enough to drive the ponies on. As we set out again, it seemed the spirit of *The People* had been revived. This, Tosahwi knew and communicated to me, was the key to survival of our band. The water had brought about a refreshing hope.

One Horse made his way toward the front of the procession, drawing alongside us. Gift followed close behind him, without a lead rope. Nadua also followed closely behind One Horse.

"I will return to the spring now for more water," he announced. I was amazed at his willingness or ability to even consider such a task. *"Gift is strong and well-watered; she will carry me to the spring. I will return in the night with more water."*

Tosahwi seemed pleased…or was it pride that I saw in his eyes as he regarded the strength of my friend Sumu Puku (One Horse). He paused a moment and glanced in the direction of Nadua. With a knowing smile, Tosahwi nodded his approval of the plan. One Horse instantly threw a leg into the air and mounted Gift effortlessly.

Tosahwi motioned for us to both come near him as he paused a moment. *"The marriage ceremony will take place on our arrival at the ancient spring."*

A look of wonder and excitement filled the eyes of my friend, a look I had never seen before, as he sped away on the back of Gift. *The People*, in unison it seemed, let out a little cheer as One Horse departed in a cloud of dust, sitting tall upon his mount.

The formality of our culture required many steps prior to a wedding taking place. Tosahwi had just dismissed all that tradition in favor of what most could clearly see on the face of Nadua as love.

The Following Day

The People rested in the shade of the gigantic trees that surrounded Mescalero Springs. We had feasted on roasted fish and fire-grilled venison. The trees swayed in the gentle breeze, even though the heat just a few yards away from the springs continued in its intensity. Here, however, in the shade and deep green grass along the edge of the cool water, the temperature was pleasant and comfortable.

The People napped, drank, feasted, and recovered from our life-threatening ordeal on the heat-scorched prairie. A sense of peace and even gratefulness infused the atmosphere within the camp. We had survived. Each of us understood this was solely due to the provision of the Great Spirit.

A council was held that night. The leaders seated themselves around the sacred fire. One Horse was now included and would from this day forward be seated at the right hand of Tosahwi. My heart rose within my chest as Tosahwi motioned for One Horse to sit next to him.

I was so proud of my friend, my brother. No words were needed, all understood One Horse was to be forever honored for his part in saving *The People*. He smiled his toothy grin, and a light chuckle arose from the group. A decision was made; we would remain here at the spring until the summer rains arrived. Then we would continue our travel toward the south and east. It was a good decision; all within the circle nodded in agreement as we passed the sacred pipe.

The women also met that night. Preparations were underway. The wedding feast would begin tomorrow. The celebration, tradition, and beauty of the ceremony was beyond compare. The feasting provided much needed strength and nourishment. Hope filled the hearts of *The People*. After the marriage ceremony, Nadua and One Horse disappeared for days within their lodge.

****

I met One Horse in the late evening a few days later as he exited his lodge. A look of satisfaction showed across his long face. He walked to the edge of the lake with the loose carry of a man who had not a worry in the world. He stood in the water and washed himself, brushed his teeth with cedar trimmings, and even combed out his hair. After a long drink he rose from the water and stared at me with a strange questioning expression. *"Well, how do I look?"* he asked.

"You look very happy, but you are still not so handsome," I replied.

"I am husband to the most beautiful woman on the earth," he said with a confused look on his face. *"I think you don't know very much about women, Dak!"* We stood together by the calm lake, a smile breaking across his face and mine.

"You should have told me sooner how much fun it is to be married."

I smiled at my friend. *"Let's go for a hunt tomorrow."*

"Dak, I am busy learning how to be a husband...this is not a good time to hunt." He grinned his toothy grin and walked away with a spring in his step I had never seen before. I laughed aloud, as did the group of curious onlookers who had gathered at his appearance. Kwanita was among the observers. She smiled an inviting smile my direction with a twinkle in her eyes.

I took her hand in mine and recognized the look of longing on her face. Or was it something else I saw in her eyes? We walked along the pathway lined with teepee lodges. The sights and sounds of our camp surrounded us, the smell of meat roasting, the sound of children playing. I heard the gurgling of the springs and felt the light breeze on my face as it swept Kwanita's shining hair across her shoulders. We paused, her hand in mine. I spoke first the thought we both must have been thinking, as I recalled the night of our marriage in her parent's home.

"Do you feel as if we missed...I don't know...I was just thinking of the circumstance of our marriage." Kwanita put a finger to my lips.

"No, I don't," she said. I looked into her eyes. No more words were needed. This woman, my woman, loved me completely. I knew that deep in my soul.

****

The fire crackled, the smoke rose, the comfort of the buffalo robe caressed us both, soft on our skin as all our senses came alive.

"It is good to be a husband," I said, as Nita welcomed me into her loving embrace.

It was again simply put, a happy blessed time that we spent beside the waters of Mescalero Springs.

Two weeks or more had passed when the gentle scratching at the flap of our lodge awakened me from a deep sleep. I stepped out into the moonlit night to a cool wind and the distant sound of thunder rumbling. Tosahwi and One Horse greeted me. I was relieved the rain was coming, but I discerned instantly it was not the news of rain that brought the two to my lodge in the night. The scouts from the south had arrived.

Chapter 39

Nita and I had spent days and days discussing what we remembered from our history classes from the year 2020, the time that we had departed just a few seasons ago. I wished I had paid better attention in those classes. The complex struggle for control of these lands we walked and much of North America, for that matter, was a blur of confusing distant facts and thoughts. We knew the final results of this tremendous struggle for control. That information helped immensely in whom we might align ourselves with as a band, as a tribe, and ultimately as a Nation of People. Communicating our knowledge of future events wasn't difficult within our little band. Tosahwi was extremely open to our input and heeded the strategy and advice we offered. Communication with the other bands of Comanche was difficult at best; it was, however, possible.

I sat in the council circle with my friends, listening. The scouts reported a large army approaching from the south. This army was not the Spaniards we had feared. It was reported the army Spain sent from across the sea had been defeated in the great city of Mexico to the south. Mexico had revolted at the rule of Spain. Those who prevailed had sent an army north. The intention was clear. Mexico would now attempt to hold the lands north of the river. The whites were beginning to occupy those lands. The scouts reported two thousand men had crossed the great river, marching quickly, intent on their mission. I knew we were quite simply in the way, a distraction. The "powers that be" did not even consider us a force with which to be concerned. I also knew this two-thousand-man army marching to claim our land might easily destroy a band of Comanche numbering one hundred souls.

On hearing the complete report, Tosahwi looked toward me. Without words, he was asking for the knowledge or information I might hold. I nodded. All within the council circle awaited my response. I paused and smoked a moment. I considered the mindset of the Comanche. It was not in their nature to allow any army to simply enter their homeland unfettered. For centuries they had brutally attacked any and all that dared to enter their lands. The Comanche People were fierce. There was very good reason that *The People* had become known as "The Lords of the Plains." I had much doubt that those within our own council might heed my advice. I perceived the Comanche Warriors within this very circle had a resolve in their hearts. They were hoping I would recommend attack. I spoke as few words as possible.

"I would say send the runners. Let us move as one into the Llano."

All within the circle nodded in agreement. Although they assumed I was advising to gather our forces and prepare for war, I was doing the opposite. I had no way to explain this march had nothing to do with us. That we were greatly outnumbered and outgunned. That this force, this battle, was not about us. If I spoke the words, *let's retreat and go hide in the Llano*, many would consider me a coward.

Tosahwi considered my words and spoke. *"Daklugie has spoken wisdom this day."* Peering intently into my eyes, I knew he understood my true intent. *"We will break camp in the morning and move north and east into the Llano. Send the runners north, south, east, and west. Let us gather our people."*

The runners were our lifeline of communication. It would take them a few days to deliver the information to the other bands; our people would be safe in the Llano.

Grunts and nods of agreement emanated from the council circle.

"I will travel to the east. I will observe this army from the south with my own eyes."

A grumbling arose from the circle at my statement. Tosahwi looked my way with a questioning concerned look in his eyes. I spoke nothing further as I sat in silence. I needed to meet with the leaders of this army from the south. I was not concerned for my life as were the others that sat within this sacred circle. I had in my possession enough gold to gain an audience with the leaders of this army. What I needed was information. I needed to know what had happened with the hordes from across the sea. What had become of the Spaniards? Had they truly been defeated? Or had they held back? Kwanita had seen things that contradicted the reports from the scouts.

****

One Horse and I traveled stealthily through the night. The trip east from our location would take days of hard travel. As we moved along the rivers of the Comanche homelands, I was amazed at the beauty of this place. The land was filled with clear water streams and springs that seemed to rise from the earth in serene hidden valleys. Game was plentiful and we easily fed ourselves with what we harvested daily. This land was immense, wild, and pristine. I could easily see why so many would enter the fight for its ownership. However, this was Comanche land…this was our land. I also understood these enemies would stop at nothing, even attempt to destroy an entire race of people in order to possess these lands.

After four days of hard travel, we began to see signs of the white man. We noted: a burned-out barn with the grave markers of those who had obviously attempted to claim a small portion of land; a few miles further the tracks of a wagon, the campfire of those who traveled in the wagon still smoldering along the edge of a small creek. One Horse became alarmed and angry at the presence and evidence of the intrusion into his people's land. He considered these people trespassers.

"*We should hunt them down, Dak.*" I had never seen the daunting look of fierceness that radiated from his eyes. "These whites are uninvited. If they die by my war club, others may not be so bold."

"I understand, One Horse. For now, we must press on." The look in his eyes told me this conversation was not over.

The following day we stood on a small hill and watched an army of two-thousand men moving along a great river. We would need to exercise extreme caution. Although our skills would allow us to remain concealed and move within close proximity to this army, we simply could not be discovered. How to gain a meeting with the commander of this force was in the forefront of my mind, along with how to make certain my friend One Horse and I would not be taken captive. I knew the history of these men; I knew what they were capable of. I knew how ruthless these men were, even though they called themselves Mexicans now. These were the descendants, the sons of Onate, a brutal man. As the leader of the Spaniards, Onate had brought unmeasured torture and misery on all Native American peoples he had encountered.

We camped that night with no fire. No moon lit the summer sky. The canopy of starlight overhead so intense it created shadows on the forest floor beneath the immense cedar and oak trees that towered above us. Here in the shadow of starlight we lay upon Mother Earth, two friends, brothers even, staring into the vastness of the cosmos. The closeness and humidity in this part of our land felt familiar and comfortable. The moisture in the air was filled with the wonderful smells of early summer. Blossoming dogwood, Indian paintbrush, bluebonnets, even the prickly cactus was in full bloom, its yellow blossoms glowing in the starlight.

One Horse and I talked late into the night. The hidden meadow and shadows offered further concealment from any scouts that might be traveling ahead of the Mexican army. One Horse said these scouts might possibly be Comanche, hired to scrutinize the route that lay before the army.

"*Our own people might be assisting this movement?*" I questioned.

"*Yes, Dak, these armies many times make great promises, promises of peace, or lands as a reward. Most scouts are often rewarded with death...after they are no longer needed,*" he stated bluntly.

"*Might it be possible to intercept one of the scouts?*"

"*Now I think you are finally beginning to think like a Comanche Warrior,*" One Horse replied.

The possibilities flooded my mind. I was quickly forming a plan and I was certain it would work.

Our eyes became heavy. The conversation dwindled. I drifted off into a light sleep, but not before I heard the words from my friend that comforted my heart in a way I would not understand completely for several years.

"*The child is a son, Dak. He is to be born after the snow flies.*"

****

We awakened as the sun lightened the eastern sky; however, the sun would not show itself for hours. A thick morning fog dampened not only the earth but also most sound in its enveloping mist. We would need to travel carefully.

"*I will lay the sign for the scouts this morning, Dak. It is an easy thing,*" One Horse said. "*You stay here. Before the sun sets, they will meet us in this place.*" He smiled his signature smile and showed his toothy grin...then One Horse, my friend and father-to-be, disappeared into the mist. He made no sound as he traveled.

I heard his voice emanate from a different direction than he had departed.

"*Hide yourself, Dak. Just be lazy this day...I know this is an easy thing for you to do. I think you are even good at it.*"

127

I smiled, thinking of his wry humor, then settled into a perfect hiding place within a massive cedar tree that had been hollowed out by animals and a huge fire that must have taken place eons ago.

I awoke hours later to a strange clinking sound—my mind sorted out the sound within a few seconds—the sound of metal rattling against metal. It took but a few moments for me to understand the sound. Swords.

Chapter 40

In the vastness of the Llano Estacado, the bands had gathered. Hundreds of teepee lodges lined a small creek. Lodge fires burned; children played within the high buffalo grass; the ponies, hundreds of them, grazed along a high bluff above the camp. The women of the bands went about their daily routines. Kwanita tended to the needs of Nadua and Topusana. Nadua was beginning to show. The beauty of the young woman seemed to radiate. Vibrance, health, even love, shone forth from her face at the gift of motherhood. The child within her womb tossed and wrestled like all unborn babies do. However, there was something special and unique happening within the womb of Nadua. Kwanita had heard and seen in her vision this unique gifting. On quiet nights within the warmth of the lodge, the two women could hear the voice of the baby boy within Nadua's womb. He hummed and sang softly. He whispered unknown phrases and words. The young child's voice often lulled them to sleep as he sang the ancient songs.

This was a miraculous sign.

The leaders and men of the tribes also went about their own duties of supplying the bands and their families with meat. Hunts took place daily. Game was plentiful. *The People* were well fed. This fact alone brought much contentment to the bands and families. This was how prosperity was measured among the Comanche People. Well fed, happy families, with no immediate threat, brought this contentment and peace, more than any other factors.

Tosahwi held a council each night. There was much talk of war. Buffalo Hump, the leader of the Penateka band, now sat in the seat of honor alongside Tosahwi. Buffalo Hump was an exceptional hunter and leader of men. The young Chief seemed to possess an ability to inspire and motivate all who followed him. Tosahwi considered Buffalo Hump his greatest friend and ally.

Buffalo Hump was an imposing man. He was tall, well over six feet. His hair was long; his skin a perfect dark red; his physique incredibly muscled. Buffalo Hump was gifted as a natural born leader. His wisdom was looked on and sought even by Tosahwi. Yet, in humility, Buffalo Hump sincerely considered himself a student. He knew he needed wisdom, and he often silently asked for this gift from the Great Spirit. Those prayers were being answered. The man was filled with wisdom and insight.

This night in the council lodge the men smoked the pipe and wondered aloud when Daklugie and One Horse might return with news.

"*It is a difficult thing to do this waiting, it is, however, the best course of action to take*," Buffalo Hump spoke. His words of wisdom were greeted with nods and grunts of affirmation.

Tosahwi allowed a few moments to pass before he spoke. "*We should send a few Warriors and runners to the south and east. Perhaps they might reduce the time of discovering and bringing this vital information to us.*"

"*This is a good plan. It is a possibility that Daklugie and One Horse may well find themselves in a dangerous situation and in need of help…or even rescue. It is a brave thing they are doing and most certainly this is a perilous mission*," Buffalo Hump said.

The men smoked and all nodded in agreement. The Warriors and runners would depart before the sunrise. It would take them a full week to arrive along the banks of the river just to the south of the great stone mission.

****

I heard One Horse call to me. "*Dak, it is safe to show yourself.*" I waited silently. Something was wrong. His voice was stressed. "*Dak, are you here?*" Now, I knew without question there was danger as I detected the break in his voice. I stood motionless inside the great tree. I breathed deeply, blowing out as quietly as I could. I was concerned the unseen enemy could hear my labored breath. What to do? I heard again the sound of metal on metal as the group seemed to move slightly closer to my tree. The fog was finally breaking as the first few rays of sunlight penetrated the hidden meadow. I heard a new sound above my head. A distinct buzz.

The bees were awakening.

I slowly raised my hand above my head and felt the side of the great tree. My hand instantly sunk several inches into the sticky substance. I drew my hand back and felt the first sting. My heart raced. It remained quiet outside the great tree; however, at my disturbance of the hive, the buzzing sound began to grow. I felt the next sting on my arm, and bit down hard on my lip to keep from making any sound. Raising my bow, I reached high into the tree and silently scraped my bow along the inside of the hive, digging deeply into the honey. The buzzing sound grew, thousands of bees began to swarm out of the tree. I heard men running, crying out in pain as the bees attacked those outside the tree. I heard footsteps, metal swords clanking as the group apparently ran toward the river.

I chanced a peek out as I was stung repeatedly. I caught a glimpse of One Horse escaping up the hill away from the river. His back was bleeding, torn open by what appeared to be whip marks. My blood boiled at what I saw.

I don't know how many arrows I fired. But all met their mark. I followed the group escaping the bees. Seven men fell. None escaped my arrows. They flailed their arms, swatting at the bees as they ran. The little bee stings must have seemed like nothing as an arrow penetrated skin, cracked ribs, pierced intestines. Arrows flew mercilessly as I fired again and again. They severed arteries, cut through flesh, shattered bones. Those who fell wounded, quickly received a blow from my war club. Skulls caved at the fierceness of my attack.

My mind went to a place from long ago. I saw the cruel man who had killed my mother. I saw his face in the face of each soldier as I lifted scalps. I brutally hacked away at the bodies of the dead men with my war club. Something within me was broken. Deep anger continued to rise from somewhere within my soul. I spoke under my breath as I took the scalp of the last man as he lay dying, an arrow protruding from his back. "What have you done to my friend?" I whispered to the man through gritted teeth. His face was white with fear as I lifted his scalp, then crushed his skull with my grandfather's war club. I reeled, looking for others, there must be more. I will kill them all, my only thought.

I heard a voice behind me. *"Dak, Dak...Dak."* An arm grabbed my shoulder, and I quickly turned, my war club raised. *"Dak, it's me."* One Horse looked pleadingly into my eyes, pain radiating from his face. Heavy chains bound his wrists and rattled as he dropped his arms in exhaustion.

"Dak, it is done." A strange questioning look appeared on his face. *"It is done. Let's go, Dak."* His words echoed within my mind. I slowly lowered my war club.

I reached for him and saw again the severity of his injuries. The skin of his back was shredded. I could even see exposed bone across his shoulders. We fled, moving away from the river. I began to cry.

I cried for my mother. I cried for my grandfather. I cried for my wounded friend. My cries welled up within my heart, and I was overcome with grief and hatred. My emotions poured out of me in a wave of seething anger and heartache.

We ran. As we moved away from the enemy army, my tears eventually turned into song; tears continued to run down my face as I sang. I cried out to the Great Spirit for my people, and for my friend Sumu Puku as he moved along the trail, struggling to walk. His back had been torn deeply from some unseen cruel whip. Skin and muscle hung loosely from his body. His hands and arms were raw and bleeding from the weight of the iron shackles fastened around them. At this moment, I had no idea how we might possibly escape. Would One Horse even survive?

Chapter 41

We moved along rapidly for one, perhaps two miles. The adrenaline dissipated from our bodies, and One Horse began to slow. He required medical attention. It was crucial that his wounds be treated and wrapped. He needed rest, food, and drink. I could offer nothing my friend required in this moment. I knew of some plants that contained healing properties from my study of the scroll. I also knew we could not stop. Soon the Mexicans would discover the bodies. I knew they would hunt us down. Possibly, they were on our trail even now.

"*Dak, you should leave me; we will both die if you do not,*" One Horse said.

"*You will never mention that thought again,*" I said with a steel resolve in my voice.

"*The irons are much too heavy; I can't go on.*"

I examined the massive chain links, and the iron lock that held them in place. The weight of the iron had cut deeply into his flesh; our running had removed the skin from his wrists.

"*There must be a way to remove them,*" I said as I struggled with the mechanism, wrestling with it a moment, but quickly seeing there was no way to open the lock. I examined the chains and knew instantly we had no tool with which to cut the iron. One Horse saw the look in my eyes; the impossibility of removing these chains must have shown on my face.

"*Dak, please, you can escape if you are on your own.*"

He slowly lowered himself to the ground below a great boulder. The blood from his wounds ran down the face of the rock, creating an image on its surface.

I stared a moment at the unintended painting my friend's blood had left on the rock. The image showed me and even whispered a message within my heart: it was not time to discuss escaping. The blood in his hair left the outline of a small, tangled crown at the top of this involuntary masterpiece. His shoulders and arms had left an imprint like that of a horizontal branch of a tree just below the image of the crown. As he slid down the face of the rock, a vertical upright column of blood was left behind. Blood drops scattered in no particular fashion graced the remainder of the rock portrait...of a cross.

One Horse looked intently into my eyes. *"Take care of my son, Dak,"* he asked softly.

I knelt and sat next to him for an hour or more. I prayed.

We talked quietly of our hunts together. I thanked him for saving our *People* with his courageous act of running through the night to the great spring. I thanked him for teaching me how to be a Warrior. We sat in silence for a few minutes, the sun on our faces. Little white clouds floated across the bright blue sky. The birds sang in the trees. The light wind caused the flowers at our feet to bow and dance in unison as if performing some unknown ballet before a king. It was all so magnificent...and painfully perfect.

Then Sumu Puku (One Horse) my friend...breathed his last.

****

I believe it was this very day that a dark cloud began to grow in my heart and mind. Perhaps the seeds of this darkness had been planted long ago. I remembered the day I had identified the body of my mother. This same darkness I had felt then. It was only momentary, a small inkling of what I was experiencing now. I had felt its shadowed presence as I had gazed on the bruises encircling her neck. I knew without doubt the day I killed the cruel man this unseen cloud had grown within my mind. I had become an Apache Warrior that day.

This day I had become a Comanche Warrior. The dark cloud of thoughts and emotion would not allow me to sing the song. This was not a victory to be celebrated. Yes, I had killed seven men. I was convinced these were the men who had allowed and overseen the torture of my friend. They had come to attempt the same cruelty on me. I knew these men would continue to press in on my people, my family, and our Homeland. My tears had ceased. I would never shed a tear again. The cloud of darkness would not allow it.

I gazed on the body of my friend. I would not leave him like this with the chains binding his body and spirit. I laid him gently below the rock painting

134

and started down the slope toward the enemy. I did not attempt to conceal myself as I moved back down the trail of blood my friend had left. I needed the key to the iron lock. I was certain one of the dead soldiers below must have been carrying it. Nothing would prevent me from finding the key and returning here to free the body of my friend from the chains. If any dared to interfere with my mission or stop me, they would die, or I would die. Within the cloud of darkness, it mattered not which possibility occurred.

Chapter 42

The vultures had already begun to circle in the sky. The bodies of the Mexican soldiers were strewn about the little concealed meadow where just a few hours ago we had spent a peaceful night. The dark cloud overshadowed both my mind and this place. I found the large key and ring on the third body. I removed the key and continued my work. I retrieved my arrows. Using one of the heavy sharp swords, I mutilated the bodies, removing manhood, arms, legs. It would not be possible to blame the Comanche for the death of these men. This site would, however, strike fear within the army along the river below me when they discovered an unimaginable massacre of their own men.

I tucked the key into my belt and moved silently away from the scene. I heard the sound of a detachment moving in my direction. They would discover the bodies within minutes. I had no concern of discovery. The detachment would report back to their leaders. Additional troops would return to investigate. It would be hours before any possible order might be given to attempt a pursuit. I was alone now. My friend was gone. I would become one with the forest and the land. Over the next few days, I would eliminate one at a time, many from this army. So many would be killed their general would seek to meet with me. I would never again think of pleading to meet with him. I would give him reason to plead for a meeting with me.

My priority, however, would be to return to the body of my friend One Horse.

I freed my friend from the shackles. It had taken the entire day for me to prepare his grave. I shed no tears as I lay his body in the grave below the large boulder that displayed his masterpiece. I transplanted flowers of all kinds over his grave; I gently smoothed the ground around the grave site. The earth showed no sign of the grave. Just an explosion of flowers beneath the cross of blood. I gathered a large amount of wood. Limbs, branches, even trunks of nearby dead trees and arranged them at the top of the giant boulder above his grave. I would light the funeral-fire well after the sun set, only when complete darkness fell on the land.

The fire would be seen by the entire army camped along the river. If the commanders chose to send troops to investigate. I would be awaiting them in the darkness.

****

At midnight I lit the fire. The blaze was massive. Flames towered into the night sky. I estimated the flames must be reaching fifty feet in height and the glow, I was convinced, could be seen for miles. I said my last goodbyes to my friend in a silent prayer and moved away from the funeral-fire toward the camp of the Mexican army. I planned to silently intercept any who chose to investigate. Once away from the sound and light of the fire, I heard alarm bells ringing and horns blowing from the distant camp. It was obvious a general quarters had been ordered. It was only a matter of time now. How many would they send?

I moved onto the hidden small rise of land. I had chosen the first location of my attack plan in the daylight. In fact, I had worked out several locations from which to attack. All the points were on a direct line between the funeral-fire and the army. Each site was easily escapable. Each carefully chosen upon a small rise of land, with a downhill escape that would conceal my location and escape route.

I had learned much of tactics from the Warriors in the years I had spent with my Comanche friends. I would put those skills to the test this dark night. I knew and had seen that a small group of well-trained stealthy Warriors using guerrilla warfare could inflict massive losses on a much larger opponent. I had spent days alongside One Horse, practicing with my bow. We had trained with the Warriors, wrestled, learned hand-to-hand combat techniques. I was prepared.

I allowed the darkness to envelope me. I became a part of and one with this dark night. Then somehow, the darkness that lurked within my mind united with my spirit. In the center of that darkness, however, burned a white-hot intense light. I would forever begin to know and rely on this inner light that dwelt hand in hand with the darkness. I cannot explain spiritually this inner presence of light. How might this light become my friend? How could this single beam of goodness and hope exist in this dark world that would consume me? And to this very day, I have no answer. But this light would guide me, assist me, protect me.

In many instances across chasms of time…I know I should have died, fallen on some unknown battlefield a casualty within my own private war. I know this for a fact. This night, as I look back, was one of those times. However, the flicker of light that I now know lives in my heart would watch over me in the darkness.

I heard the detachment approaching from hundreds of yards away. Their heavy boots broke limbs and snapped twigs as they moved toward the fire. The swords they carried clanked noisily. Perhaps they felt no need to conceal their position. I waited until they had passed my position on the slight rise. The troops even carried lanterns, allowing me to count them. Sixteen men heavily armed with swords and muskets. I attacked silently.

My arrows flew true. The first man at the rear of the procession fell unnoticed, my arrow piercing his neck. The group moved ahead without him, unaware he had fallen. The second shot had the same results; the man fell to the ground silently. I held my ground and launched another arrow. This time the man cried out. The remainder of the soldiers stopped. Confusion overcame the group. Some retreated, thinking the attack originated from the front of the group; others fired their weapons haphazardly in the direction from which they had come. The gun shots killed two of their own men. Others fired blindly up the hill in the direction of the fire. I simply stood and watched. The leader ordered a halt, attempting to restore order. Four of the sixteen died in this first little skirmish. I heard them speaking in Spanish. It seemed strange after so many years, to hear this language. As the captain discovered the casualties, he ordered his men into a defensive column. The group now numbering twelve began again in a much more cautious fashion to move toward the funeral-fire. I killed another man as they began their march. The arrow sank deeply into his chest from the side shot, evidently penetrating between ribs. He fell to the ground with a loud grunt.

The captain called a halt again; his troops obeyed. He held his light toward me and ordered a few men forward in my direction, pointing into the deep night. It was the last command he would ever give. My arrow pierced his throat and he fell in a shower of blood. The darkness whispered to me, *time to move, Daklugie.*

I calmly moved behind the little rise of land I had been standing on, then traveled another one hundred yards or so in advance of the soldiers. Taking up my next position on a similar rise of land, I waited. The men moved erratically. Some wanted to return to the camp by the river; they argued about what to do next. Two of the soldiers lingered behind, then turned and ran, escaping into the night back toward the massive encampment. I smiled at my good fortune. Only eight remained, and there would be survivors to report the fate of the group.

The men moved cautiously, slowly making their way closer to the fire. I waited for the right moment when they were again beyond my hidden location. I launched another arrow. The man in the rear of the procession fell. Panicking again, the others fired wildly down the hill behind them. This time the men gathered in a circle and lowered to the ground, reducing the target size. The lamps shone brightly, illuminating the targets. I fired again and again. Arrow after arrow flew into the group. I heard screams as men cried out. I was unsure how many were wounded or dead. All remained on the ground. I obeyed the dark whisper and moved again.

This time I returned to the funeral-fire. It was beginning to burn itself out, the flames rising only a few feet yet casting an eerie glow. The Cross of One Horse could be seen clearly, reflecting in the firelight. I moved to the opposite side of the flames from where I had been firing. I hid away in the night just outside the circle of light. I waited.

I heard them before I saw them. Fear permeated the darkness they traveled within. That fear grew as the men made out the masterpiece of blood on the rock. The soldiers had extinguished their lamps. However, the light of the funeral-fire glowed against their swords and muskets. I could easily make out the targets and kill zones. I killed three men inside of three seconds. The lone survivor knelt to his knees in prayer…and begged aloud into the darkness for his life.

I showed myself in the edge of the firelight. The man fell prostrate before me. He cowered in fear and held to his rosary. I calmly walked toward him.

"Tell me the name of your commander," I asked quietly in English.

"His name is General Joaquin de Arredondo," the man replied in perfect English.

"Tell General Arredondo…Daklugie will kill more men tomorrow and the next day, and the next."

The death toll within a few days would be alarming to the general.

Chapter 43

The following day I stood on a little hill within a sandy oak forest and observed the Mexican army from the south obliterate a slightly smaller army that had intercepted them. This slightly smaller force was comprised of those rebelling against the rule of Mexico, previously referred to as Casas. I estimated well over one-thousand men from the northern force had lost their lives. This was a great reminder to me of what I already knew and had communicated to Tosahwi. The Comanche, the Apache, and so many other tribes were but…a distraction, an inconvenience, and in their way. The true prize and reward for these armies were the lands of Texas and the entire western United States, and the riches and power that would certainly come to those who succeeded in possessing those lands. How might we as a people survive against such a hostile, bloodthirsty, power-hungry, greed-filled enemy? What I witnessed this day taught me a valuable lesson, or perhaps reminded me of something I already knew. These men would stop at nothing in their lustful attempt to gain the wealth these lands held.

But I also knew something about greed and those that were consumed by such. They would perhaps negotiate at the sight of that wealth being laid at their feet. Gold had a mighty unexplainable influence on the greedy.

I placed a ten-pound gold bar along the riverbank, then started a small fire near the shining gold. Prior to our journey east, One Horse and I melted the forty-pound bar I had removed from the cave in the high mountains. We poured the hot liquid into clay molds we had fashioned in the ground. I had carried two of these bars with me on the journey east, knowing it might be needed to gain an audience with the leaders of the army.

It only took a few moments for the soldiers to investigate the smoke. The note I wrote in the sand to General Arredondo was simple and to the point: "If you want more of this, meet me tonight at the fire rock overlooking the river. Daklugie"

I hid myself in the oak forest and observed from a distance. The men literally ran toward the camp after discovering the gold bar near the signal fire. I killed one of them with a perfectly placed arrow.

****

Santa Anna stood in silence; a storm of hatred contorted his face. Though General Joaquin de Arredondo, his superior, appeared calm and casual at our meeting, I could see the lust and greed that burned in his eyes. The second gold bar gleamed in the firelight, the Cross of One Horse clearly visible. I sensed the men were intrigued by its presence, perhaps even frightened, but neither spoke of the masterpiece overlooking our meeting.

"You and your warriors have killed many of my men, Daklugie," the general said with a look of hatred and revenge on his face.

"Those men tortured and killed my friend," I said defiantly. "Perhaps you have the power to end the killing of your own soldiers."

"What you possess has the ability to change the course of what my plan might be in dealing with you and your warriors. I assume there is more gold?" Arredondo said, a questioning look of lust in his eyes.

"I have more gold than you can carry, General." His eyes seemed to brighten at my words. "However, you will see it only if I receive that for which I came."

The general regarded me for a moment and considered his options.

"As I am sure you are aware, Daklugie, my men can take you captive at any moment."

"Possibly. But you will never have the gold if you allow that to occur, as I'm certain you must know."

"I am very intrigued by you, Daklugie. How is it that you speak perfect English?"

"There are many things about me you may not be able to comprehend, my gifting of language is the least important of these gifts. What you might be interested in knowing that may be more revealing to you is, there are no warriors with me. I act alone."

"Lies!" Santa Anta screamed, his voice rising in hatred. "You have killed forty of our finest fighting men, alone?" He spit on the ground in disgust near my feet.

"Forty-three," I said looking directly into the eyes of General Arredondo. I could see he believed me. A slight twinge of his mouth revealed his belief in the truth of my words. He knew I was speaking the truth.

"What is it you are asking of me in exchange for the gold, Daklugie?"

"Simply information," I said.

The man regarded me for a moment then replied, "First, you will share with me where this gold came from and how it is that you possess it."

"No, I will not."

"How dare you speak to the general in this fashion!" Santa Anna moved a few steps toward me, drawing his sword.

I stood my ground but kept my eyes on the general. He was still attempting to read me, determining what kind of man I was.

"Sit down, Colonel," the general reprimanded Santa Anna. The defiance in his eyes and the disrespect for the general radiated across the face of Santa Anna. I remembered my history on Santa Anna. I knew he would soon become president of Mexico and would defeat a brave group of soldiers at the great Stone Mission known as the Alamo. I also was aware it would be a temporary victory.

I said nothing for a few minutes as the fire crackled. With a sudden shift of the light wind, the smoke drifted our way. I followed the general's gaze as he observed the Cross of One Horse. With the change of the wind, I also heard a light disturbance in the trees above us. Someone was watching…waiting. Had he heard it also?

"My request is simple, General Arredondo. What has become of the armies of Spain? I know they have attempted to take back what their fathers claimed. I know also you have resisted and defeated the armies from across the sea. However, many remain; is that not true?"

Again, the general regarded me. I saw the wonder in his eyes. "Daklugie, your question brings many questions to my mind. Why do you ask of this? You are Comanche. Why does the Comanche value this information?"

Again, I waited a few moments. In the silence, I heard the call of the night bird…and a reply from across the hill. This was a tactic of the Comanche. Warriors had arrived!

"Why is a question that never has a complete answer, General. Why are there more than one-thousand dead men in the field below us? Why is my friend's blood on this rock behind me in the shape of a cross? I ask a question that has an answer; you ask a question that has no answer."

"Enough of these games! Let us see if you bleed red blood just as your friend did!" Santa Anna said.

"Silence!" the general commanded.

The anger and temper of one Antonio de Lopez de Santa Anna permeated the scene, a cloud of turmoil and rage surrounded the man. I began to understand the single overarching reason this man would be defeated. Pride.

"Daklugie, I will answer your questions, then you will direct me to the gold."

I nodded.

"The armies of Spain were defeated. There were very few survivors. A few soldiers escaped to the west. They had ships upon both shores of Mexico. Those who landed to the east on the Atlantic coast were routed. Those who arrived from the Sea of Cortez in the west were also defeated. Most of the western army never made the trip across the mountains. They were attacked by the French, the Natives, and finally by me. These armies are no more."

I looked deep into the eyes of the general as he spoke. I now had my answer. I knew where they would come from and how close they were to my Homeland. I also knew he had lied. I nodded in agreement.

"And now the gold!" Santa Anna moved toward the gold bar gleaming in the firelight. As he reached for the bar an arrow pierced his arm. He fell, crying out in anger. General Arredondo blew a whistle as his men raced up the hill. I heard him call out his orders. "Seize him."

But I was gone; in an instant I disappeared into the night. I ran in the direction of the arrow shot. The Warriors ran with me. In the blackness of the night, we escaped. We would not stop for miles. They would never be able to catch us. I tapped a Warrior on the shoulder. I held the gold bar I had gathered in my hasty departure toward him, indicating I needed assistance. "Your turn, my friend. This is quite heavy."

We ran through the night.

Chapter 44

We reached the horses just prior to the sunrise. Dried meat and water were shared in the few moments we rested along a clear running stream. Storm clouds filled the summer dawn and thunder rumbled through the countryside from all directions. The rain began as we departed the stream. The horses were fresh and took to the challenge, galloping through the beginnings of a glorious downpour. The storm would cover our tracks within a few hours, making it impossible for any pursuers to track us.

We were joined by the young boys who had tended the horses. We now numbered fifteen in total, twelve Warriors and three young men. Each man tethered an additional horse alongside his mount. I understood the purpose. We would ride out the first mounts, driving the animals until they foundered or simply came to a standstill. The war ponies were strong. They carried us along for hours. We slowed late in the afternoon along a beautiful clear running river, the San Saba I was told. We watered our original mounts, and the young men did their best rubbing them down for a few moments. The storms had helped in keeping the animals cool; perhaps the ponies would survive. We released them and took to our new mounts.

The fresh ponies again took up an unbelievable pace. We must have covered another twenty miles or more before the sun set. The rain continued, giant drops driving in windblown spray. We were soaked, everything we carried saturated with water. We continued to follow the river, and as the sun lowered below the western horizon, we slowed to a trot. The Warriors dismounted, and we started up a little canyon above the San Saba. I paused a moment, taking in the serene setting. Enormous oak and cedars lined the river, even some enormous native pecans. Deep rich grasses filled the meadows. This was a special place. I had no way of knowing this would become my home for decades to come. The Warriors motioned for me to follow as we entered a cavern, its entrance hidden in the bottom of the little canyon above the San Saba.

The way was difficult at first with a ceiling that was near only three feet in height. We crossed several small streams as I was warned not to step into the water. The men took up torches that had been prepared in advance. Eventually the cave began to open. Massive rooms appeared before us. Stalactites hung from the ceiling. Water flowed along bold little streams. I could feel a light wind against my skin. I was in awe.

A light appeared before us. Faint at first, the light grew as we neared its source. Within a hundred yards or so I could see men moving about the firelight. I smelled the aroma of meat cooking. As we drew near the firelight, Tosahwi moved forward and greeted us. He peered deeply into my eyes with an understanding look. I approached him and he reached for me. With his hand upon my shoulder our eyes met. "Daklugie, I am sorry beyond words at the loss of your friend. One Horse was a brave man." Tosahwi then embraced me and held me like a father would hold a child.

This act of kindness transported me to a different place and time. I was standing outside a gymnasium, my coach embracing me, comforting me at the loss of my mother. My thoughts wandered a moment, my mind focused on the image of my friend's cross of blood. I took in a deep breath and stepped away from Tosahwi, a dark pain rising within my soul.

These acts of kindness these great men imparted on me and so many others, allowed a soul a brief moment of comfort. Memories of my goodbye with Mr. Natchi flowed across my mind. I remembered again his prayer that he had spoken over me. Even though I could feel the love, compassion, and heartfelt sympathy my friend Tosahwi brought to my soul in this spiritual moment… this time I would shed no tears. The dark cloud would not allow them. I simply nodded. Those who had killed my friend would pay. I believe, as I look back on that moment, Tosahwi must have seen and known the look that arose from my soul and shone forth in my eyes.

****

The following morning, we exited the cavern along the banks of the San Saba River. The sky glowed a pearl blue and appeared washed clean from the rain, as was the earth. The grass glistened a deep rich green; the river flowed below us, clear and clean. The Warriors had feasted and rested soundly within the protection of the hidden cavern. As we mounted for our journey into the Llano, I thought how fierce and deadly this group's appearance seemed. We now numbered twenty-four warriors. Lethal, equipped, and able to protect, defend, and destroy any who dared enter our homelands. It suddenly occurred to me…this was a first. I was riding with and within a Comanche war party.

We found the wagon tracks only an hour into our journey. I knew these were the whites One Horse and I had stumbled on in our travel east just a few days ago. I remembered his words, "Dak, we should hunt them down." I recalled the look in his eyes and his intent. I would make certain whoever these trespassers were, they would feel the arrows of my friend One Horse. Those arrows I now carried within my quiver.

Tosahwi called a quick council. The Warriors gathered in a tight circle while we remained on our mounts. *"Three will trail them. Three more will follow yet remain hidden. The rest of us will wait here. Daklugie, you will lead the Warriors."*

My heart rose at his instructions. As Tosahwi selected the remaining force to accompany me, I removed an arrow and tested its edge. I knew they were all razor sharp. My grandfather's teaching created rote acts of preparedness that I executed sometimes knowingly in full awareness. This act was purely for show. The Warriors watched as I checked the arrows and the remainder of my gear, my war club, my grandfather's knife, the strap of my quiver.

The wagon was easy to follow due to the tracks left on the land. The smell gave the proximity away as we neared the whites. We stalked low in the buffalo grass. I could not believe the stench. The rotted flesh of twenty or thirty deer carcasses wafted along the trail left by the wagon. The wagon was loaded with the bodies of the dead bucks. *"Why so many?"* my fellow Warriors asked, a questioning sickening look on their faces. In disgust, I simply rose from the knee-deep grass, nocked an arrow, and strode intently toward the men in the wagon.

"You there. What have you done to the Great Spirit's animals? What are you doing to the land with your wagon wheels?" I spoke in perfect English. The three men rose from the seat in the front of the wagon, shock and disbelief on their faces. One man reached for a rifle. My arrow embedded deeply into his chest, and he fell from the wagon. The others jumped and attempted to draw weapons from their holsters. The next man fell with an arrow from my bow penetrating his torso.

"What have you done with these animals?" I asked again.

"We're tradin' um," came a terrified reply.

"To whom?"

"The Rangers need um; they pay good," the man replied as he rose from the ground with his hands in the air. I noticed the other Warriors rise from the grass behind the man.

"Rangers are buying rotten meat. Sacred animals stolen from the Comanche people?" I replied.

"Please, sir, we don't mean no harm." I saw the man move his hand behind his back as I neared him.

"My name is Daklugie. This is our land. You do not belong here. You will pay for the animals with your life." I spoke through clenched teeth, a heat rising from within my heart. The man brought the knife from behind his back as my first arrow penetrated his shoulder. The next arrow broke bone in his leg; the third, pierced his liver I was certain. The man fell to the ground, writhing in pain. I stood over him, my war cry echoing along the small hills. My grandfather's war club met its mark. My grandfather's knife lifted the man's scalp. Within seconds I held another two scalps in my hand. The knife and war club working quickly, skillfully. The dark cloud within encouraged, whispered, possibly even rejoiced at the elimination of this evil from our land.

The Warriors set fire to the wagon. We knelt together and prayed our sorrow to the Great Spirit at the careless waste and loss of the beautiful deer.

Tosahwi and the others watched the smoke rise from the bloody scene where vengeance, skill, and razor-sharp arrows had meted out complete and total justice. The words of One Horse rang in my heart as we resumed our journey north and west. "Others might not be so bold, Dak."

Chapter 45

One month later

Nita and I stood on the outcropping of rocks atop the ancient trail. Several seasons had passed since we had left the high mountains. Being back here among the high peaks brought to our minds the life we had left behind so many years ago. I held Nita's hand as we peered into the distance. The white sand desert shone brightly in the afternoon sun five thousand feet below us. There was no sign, nothing out of place from our vantage point. However, I could imagine the ominous cloud of dust rising in my mind's eye at the rear of the large army that was out there somewhere...advancing toward us.

"This was my point of view from where I saw my vision, Dak. The army was crossing the desert below, a gigantic cloud of dust trailing them. They may number in the thousands. However, you will succeed. The scales of wisdom are in your hands, husband." The ominous cloud of dust rose again in my mind's eye. I, too, could envision the storm rising as the large army advanced toward us.

I took a deep breath and paused, taking in the scene. I knew my purpose. I would make certain they never arrived here within our Homeland. I turned to Kwanita and simply gazed into her understanding eyes. I believed her vision was true and accurate. I thought of how best to turn the horde away. How we might best protect and defend. Gaining an audience with the leaders might cost men their lives. I thought of my friend One Horse.

"I must make certain they never arrive upon these mountains. They must be stopped in the deserts they are crossing. I am sure the trip has been difficult, and to this point they have no doubt wondered why anyone would value the land they have traveled. If they march into the mountains and discover the beauty of our homeland…they may desire what they see." I said these words aloud; however, I was speaking more to myself than to my woman. Nita nodded, an understanding look on her face. We turned and began the walk down the ancient trail.

The tribes and bands of Comanche and Apache had gathered along the banks of the Bonita River near the lower entrance to the snowy river cavern. One thousand fighting men ready and able, along with their wives and families, made an incredible sight. I could see evidence of the camp even from thirty miles away. The army of the Spaniards was out there moving toward us. How many miles now separated the two groups? I would need to act quickly.

The council convened that night, outside under the stars. Leaders from all the bands were included.

Tosahwi and Buffalo Hump took the places of highest honor. Buffalo Hump motioned for me to sit next to him. This was also a great honor and a great burden. With so many in attendance there were simply too many words. I sat in silence as Chiefs and Warriors alike spoke of attack and certain victory. I held my tongue, remembering what I had witnessed along the river lands far to the east. I had seen an army of 1,400 men slaughtered by the great guns on wheels, and rifles. I was convinced the Spaniards were so equipped. I waited.

The fires began to die out. The night grew cold, yet the fire within many of the Warriors and Chiefs remained white hot. The wind whispered in the trees along the riverbank. The stars seemed to twinkle in rhythm to a tune playing in my mind. The smells of the fire, the sound of children playing, songs of our people being sung by our women, moved my spirit in a way I had not felt in many moons.

Our travel into the Llano with the war party, the rendezvous with our people, even my uniting with Nita had left me empty. I felt a void and disconnected from my heart somehow. The mourning of Nadua at the loss of her husband, my friend One Horse, had added to this separation and pain I felt within my soul. As we traveled along toward the high mountains, Nadua sang the songs of mourning daily. Her pain and loss made the trip west unbearably sad. Even the swelling of her belly with the son of One Horse and the joy that should have brought was drowned out by the mournful songs she sang daily. This void within was somehow filled with the darkness that lived in me. Its presence ever near my thoughts. The darkness was quiet this night.

The sights and sounds before me tonight brought about the sorely needed reminders of my purpose. I must protect these people. My *People*. In an instant the plan took shape in my mind.

****

As I sat that night within the Council circle contemplating the news the scouts had delivered, I was amazed at the gifting of my wife. The scouts reported to the council the landing of many ships on the western shore a mere two hundred miles south and west of the Tucson Mission. Kwanita's vision had been true and correct; the army from across the sea was coming.

Buffalo Hump, Tosahwi, and the other Chiefs present regarded the news with some level of calm. We had known for months of their coming. But when would they arrive? The scouts had now confirmed the time frame. How best to respond to the army from across the sea was the question that rolled and twisted like an ominous storm within my mind. I smoked and listened, giving my full attention to each speaker. The suggestions offered to this point I knew would not succeed. After seeing the tactics and abilities of the Mexican Army along the river to the east, I believed none of the plans suggested would be successful, nor survivable.

I was also beginning to dismiss my thoughts of delivering the gold to the armies in an effort to appease them. The dark cloud within my soul suggested defending our families, our way of life, our land from these foreign hordes that had no right whatsoever to be here. A subtle burning within my mind and heart would not be damped by any peaceful offering. I wanted to drive these armies from our land, wounded and suffering. The death of my friend One Horse was due to these invaders. His life called to me, and his words echoed in my dreams. *Dak, perhaps others will not be so bold.* The talk of the council waned. Tosahwi spoke. *"Daklugie has been silent. What thoughts are within your heart, my friend?"*

I rose to speak. *"Brothers, these men have the ability to defeat us easily with their modern weapons. The cannon and the musket are far superior to our bows and spears. Understand I have seen these weapons of war in use. I have seen over one-thousand men fall in one day."* A wave of mumbling spread within the council circle. *"We must, however, fight."* Again, a round of positive, subtle cheers arose from the group. *"I have learned from my experience with the Mexican Army. There is a way to inflict serious casualties on this huge army. It is not with a show of force or a full battle. Let us attack them upon the ground we choose. We will choose wisely. We know this land. The Apache, the Comanche working together in small groups will pick at the edges of the hordes. Small groups of warriors under cover of darkness can kill three or four then quickly escape. In hidden canyons we can kill six or eight, then evade any pursuers. We can ambush any small groups of pursuers, intentionally leading them into traps...and kill all of them. In the passing of one moon, five hundred men, possibly more, will fall. This will discourage the others. Further, we must stop up the hidden springs that lay ahead of this army. The scouts have reported the leaders somehow know of the secret watering places.*

"*This has been done before. This is a plan that will remove the fight from the heart of this army. They will awaken each day to find their friends dead. They will arrive at a spring thirsty and find no water. They will be suffering terribly by the time they arrive here.*"

A silence fell over the council as the Chiefs considered my words. After a few moments, Buffalo Hump spoke. "*Daklugie, the war party reported you used these tactics on the edges of the Mexican Army. What were your results?*"

I paused for effect, then replied with a fire in my eyes that all could see. "*My bow killed over forty soldiers within three days. None of these enemies knew my well-chosen locations. None even fired a shot in the proper direction. Many retreated in fear at the death of their companions.*"

Silence fell on the Chiefs within the sacred circle.

Tosahwi stoked the sacred fire and stood. He began the song of victory. Indicating for me to kneel, I did so. Buffalo Hump also rose. As Tosahwi and the other Chiefs sang, Buffalo Hump placed his hands upon my head. The ceremony to become a Comanche Warrior began. Prayers for wisdom, prayers for victory, prayers for the safety of all Warriors were offered. The fire glowed brightly as the wives of the Chiefs entered the edges of the firelight. Kwanita moved alongside me and took my hand.

With his hands still upon me, Buffalo Hump gave me my new Comanche name.

Tenahpu (The Man) was now officially a member of the Comanche Tribe. I was now a protector Warrior of the NuMuNuu (*The People.*)

"*May the war plans of Tenahpu succeed!*" Buffalo Hump, the great Chief of the Penateka Comanche, proclaimed.

A loud cheer erupted from the group and the celebration began. I, however, was troubled deeply. The darkness continually reminded me of the vision I had seen in the still of the night along the banks of the Pecos River. I prayed I was wrong. I prayed I had not heard.

I could possibly protect our entire people. But how could I protect my wife, the mother of my child...the love of my life?

Tosahwi gazed into my eyes and saw. I knew that night...he had also seen.

Chapter 46

One year earlier

General Isidro Barradas stood on the bow of his flagship *Sovereign*. The trip through the Tierra del Fuego archipelago had been dramatic. The sea was angry and filled with waves larger than he had ever scene. The *viento*, or wind, sent a blinding sea spray across the bow of each ship. They had signaled repeatedly for the smaller galleon *Santiago* to move away from the coast. The captain of the *Santiago* ignored the signals, mistakenly thinking he was safer near the shoreline. Eventually the lee shore blocked any navigable wind. The ship, along with its crew of fifty men, was drawn helplessly into the protruding rocks along the coastline. Within minutes the massive waves splintered the galleon into small pieces of floating debris. General Barradas was fairly certain none had survived. A rescue would have endangered the other ships. It was an easy decision to press on.

Still, he knew they had been blessed. The loss of but one ship to the treacherous waters was a success by any measure. The men were recovering from the loss of their fellow sailors. Perhaps the sailing on the Pacific would be much more hospitable. Indeed, the sun shone brightly on the remaining fleet. The sea had calmed, the air already beginning to warm slightly as the small fleet bore to the north and west, moving away from the coast of South America. "Steady as she goes, *Capitán*," General Barradas ordered.

"Aye, aye, General," the captain replied.

General Barradas strode along the deck of the schooner, examining every detail of the ship. The *Sovereign* was still sound despite the beating the sea had dealt her. Descending the steps to his cabin and entering, he settled into the

comfort of his desk and opened the research logs again. He knew the gold…
must still be there.

The trip from Spain and the orders he had received were futile at best.
Moving three thousand-plus men across the sea to attempt to regain control
of Mexico he considered a foolish undertaking. The powers that be could not
quite let go of the lands of North America. Two hundred years of attempting
to rule…from across an ocean were at last failing. The men who now ruled
were indeed the descendants of those who had explored and conquered the
land. However, many of these men had been born in North America, educated
there, and raised their families there. The leaders of the New Spain had very
little connection to a crown across the sea that demanded taxes, loyalty, and
submission. The general believed this continent would never remain under the
control of Spain…nor France or England for that matter. He also understood
this mission to seize control militarily was destined to fail. Military success
was not why he had agreed to lead such a doomed undertaking. His years of
research, however, were the deciding factor in accepting this mission.

He had spent his life savings to acquire the logs. The writing seemed to leap
from the pages. He had studied the detailed maps for years. Most of the map's
features were burned into his mind. The handwritten treasure of information
penned by Juan De Onate himself revealed that Onate had in fact discovered
the *Casa del Cueva de Oro*, the House of the Golden Cave.

Details of the enormous deposit of golden bars and treasure were even logged
daily as the booty had been inventoried and stored within the cave. The general
was also aware the enslaved workers had been left to die within the cavern on
completion of their grueling work. Most had been chained and left to die with
the secrets they were privy to. Onate was a brutal man. His enslavement and
mistreatment of the Native Americans living in the deserts of southwestern North
America had eventually reached the ears of the King of Spain. The logs revealed
Onate had been charged with cruelty, dereliction of duty, and immorality. He had
overseen the killing of more than one-thousand Acoma Pueblo Native Americans.
He had ordered one foot cut off any Acoma Warriors that had reached the age of
twenty-five years. The remaining tribal members were ordered to serve twenty
years of forced servitude. The results of his trial for these cruel acts were two-fold.
Firstly, banishment for life from the territory of New Mexico. And secondly, he
would never reveal to his superiors the details of the treasure he had discovered
and hidden away. Nor would the enormous cost of thousands of lives lost while
attempting to keep the treasure a secret be revealed.

The code he recorded in his personal logs had taken years to decipher. The scholars the general had hired eventually had cracked the code using an ingenious tool. The transcription became quite simple when navigation points on the globe were sorted and the text reorganized based on known points on the globe. The math equations revealed the precise location of the gold.

The scholars had met with unexplainable deaths after solving the formula to decode Onate's logs. Their deaths were added to the innumerable life toll this gold had caused. General Barradas breathed deeply and closed the 200-year-old handwritten logs. He was drawing closer to the Cueva de Oro. He could picture in his mind this unbelievable treasure within his hands. He could even imagine what his life would become…after its recovery.

The trip north would be difficult to conceal. He had departed the Indies to the east toward Spain. However, once out of sight of land he had taken up a heading to the south. His superiors in Spain would believe his fleet to have been destroyed or sunken in some great storm on their failure to arrive home on schedule. His men were awaiting him on the shores of the Sea of Cortez. Those who had made the halfhearted effort to retake Mexico City had moved away from the battle to the south and west and would await his arrival. The general was aware the upcoming trip overland across the southwest deserts would be difficult at best. The knowledge contained within the logs of Onate would prove to be invaluable. The water sources and routes were clear in his mind. Patience was a difficult thing for many. He would not repeat the mistakes of Onate. Moving a fleet in complete concealment was possible. They would travel hundreds of miles between landings. Resupply would only occur under the protection of nightfall. After each resupply, the ships would be well offshore prior to day light.

The plan was intact and being executed with precision. As he reviewed each integral step in his master plan, the only unknown factor that haunted his nights and troubled his mind was what had happened with Onate himself. He was aware of the historical facts, the Native Americans had in the end… defeated Onate.

Would there possibly be resistance once again from the Native Americans? Apaches, Acoma peoples, Comanche even. It was impossible for him to know their numbers or their military capabilities. He was confident he would have the upper hand militarily. He was certain of his superior intellect. In Onate's logs, he constantly referred to these people as "uneducated heathens." He believed the logs would prove to be true and correct.

Why, then, was his mind so troubled concerning the savages?

The Cross of One Horse

Three Months Later

General Barradas spied the jagged shoreline of the island that appeared eerily out of the lifting fog just two kilometers ahead of the ships. The fog dissipated just enough to make out the sound they would sail into and anchor within. Using the maps and writings of Father Eusebio Francisco Kino S.J., he was amazed at the accuracy of the map details. It seemed appropriate, this chosen hidden location being used as his last resupply point…was aptly named after the man who had spent his life detailing the coast of what was then New Spain. Kino Bay, located along the western coast of mainland Mexico, was small and well hidden from view due to the large island of Tiburon just offshore. Any other ships sailing the Sea of Cortez would most likely never have the vantage or ability to spot his ships as they lay at anchor in the small inlet. The general knew they were again fortunate they had not been intercepted or even spied by any of the French cargo and war ships that plied the waters of the Sea of Cortez. He was aware a mere ninety miles west of his present location the French maintained a stronghold on the peninsula of California within the small harbor of Santa Rosalia. His good fortune was a sign to him that his mission would indeed succeed.

The ground troops had successfully navigated the Sierra Madre's and had spent a full year along the shores of Kino Bay. The men were well supplied and had befriended the local Native population of Yaqui Indians living in this desolate harsh environment. This also proved to be a positive sign to the general of his assured success. His commanders expressed the certainty that without such assistance from the natives, the Sonoran Desert would without doubt have cost many lives. However, the general could not allow these natives to live. At the objection of his commanders, the Yaqui were chained and orders for their execution given and carried out. He did not need any witnesses that might report the location of his army. More innocent lives had been added to the death toll relating to the Casa del Cueva de Oro and the gold that it contained.

General Barradas allowed a full week of rest and recovery for his troops and commanders. He knew without doubt the difficult journey they had all endured was a small victory. The vast wastelands of the North American southwest lay before them—wastelands that could prove to be more difficult than crossing oceans and mountains.

The men were well-fed, healthy, and ready for adventure. On the eighth day after their landing in Kino Bay and reuniting with his army from the west, three thousand men began the long trek to the north and east. Casa Del Cueva de Oro lay possibly only two months of hard travel ahead.

The cannons rolled along well. The supply wagons were filled with ammunition, cannon fire, musket balls, and gun powder. The men shouldered the loads eagerly. The promise of gold was a quite unique motivation. Although, most of these men would never see or share in the bounty that lay ahead. A pity on some level, he thought.

****

The Apache scouts observed the scene below them from the mountains above Kino Bay.

A great army from across the sea moved along the desert floor, creating a huge column of dust that rose hundreds of feet into the clear blue Sonoran sky. The scouts would carry the news to their homeland quickly and efficiently as they rode tirelessly across the endless expanse of desert. They would arrive along the high mountains of New Mexico Territory a full month ahead of the army from across the sea.

Chapter 47

One Month Later

The first skirmish came at an inopportune time, General Barradas thought. "A small band of Native Americans," his commander reported. "I am certain we stumbled on these Natives by pure accident, sir."

"And the result of this so-called accident?" General Barradas questioned. The commander swallowed hard.

"We lost seven men to their arrows." The commander lowered his head and stared at the ground as the fury in the eyes of his general bore through him.

"And did you pursue and kill the savages?"

"I am confident we killed several of them. However, we were not able to recover any bodies."

"And why is that?" General Barradas rose to his feet in rage, his voice high pitched with anger and tension.

"The savages move like ghosts; they are there by a boulder…only to vanish. We spot them in the brush…and then they are gone," the commander replied.

"Silence! Enough of this deceit! Did you fire a musket or unload a cannon on these savage ghosts?"

"The savages do not allow time for cannon fire, sir. Most of my men were killed while attempting to position the cannon. The arrows flew relentlessly. We had to retreat, lest all of us would have died."

****

We disappeared from their view, escaping along the hidden arroyo. The small advance party of Spaniards had felt our arrows enter their bellies. Many fell dead, several others wounded; none of our warriors were injured.

Buffalo Hump walked beside me as we made our way along and within the deep crevasse in the desert floor.

"The strategy is good, Tenahpu." He gazed into my eyes with a look of admiration. I nodded.

"The secret watering place will be an even greater victory." He acknowledged the thought, knowing the location and natural cover within firing distance would cause many more of the horde to fall.

The following day we observed a detachment of forty men depart the main army for the resupply and filling of the water barrels that were carried along by the wagons. General Barradas ordered two cannons to be positioned prior to the resupply, along with the doubling of troops to escort the wagons to and from the hidden spring clearly marked on his map.

He was troubled within his mind. The previous night he had found no sleep into the long restless night. Perhaps his commander was correct. Certainly, the previous day's skirmish was but an unfortunate, chance encounter with the savages. He would, however, take no chances this day. His bravest commander would oversee the water resupply. They had only two days of water reserves. It was imperative the supply barrels within water wagons be filled. The heat was becoming unbearable.

Yes, he was convinced it had been a chance encounter.

****

The ground we occupied was elevated, concealed, and provided an easy escape into the arroyos of the desert floor below us. We waited. I observed the cannons being moved into position. Each cannon was positioned within firing range of the spring and behind the main group of soldiers. A two-man detail remained with each cannon. Buffalo Hump understood my hand signals instantly. He departed with two Warriors to dispatch the cannon crews. We waited, observing the soldiers falling around their cruel arsenal within the next few minutes. None were able to fire a warning shot. The water wagons were drawn up alongside the spring, or rather where the spring had been flowing. Now the ground was but a puddle of mud where just the day before fresh water had flowed. There would be no water stores for the horde from across the sea found here this day. The poison herbs we had buried within the head spring would bring great sickness on any who attempted to reopen the spring and drink of its fouled water. The ambush was set. Surprise, our greatest advantage, was still on our side.

The wagon crews seemed confused. Unable to locate the free-flowing water, they signaled for the leader to come to them. The commander unknowingly allowed his entire troop to follow him to within bow shot of the wagons. I paused a moment and saw in my mind's eye the scales Kwanita had seen in her vision. The scales were decidedly tipped in our favor this day. On my signal the arrows were released. I released my arrow from the string nock of my grandfather's bow. The leader of the detachment fell in a shower of blood. Within seconds, the arrows of my Warrior friends and brothers also found their mark. A dozen men lay dead. The retreat of the soldiers was met with a rainfall of arrows on them from our flanking movement at the rear of the group of Spaniards. Many fell in the volley of wooden arrows, sharpened stone arrowheads, and lances. The great guns of the Spaniards sat in silence, overlooking the bloody scene like frozen impotent soldiers unable to advance on their enemy.

A few musket shots were fired at no particular target. This was our signal to retreat into the arroyos. Many soldiers would respond to the firing of the guns. They would find nothing but light footprints in the sand…and more than thirty of their men dead.

We paused after an hour of travel. The twelve of us drank deeply from our water carriers. Our stronghold was less than one hour of travel from here. None from the hordes had followed. The small foothills that rose from the desert would conceal our position. The stronghold was stocked with food and supplies. We would be well fed and refreshed as we planned our next attack. Upon our arrival at the stronghold, Buffalo Hump struck a small fire and began the songs of victory.

****

General Barradas fumed inwardly. He had questioned the survivors personally. None were able to answer his questions. They had no idea how many Natives had attacked, nor did they have any indication of which direction the natives had fled. Nor for that matter could he obtain from the men any explanation or description of what group, or tribe, the heathens hailed from.

He studied his notes, knowing full well the next water was more than five days from their present location. He immediately ordered the rationing of all water and supplies. He had his men dig into the earth and fill but three water barrels. As the sun lay on the western horizon, the heat of this day failed to subside. General Barradas stood and moved to the large water barrel he kept within his private tent. He drank deeply from the store. The men were already beginning to grumble. The next five days of travel would be torturous…for most. Realization dawned. The previous day's attack had not been a chance encounter. Nor had this attack been unplanned. In fact, it was a well-planned military operation that by all accounts was quite successful.

Sleep would evade him again this night.

****

The captain who had survived the attack with but a shoulder wound from an arrow sat in the circle with his comrades. The tale of the attack was both captivating and gruesome. More than any other detail, the retelling of the arrows from the ghost warriors hitting their marks, planted fear in the hearts of the men whose ears the information rested on. Fear spread each night around the fires, and each day along the hot, dry, thirst-filled column of Spaniards as they made their way across the desert in this miserable land far from their homes and families.

The following day many of the men became sick with dysentery. Many of the afflicted could not continue and were left behind. Most understood this was a death sentence. The men of the horde scanned the horizon and the brush with each step they took. They knew "Ghost Warriors," might appear and attack at any moment.

****

The following morning after a full restful night, we arose within the safety of the stronghold. This day would be spent in resupply and planning our next attack. I knew without doubt our victories of the last two days would have an enormous effect on both the leaders and the men of the armies from across the sea. I sat alongside my Warrior friends and imagined an unseen enemy attacking our Warriors from what seemed like nowhere. It would cause much fear. I was proud of the Warriors. I also knew the seed of fear had been firmly planted in our enemy.

"*What is in the mind of Tenahpu,*" Buffalo Hump asked as we sat in a circle around the sacred fire, savoring and recalling our victory.

I thought for a moment before speaking. I smoked deeply from the pipe. "*Fear,*" I stated. "*Fear has been planted in the hearts of this army.*" All nodded in agreement.

"*We must choose wisely. We will now change our tactics. They will expect an attack at the next water source. That will not happen. We must never respond in the way they might anticipate. We must remember their abilities with the guns and the number of fighting men they have. We will attack again when they are out of water. This time let us find an ambush at the rear of their column. We may only kill a few...but it will be enough.*" The men all nodded in agreement.

The Spirit had spoken in and through me. My "Time of Quiet" was becoming increasingly fruitful. I saw the scales again two days later.

****

We sat unmoving, hidden stealthily within the boulders along a small uplifting of the earth. The rock outcropping stretched for ten miles along the desert floor. The heat was stifling. However, each Warrior was able to conceal himself within the small shadows the boulders cast. We observed the horde as the heavy guns, uniforms, and powder horns hindered their march. Shoulders slouched, arms drooped, heads bent low. We waited while the entire army passed us by. I counted soldiers as they passed. My estimate: at least three thousand men paraded before us. I listened to the talk as groups of men drew near and stumbled by our hidden location. I heard the term more than once as several of the men peered into the shadowed outcroppings.

"No ghost warriors here, amigos."

Ghost warriors? We had been named!

I suddenly had an idea. I began to draw a rudimentary picture of a ghost on the rock nearest me. It was holding a drawn bow and floating in midair. I hoped they would find it.

Toward the end of the procession, we readied our bows. Twelve Warriors each took aim. The arrows were released simultaneously. Each man had chosen one of the last twelve men in line. All arrows met their mark. Twelve men fell as we disappeared into the boulder field. A volley of musket fire followed within a few seconds; however, we escaped and were well out of range by the time any responded. Moving rapidly and now concealed by the uplift in the desert floor, we simply disappeared. The cavern was half a mile from our location. All Warriors reached its safety within five minutes of our attack. We skillfully moved the gigantic boulder into place. I, being the smallest, smoothed the sand below the boulder, expertly removing any tracks and sign. I entered last. From within the small cavern the Warriors moved another large boulder over the entrance. It would take at least six men to move the boulder again as it settled snugly into place. The *ghost warriors* had vanished within the boulder field.

****

General Barradas swore as he interrogated the witnesses of the attack on the rear of the column. Each time a witness used the words *ghost warrior*, he swore again. He ordered the term never to be spoken within his hearing again. His order insured it would be spoken repeatedly, day and night among his men.

He sent one hundred men into the boulder field. He surrounded the edges of the field with another two hundred men. The army wasted an entire day attempting to find the attacking heathens. His men found nothing, not a trace, with one exception—an image of a ghost warrior was discovered scrawled on a rock. The story of the image was reported around each and every campfire that night. Ghost warriors had attacked the army from across the sea.

****

We exited the cavern the following day. Rested and well fed, we observed the army of three thousand men separate into two columns. One column continued east, the other hastily moved south. We heard the thunder of cannon fire as the northern army evidently fired upon their own escaping men.

Chapter 48

Kwanita

It was peaceful, Kwanita thought. Life here within her homeland, among the lifelong friends she had made was peace-filled. With Dak away leading the small group of Warriors, the days were filled with caring for one another, praying together for the men, feeding, and caring for the little ones. Nadua would give birth at any moment now, though it was early for her. The child within her womb continued to grow and wrestle...and sing. Kele, wife of Tosahwi, had prophesied over the child within the womb of Nadua. She had seen. He would become a great leader. The nights spent within our own lodge were the most amazing. The child would sing for hours, or simply hum the tunes of our people. The voice was pure and clear. The voice seemed to bring light into the mind and heart of those who heard.

I rose early as was my practice and prepared an early morning fire. I warmed the antelope meat over the open flame. Each day I brewed the special tea I had learned of from Kele, preparing the soothing drink for Nadua. On her rising this day, I saw the look within her eyes. Today her son would enter this world.

The women were awaiting outside the lodge, birthing equipment in hand. We made our way along the high ridgeline, traveling slowly along the spine of our high mountains. All within the sacred gathering knew this day would be a special day, as all birthing days were.

We all seemed to sense this birth would be different and unusual.

****

Nadua scarcely made a sound. The pains came on her full sharp. I knew what she was experiencing and was amazed she never cried out. For hours, the midwives consoled and comforted Nadua. She struggled under the task ahead; well into the day she began to speak in a tongue none of us understood. The baby would sing and cry and wrestle. It seemed as if the child resisted his birth. I saw. With my eyes closed. I saw the vision of reunion.

I moved to Nadua. My hands caressed her face. I whispered of the greatness of her child's father. I spoke of the courage of One Horse. I reminded her of his action in saving the people. I whispered of his love for her into her awaiting eager ears. I spoke blessings over her boy child.

I spoke the secrets that had been revealed to me. Her son would indeed become a great leader of our people.

Nadua, for her part, gave all her life energy to the process. The hours floated by like a great storm cloud of summer that watered the dry places of the earth. Time was a tempest that moved slowly across the land. I saw the look in the eyes of the midwives and even the concerned expression on the face of Kele. Still the hours rolled by like a wave of slow-motion wind across a prairie filled with bowing buffalo grass.

With my hands on her face, the women singing the ancient songs, the prayers of Kele, the flood gates of her womb eventually opened. There was much blood. The boy child was wrapped in swaddling and placed upon her breast. The songs began softly. The women tended Nadua as best they could. The boy child sang the songs of new birth.

Nadua gazed on her child and spoke her only words of the entire day, "*His name shall be Tabbananica…Voice of the Sun.*"

I have witnessed a few of *The People* depart this earth, older ones whose time had come, others who simply grew sick or were injured. Always a mystery, this moving from one world we inhabit daily, into the next where we are forever comforted and blessed by the presence of our loved ones. There is, if a person is listening, a peace in the passing of a loved one.

My friend Nadua, the most beautiful maiden, now a mother, one of the bravest women I have ever known…breathed her last that evening as she lay upon the breast of the high mountains.

Within that last breath she spoke with her husband, Sumu Puku (One Horse). The two had a blessed, intimate conversation. He acknowledged how proud he was of her. She spoke to him in song, blessing their child with notes of a tune composed by the Creator that only the two could hear and understand.

Nadua gazed into my eyes and said goodbye. She reached for her unseen husband, One Horse, and the two strode away hand in hand into the Great Land. I know without doubt, they both now walk with our people. They walk with our Creator. I know they are both very happy…as am I.

Tabbananica began the song of mourning. His voice was like that of the sun on a soft springtime day, bringing a slight warmth to his listeners.

Kele, wife of Tosawhi, became the mother of Tabbananica that day.

The following day the funeral fire was lit on the breast of the high mountains. The celebration was reverent and filled with hope. Some tears were shed; however, all who attended seemed to know deep within our spirits that the uniting of Nadua and One Horse in the afterlife was a joyous occasion. I have never to this day felt the peace at the death of a friend as I experienced that day.

****

One of the things I missed most about my old life was pen and paper. As a young girl I often journaled my days and life experiences. That simply was not possible in the time we now walked. I began a practice each evening of journaling in my mind. Some evenings I recited the days gone by to myself. Topusana sat listening intently at my feet. Other evenings, I would take mental notes of my day and my life among *The People*. I realized after several weeks following the death of Nadua, how close we were. Nadua was my friend. I missed her terribly.

I was beginning to understand my husband and his suffering at the loss of his friend One Horse. Dak had changed so much since our travel into the past. He was no longer an innocent young boy. With Nadua's death, I now understood why Dak had withdrawn from me and become so distant. It was his way of dealing with the loss. I understood how his spirit could be directed to seek out and punish those who had brought about this heartache.

My loss was different. The death of Nadua had not been at the hands of an enemy. I wrote in my mind that her death was a picture of mercy, a freeing of her spirit, a reunion of her love. Though I was alone again and some days I wanted to feel deprived of the time we as young mothers would never live out together, my mind simply would not allow the bending of truth to fit into my own emotional needs. Yes, I missed her. But the death of Nadua was ordained… and a beautiful thing.

I wondered if I might ever convince Dak that the same was true for his friend One Horse.

I understood the darkness had taken hold of his emotions. I felt it many nights as we lay together within our teepee lodge. He was miles away from me; we lived a universe apart. Any and all who knew Dak sensed the fierceness of who Dak had become. The light that lived within the center of that darkness was still very much there, a small flame that brought hope to his soul.

How was I, as his women, to kindle that light of life and love?

I journaled in my mind how I might encourage, support, and draw out the light that burned ever so dimly within the heart of my man. The things we must walk through in life that bring us to the places of knowledge and understanding are never the easy path. I wrote this in the sand beneath the buffalo robe lining the floor of our lodge.

Sana settled near me in her sleep. As I watched our child sleeping in peace, I was reminded by the Spirit that I was not so alone, that I was blessed.

Chapter 49

Daklugie

Divide and conquer. I am not sure where I had read the statement. But what I saw in the distance across the shimmering heat-soaked desert was exactly that. At a minimum, one thousand men departed the army from across the sea and traveled to the south. Within the next sunrise, there was no trace of those who had moved south. The dust cloud ahead of us that trailed the main army continued to rise across the vast wasteland. They had no water. Morale was obviously at a breaking point and the river lay two days travel ahead. The Rio Grande was within reach. I was certain they were aware of this fact. We trailed the army, observing the men left behind to die. At first sight, it was just a few stragglers. Then a dozen men lay in the sand. Then in another place fifty or more. We simply passed them by without words. Ghost Warriors. We would allow the desert to take their lives.

The light within the darkness called out to me as were passing by a small group of men. A young man raised his hand, pleading for a drop of water. "Just a drop, sir?" his voice broken and dry. I looked his way. He must have been only sixteen or seventeen years old. I stopped, observing the other men attempting to grasp their weapons. The suffering these men were enduring was immeasurable. My anger at their leader rose within my heart. The light within flickered as I moved to the young man and offered him a small drink from the palm of my hand. He did not have the strength to raise his head and receive the water. I poured the small offering across his lips. A few moments later he died, with a look of relief on his face.

A true leader will never gloat when his enemy has fallen. The voice of

Grandfather echoed in my mind.

We pressed on, the other Warriors staring after me in wonder. The enemy ahead still had many healthy, willing fighting men, and they were nearing our homeland.

That night within the safety of a hidden arroyo the fire burned as the Warriors discussed our next move. "*The army will surely gain strength as they water along the river,*" Buffalo Hump stated. We all nodded in agreement. I was not quick to speak this night. I listened to the others, my mind distant. I had no plan to attack. I thought and pondered and prayed. I, simply put, had nothing in my heart about what our next move might be. "*Tenahpu is quiet this night,*" Buffalo Hump said.

"*When there is no clear path, should a man force his own way? His own will? Sometimes it is good to wait when direction is not clear.*" Nods and grunts greeted my words. I rose and moved to my sleeping area in the soft sand. Buffalo Hump did the same. The voice and wisdom of my grandfather had spoken to each of us.

The following morning, I still had no plans within my heart. I knew we should not act but rather observe. As we readied for the day ahead, all looked to me for advice. "*Let us observe this army. Let us see what their plans may be. We will move north and cross the river well away from the missions of Las Cruces (The Crosses). From there we can observe from the high ground along the mountains.*" I turned and began the long walk. Quickening my pace, we were soon a band of fierce Warriors running across our land, brave, wise, filled with fierceness beyond compare. Twelve men who had turned an army of more than three thousand into a defeated divided group of fearful men simply attempting to survive. Where were they going? Why the drive to press on? I needed information.

The two soldiers we stumbled on as they lay concealed in the shade of a small boulder revealed exactly what I needed to know. I froze as the first aimed his musket at the center of my chest. He pulled the trigger and a puff of smoke and flame exploded in his face. The weapon had miss-fired. The Warrior behind me fired an arrow that had deadly consequences. The man fell forward, dead, the arrow piercing his heart. The second soldier quickly threw his weapon to the ground and raised his hands.

"You have been left to die," I stated matter of factly.

"You speak English?" The middle-aged man said in wonder, an expression of fear and surprise on his face. His accent seemed strange and out of place, definitely not Spanish.

I paused, contemplating what had just happened, knowing that I, but for a dirty weapon, might easily have just been killed. The darkness within smiled on me. "We will spare your life based on what you can tell me right now about this army and the intentions of your commander."

The man, again with an expression of wonder, sat with his mouth agape. I dropped a carrier of water in his lap. "Go ahead, drink your fill. I will wait for your decision to live or die."

The man drank greedily from the container. I then dropped a generous supply of dried meat into his lap. "Yes, I choose life. I can tell you everything."

"There is no need to rush, you have chosen wisely." I sat in the shade beside the man as he revealed the true mission of the army from across the sea.

"Gold. It is all he can see. No matter how many lives it may cost. The general can only think of what is called the Casa de Cueva de Oro (The House of the Golden Cave). He possesses the logs of Onate. He knows where the gold is."

"And his name?" I questioned.

"General Isidro Barradas," the soldier answered.

"And you were defeated in the great city of Mexico?"

"We never mounted an attack; our mission was to survive and travel here for the gold."

I regarded the man. The information I had just received was priceless. We left him with much food and water. "Your army has divided. Those in revolt have moved south. You would be wise to join them after you recover. The river is but two days from here. Rest, move south and east when you are able. There are missions along the river. You will survive."

"Thank you, sir. I am Thomas Coulter.* Physician, botanist, and explorer. I have no interest in the gold. I joined with this army purely for educational and explorational purposes. I am in fact a naturalist and explorer by trade. And your name?" he questioned.

"Ghost Warrior," I answered as fear—or was it simply a questioning look—flashed across the man's face.

I would learn much of this Irishman's survival and work throughout the deserts of the southwestern United States later in my life.

Now I knew where the destination was. I knew the purpose of the mission, and I knew the gold was no longer hidden in the Casa del Cueva de Oro located within Victorio Peak. The gold these men had crossed the world to find…was in my little home upon the high mountains of our homeland.

Wisdom is what I would seek now. I could simply surrender the gold and the struggle and threat to our people would end. It seemed a simple solution. However, I considered the result of armies from across the sea becoming wealthy beyond their wildest dreams, and what that news might influence others to consider.

"*Let us return to our home. We will need the counsel of many to turn these men away from our homeland.*" The other Warriors agreed. We left the man with food and water. If we moved swiftly, we could arrive along the high mountains within two or three days.

The following day we crossed the Rio Grande a mere ten miles north of the army from across the sea. The day after, we observed the army setting camp at the base of Victorio Peak.

We moved across the desert floor of White Sands swiftly. I wondered how many days of exploration it would take before the general discovered the gold was gone.

*Dr. Thomas Coulter (1790-1843)

Chapter 50

The news of the death of Nadua caused the dark cloud within my heart to boil and swell like a storm riding across the mountains in summer. I spoke no words at the news. Kwanita held me that night within our tepee lodge. Sana settled close to me, my young daughter so obviously happy to see and be with her father. She needed my attention and assurance and love. As I look back on the time, it is my greatest failure as a father and husband that I gave none of what my little family needed most. It seemed I was consumed with the storm clouds of darkness.

The council met the following night. From the top of the ancient trail, I had observed the armies working along the base of Victorio Peak. Although the small mountain was more than fifty miles away as the crow flies, the vantage from the high mountains allowed a view across the White Sands Desert. The cloud of dust suggested the armies were working, digging, perhaps, searching the peak. Soon they would discover the hidden rooms within Victorio Peak were empty. I had no way of knowing if directions had been left within the hidden rooms as to the present location of the gold, as was the case in what I had discovered within our cave on the high mountains. We set watches on the ancient trail to observe continuously. The watchers would report the instant any movement of the army was detected.

"*These armies have invaded our land. They should pay with their lives,*" Chief Palanquito spoke firmly.

"*I agree,*" Buffalo Hump spoke next. All within the circle agreed with grunts of affirmation.

Tosahwi looked toward me for a response. I felt it would be difficult to continue my efforts at warning of the dangers this army posed. Many of the

Warriors and Chiefs were becoming frustrated at the lack of aggressive action they wished to take. Tosahwi gazed into my eyes with a faraway look.

"I agree, my brothers," Tosahwi said. *"We should, however, continue to set ambushes for this army. We should triple our efforts. Let us send out three groups of fighting Warriors. Twelve in each group. We will attack them day and night. The words of Daklugie must be regarded. Wisdom is within what his woman, Kwanita, has seen. This is a dangerous army. The scales must be in our favor prior to each attack."*

A silence fell within the council lodge. I knew this was not the action the Chiefs wanted. They wanted blood. I prayed for calmer voices of reason to speak. I knew it was not my time to repeat again the dangers.

"The Apache will send one hundred Warriors," Chief Palanquito spoke vehemently. *"We will test the capabilities of the army. Let us see if we cannot raise many scalps."* A cheer arose from the council at his words. I caught the look in Tosahwi's eyes. I understood we could not affect the decision proposed. I sat in silence, fearful we were soon to lose many friends and Warriors. The time had come for me to meet General Barradas.

****

The Warriors were all mounted with the finest war ponies. War paint covered their faces and their mounts. Fierceness, resolve, and confidence radiated from the faces of these brave men. I understood. I even wanted to be a part of the warring party. This was our homeland. Our people's lives were in the balance.

That night the fires of the War Dance burned brightly. *The People* offered prayers for wisdom, victory, and protection during the simple ceremony. Chief Palanquito's Warriors were filled with confidence, resolve, and fierceness. The songs of victory echoed across the high mountains late into the night.

Later, in the dim light of our tepee lodge, Kwanita and Topusana also prayed fervent prayers of protection and victory. Kwanita shared with me in the small hours of morning what she had seen. The scales above the armies from across the sea appeared in perfect balance.

Kwanita and I struggled with the sleep that night. Even Topusana lay awake well into the night. She seemed to sense our worry and concern. I listened as she prayed for the success of our Warriors. A hard lump filled my chest at the prayers of my three-year-old daughter. I wanted to cry. However, the dark cloud quickly overcame my emotions. There would be no tears shed from within the dark cloud.

The following morning *The People* watched with pride as the war party departed. They would move north and west, crossing the mountains just north of the Bonita River. They would attack on the second night from today. Six hours later the watchers reported the army beginning to move across White Sands in our direction.

We knew Chief Palanquito and his Warriors would not have arrived at Victorio Peak yet. Tosahwi and I raced our mounts up the ancient trail. Perhaps from the high mountains we could observe the movement of the army and our Warriors.

****

From our vantage point, we determined the army was on the move. A trail of white sand dust rose behind the column as perhaps two thousand men, wagons full of equipment, and cannons slowly made their way across the desert floor. The answer to my question appeared to be obvious. Why would they move toward our location? Even if they had discovered the cave to be empty, survival would be much easier to stay close to the river. To depart from a good food source and the fresh water along the Rio Grande did not make sense. A compelling reason must be driving General Barradas to cross the White Sands Desert. Had they found another log within Victorio Peak? Perhaps it contained similar information as I had found in our cave on the high mountains.

As we observed the cloud of dust below us, a smaller nearly indiscernible cloud appeared to the north of the army column. The Warriors were shadowing the movement of the armies from across the sea. "*Has Daklugie a plan within his heart now?*" Tosahwi asked with a questioning look on his face.

"*Yes, I do,*" I replied.

Chapter 51

General Barradas burned with anger. They had searched the peak for two full days and had discovered the rooms purported to be filled with gold. But there was nothing. No gold, no treasure. Nothing but dozens of skeletons. He had personally entered the caves within the peak. He had scoured each passageway and room. He could not quite reconcile in his mind that this was all a lie. The story could not be some fabricated fairy tale. Onate would never have kept such an exact log, such precise locations, killed so many...if the story were false.

There were only two possibilities. One, the gold had been discovered by others, perhaps decades ago. The other possibility, the treasure had been moved.

Turning over in his mind what could have occurred, the likelihood that the treasure had been discovered by others surely would have been reported. It would have been too great a find for the news to not have traveled the world. Yes, he thought the largest gold discovery in human history could never have been kept secret. That left the second possibility as the most likely. The gold had to have been relocated. He studied the logs of Onate long into the night. Onate had moved several hundred miles to the east of their present location. There were other locations within his writings marked with simple crosses. What might these mean? His first thought was the crosses indicated a place of death. Perhaps the death of enemies, perhaps the death of his own men. Perhaps the crosses on the map indicated where Onate had hidden the gold away in separate secret locations. Each of the crosses had one thing in common. They all fell along or near water sources.

Now that he knew the gold was no longer within Victorio Peak, he really had no other choice as to his next movement. He would follow the map. He would march his men to each location. He knew the trip to the east would expose his army to many more Native American tribes. Surely, he still had an immeasurable military advantage over the heathen tribes. Even though morale was low, he had reasoned with his commanders and could see in the eyes of his men…what choice did they have? Turn back to the Ghost Warriors and attempt to cross the southwest deserts? Or press on in hopes of locating the treasure? It was an easy decision for most.

The general swore as he rubbed the white dust from his eyes. The sun was beginning to set as he called for all to stop for the night. Tomorrow they would ascend into the high mountains and perhaps reach the location of the first cross. Then General Barradas watched in horror as the man riding nearest him fell with an arrow protruding from his back. A few muskets fired near him, his ears ringing from the gunfire. His own mount fell from under him a moment later, a lance penetrating the animal's heart. As the horse rolled and thrashed, its blood instantly coating the white sand beneath him, he heard his own bones breaking under the weight of the horse as it rolled over his body. He thought it an odd sound, like the sound of small branches shattering at the blow of an axe. Men began to fall, then the daylight in his vision faded into nothingness.

****

Attack the cannons and wagons. That is what I saw in the scales that suddenly appeared over the army from across the sea. If we could disable the cannons, we would have a fighting chance. The scales would tip in our favor.

We had moved through the heat of the day. Runners had reached Chief Palanquito. He now knew we would flank his force on two sides. The enemy army was surrounded by one-thousand fighting Warriors. We intentionally left the rear of the army open to retreat. Each cannon detail had been identified in the trail of men and equipment. Ten Warriors would attack each cannon. Every wagon in the procession had been targeted. Ten Warriors would attack each supply wagon. Our locations were concealed as the enemy came to a halt at dusk. The attack was a complete surprise. Hundreds of the hordes from across the sea died within the first few minutes of the battle. Hundreds more simply fled. Men dropped their weapons and ran for their lives as one thousand Ghost Warriors appeared from nowhere. Our faces painted pale white, our war ponies covered in images of ghost warriors.

****

The funeral fires burned long into the night the following evening. We had lost forty Warriors. The men were husbands, fathers, and friends. Although the victory had been decisive, this was a solemn ceremony. Tomorrow we would move back into the high mountains and a celebration would begin that would last for days. This night, however, I would never again wish to re-live.

****

The following day, the cannons were smashed into pieces and scattered into the ever-shifting White Sands Desert. The wagons likewise were burned, and their contents destroyed. The hundreds of bodies were left to be covered by the sands within the next windstorm. Chief Palanquito and his Warriors trailed and pursued survivors for days. Most were left scattered across the desert with no scalps. The armies from across the sea had been routed. Their plan of destroying our people in pursuit of riches had failed.

My purpose—the reason for moving through the *Dream Time*—had been completed.

Part 3

Chapter 52

I stood above the ridge to the north of the camp nestled along the banks of the San Saba and observed. The bounty of the earth in this special place was still incredible to me. Deer, turkey, rabbit, quail, dove, small game of all types were plentiful. Even the buffalo occasionally wandered this far south. The river brimmed with fish. The water was fresh and cool year-round. *The People* even grew corn and beans in large meadows along the river. The setting I observed this morning was one of peace and plenty. The camp itself stretched along the river for more than a mile. Hundreds of teepee lodges fit neatly along the river. Smoke rose from the lodges and gently floated along the river bluffs. I spied Nita and Sana outside our lodge, little Sana following along, clinging to her mother's hand; she was growing so quickly. I breathed deeply, the sight before me was more than I could have ever imagined my life would become.

As I stood at a distance observing our tribe and my little family, I remembered the night I sat at the table observing Kwanita's family. I remembered longing for the blessed family life her father, David Runningdeer, had been granted. Those wishes and hopes and dreams had come true for me in a way I would never have thought possible. I was a blessed man. I was protector over all that I saw, and I would do my absolute best to safeguard those I loved...I was now a Comanche Warrior.

After the battle and our subsequent move to the east with the Comanche, the name that had been given to me, Tenahpu (The Man), was now how I was referred.

The other life I had lived as an Apache was far from who I was at this place in time. Yes, I still remembered. I would always remember...Daklugie, the young man from another time.

We lived along the banks of the San Saba for fifteen seasons, although, our tribe had wintered in this place for many generations. Each year the entire Tribe would migrate north in summer. The fall and winter buffalo hunts kept our little band well fed, and the hides added to the count of our teepee lodges. Our families grew; our relationships deepened. Tosahwi and his wife, Kele, were the spiritual leaders of our *People*. Buffalo Hump became leader of the enormous Penateka Band. Maguara (Spirit Talker) became our Chief, and his wife, Kota, (Friend to everyone) was a great comforter to all. It seemed the years spent along the banks of the San Saba with our tribe and families might possibly stretch well into the future.

But I knew otherwise.

The land we lived on and called home was in constant struggle. Forces beyond our control fought and negotiated for our homelands without a single consideration of the Native Americans living within those lands. Yes, we were in an isolated place and far from most of the battles being fought. However, things were changing. Signs of the white man attempting to move into our lands were ever present. We no longer hunted or even moved small distances without a wary eye on any possible sign of white settlers, or worse, soldiers, or even what the whites called Rangers. My responsibility as protector grew daily. I was ever vigilant. I scouted continuously. I silently killed many who dared penetrate our homelands. In my scouting, I was amazed at the numbers of both Spanish and whites moving into the lands that had been ours for centuries.

As the years passed, Topusana grew into a strikingly beautiful young maiden, although, she was anything but what some might consider a traditional woman of the camp. Her training, initiated from her infant days, served her well. She was an excellent hunter, a student of our faith and history. Sana, as her mother called her, understood much of the medicine of our Shaman Tosahwi. Many a young Warrior often attempted to catch her eye. Sana rejected all their advances. If a young man had enough nerve to approach her, she would often challenge the young Warriors to physical contests. Running or shooting the bow, even perhaps knife throwing. The few that accepted went away heads hung low, having been outrun, or out shot, or losing a rock sling contest or bow challenge to our beautiful Sana. The young men were often embarrassed and accepted the fun joking from their friends at having been defeated by a woman.

There was one exception to her responses to the young men.

Tabbananica (Voice of the Sun).

The two had been friends their entire childhood. They hunted together; our families prepared meals together, and the two seemed more like brother and sister to me for most of their childhood.

However, I was beginning to see. Kwanita was aware and understood what was happening with our beautiful daughter. Topusana had become a woman. The brotherly love she had for Tabbananica was growing. I sometimes noticed the two staring into one another's eyes…just a bit too long.

The fall movement to the north and the ensuing buffalo hunt were upcoming. It was odd I was called into the lodge of Tosahwi on a fine spring afternoon with no particular threat or reason for a council. On entering it was not the usual council members that greeted me. Tosahwi sat with Kele. Maguara and Kota sat within the circle. Kwanita was seated near Topusana. She indicated for me to sit beside her. Tabbananica, or Tabba, was seated alone on the opposite side of the circle. The young warrior was himself a handsome man. Muscled, brave, and even fierce, I often thought.

The request caught me by complete surprise.

"*Yes, I am asking for the hand of Topusana,*" Tabba said again.

I suppose my reaction, like that of many fathers, was impolite at best. I simply sat in disbelief. Sana was just a child. What was Tabba thinking? They were but playmates. Marriage? I sat with a confused look upon my face. Kwanita cleared her throat, catching my eye.

"*Husband?*" she said to me and indicated Tabba's presence. I sat in silence until Kwanita poked me sharply in the ribs. I still said nothing. I sat in dazed wonder, scenes of Sana's childhood flashing through my mind. Tosahwi spoke, disturbing my thoughts and memories.

"*This is a good match. I have seen. This marriage will ensure the future of our people; the future of our grandchildren will be in the most capable hands.*"

Kwanita again indicated for me to say something. I spoke, although it seemed like another person was speaking and I was simply an observer watching this scene play out while everything within me was in complete denial of what was taking place. The sound of my own voice seemed out of place and I wanted to object.

"*Yes, Tabba, her mother and I both approve, and you have our blessing.*"

Tabbananica, Voice of the Sun, stood, nodded in our direction, and exited the lodge.

"*She is a woman now, Dak,*" Kwanita said with a sparkle in her eyes. I stood and exited the lodge without words. The few words I had spoken still rang in my ears. She had used my old name in an attempt, I was certain, to awaken my mind to the realities of time and life. I wandered down to the river alone. The setting was peace filled and serene. The gurgling of the river, the shadows the trees cast on the water, the sun on my shoulders caused me to pause. I thought of Kwanita's father. I thought what a brave strong man he was. How could he have ever let his daughter go. That day I discovered the difficulty of letting go. I turned the events of the last few minutes over in my mind. I saw Topusana as a young girl again for a moment.

I sensed her presence, then she touched my shoulder.

"I am in love with him, Father."

"I understand, Sana. You will be a beautiful wife and mother. I am proud of you both."

She smiled at me and kissed my cheek.

The light within my heart that day overcame the darkness for a moment, and I am certain a tear made its way out of my soul and rested on my face as we strode hand in hand to the home camp along the banks of the San Saba. The perfect picture of a father letting go was painted within the canvas of my mind as I released her hand, and she joined a group of maidens awaiting her arrival.

It was, as Tosahwi would say, *A good day.*

Chapter 53

I sensed the danger long before I spotted the enemy. I had seen the signs for days. We had moved to the north at the first signs of spring. The Llano seemed forever to be an impenetrable ocean of grass and secret springs. The wagon tracks across our land, however, were an eerie sign of the white man invading our lands. I scouted two days ahead of our band. This was not just a few whites exploring. The men were mounted, in uniform; they traveled as one, the supply wagons following at a distance. At least fifty well-armed soldiers cut an obscene swath in the grass across the Llano. The trail of litter and wagon tracks that rutted the prairie gave silent testimony to trespass and invasion. I crawled away from the group, hidden in the knee-deep grass. This would be a difficult enemy. A trained military force lay in our path. I knew only one way to deal with them. I prayed for wisdom. My people were much too close.

Two nights later, the lodge fire burned in the center of the council. My report met with much anger…and a level of fear I had not sensed before. Tabba appeared to be the only Warrior unafraid. He seemed determined and intent on simply attacking and destroying the invaders. The big gun in the wagon troubled me most. The enemy was obviously in possession of a new weapon.

"I am proud of your courage, Tabbananica. However, we must determine what this new weapon is and what it is capable of. Let us take a few Warriors. We will locate a favorable piece of ground to attack and escape. We will mount our swiftest war ponies. They will have no chance of catching us. Discovering our enemy's capabilities is what is most needed," I said.

Tabba stood and exited the lodge, a fierceness in his eyes I easily recognized. I also saw understanding on his face. Tabba was learning.

The canyon country on the northern extremity of the Llano was a broken and rough land. The prairie abruptly ended in a complex tangle of deep canyons, creeks, and rivers. Many of the canyons were impenetrable and boxed with steep cliffs rising from what might first appear as an easy exit with gently sloping rises in the land. There was simply no way out once a box canyon was entered, other than backtracking. The plan was to show ourselves, then lead the white soldiers into a trap within any of the dozens of box canyons. Our war party would remain atop the canyon edges, traveling easily. Keeping a vantage point above the white army. The Warriors who showed themselves would then scale the cliffs with the ropes we had woven and tied to our war ponies. The ponies would pull the brave men up the cliff faces. It seemed a good plan.

We followed the white soldiers at a comfortable distance. The first sign of concern were the Native American scouts we sighted who led the invaders across the Llano. I remembered the words of my friend One Horse, *"Dak, these men are promised many blankets and rifles in exchange for their assistance. Most are imprisoned or killed on completion of the missions."*

It angered me, knowing the fate of the Native American guides. The dark cloud considered them enemies and traitors.

The following day I observed again the speed in which this group moved. They broke camp quickly each day and moved at a driven pace, stopping briefly for water but pressing on until near darkness. Why the rush? Why the pressure on the animals and soldiers alike? I determined the obvious reason and reported to the council that night.

"These soldiers have been ordered to the north. It is evident they are needed elsewhere. Perhaps a runner will arrive from the north soon. It may be our bands to the north are under attack, or even perhaps another tribe."

The Warriors and leaders considered my observations. *"Tenahpu, I believe you are correct,"* Maguara spoke. *"However, the big gun will certainly be used against us or our peoples eventually. I think it wise to destroy these soldiers and the weapons they carry."*

I said nothing, awaiting others who might comment. There was a steely atmosphere, a palpable resolve and edge within the council lodge. The fire burned brightly before us. The fire within the Warriors' hearts burned even brighter. There was no further need for words. Tosahwi began the songs, drumbeats were taken up outside the lodge. The war party would mount our war ponies, and at the most advantageous location, we would ambush the white soldiers with the big gun. I prayed for success.

That night Kwanita did not sleep.

We traveled swiftly along the edges of the canyons. The soldiers remained within the canyons along the streams of water. We moved ahead of them late into the day, and in a small gently sloping draw two Warriors descended into the canyon. It was but another two miles upstream to a huge box side canyon. The Warriors within the canyon disappeared. The remaining war party rode swiftly ahead. We would reach the top of the box and set the ambush within minutes. Although we could no longer see the Warriors below, we knew they were there. The soldiers continued their breakneck pace. When precisely below the box canyon, we saw the leaders and native scouts signal *stop*. Our Warriors had been spotted.

The leaders gathered quickly and consulted with one another and the guides. I wondered what they might be considering. I put myself in their situation, imagining the conversation taking place. They had spotted but two Warriors. Would there be more? This must be their thoughts. Would the Comanche escape to report the movement of the soldiers? Would no action invite attack? I considered their mindset. It was no certainty they would pursue the Warriors they had just sighted. A flurry of activity took place within the ranks. The wagon gun was brought forward and positioned. The barrel was rotated within the wagon and trained on the box canyon. I knew the war party, even those on the rim above the canyon were all in danger. The weapon began to fire. The sound seemed to shake the ground around us as we took whatever cover we could find. I prayed the Warriors in the box could find shelter. The number of rounds fired was unending. Forty then fifty then one hundred. Although the rounds fired hit no targets along the top of the canyon rim, the effect the weapon had on the war party was definitive. The gun silenced for a moment. The echoes of the gunfire rolled through the canyons for several minutes. The troop below us reorganized and began their drive to the north again, moving rapidly away from the ambush we had set. Within the hour they were out of site. We lowered the ropes and pulled the men up the face of the cliffs.

"*We will return to* The People *now*," Maguara ordered. As we mounted our ponies and began the long trek back to our tribe, I wondered how we might possibly fight this enemy with the wagon gun. I wondered how many might die attempting to do so. Their leader had not defeated us physically; he had, however, attained his intended goal. He had struck fear in our hearts. Not of the soldiers he led across our lands, but rather fear of the power of the weapons they possessed. I knew it was imperative we find a way to disarm the wagon gun.

After we had traveled a mere five miles or so we saw smoke darkening the sky in the direction of *The People*. We raced our mounts through the night toward our loved ones.

Chapter 54

The smell of burning lodges and animal skins afire drove a sickening ache deep within my soul. The dark cloud within raged at the scent… well before the massacre appeared in my sight. We raced into the camp, dismounted and searched frantically for our loved ones. It was difficult to identify individual family lodges among the burning camp. I located what I thought was our lodge.

The darkness of the night was dampened by the glow of the few lodges that still smoldered. The smell of flesh burning hung in the air. Cries of the wounded filled the atmosphere. The air was hot and close. I was surrounded by scenes of death and the dying. The realization of the nightmare that had occurred played across my mind. The massacre unfolded before my eyes. I fell to my knees in shock and disbelief. How could this be? Who had done this? My heart sank, my mind grew numb, I screamed a war cry. The darkness raged. The light that glowed dimly within the darkness in my soul flickered and disappeared as I located her body. She lay covered in what appeared to be burned blankets. Kwanita, my life love, was gone from this world.

I sat in the dust and ashes of what just this morning was our life, our home. Tosahwi touched my shoulder gently. I rose and stared into his eyes with a blank expression. The smoldering fires reflected a brokenness in his vision.

"*Kele?*" My voice echoed in the darkness. A question of life or death in one word.

"*She now walks with the Great Spirit, as does Kwanita. They are safe and happy now, Tenahpu.*"

Suddenly I became aware as the fog lifted from my heart and mind at the truth his words contained. "*Topusana?*"

"There are many survivors to the north in the canyon."

I ran. The prairie flew by, my feet scarcely touching the ground. The canyon rim was one half a mile away. I felt what those escaping must have experienced. Bullets zipped by me. Dust flew as the horses of the enemy pursued me. Little puffs of Mother Earth sprang from the ground to my left, then the same puffs exploded on my right, evidence of the musket balls striking the prairie floor. A quarter of a mile to go. I ran. The safety of the canyon was in sight. I imagined cannon fire exploding around me. Friends must have fallen at the blinding flash and report of the huge gun. One hundred yards to the edge. I ran with all that was within me. Would Topusana have been swift enough. I leapt into the small crevasse that began the drop into the deep canyon, landing in the soft sand at the bottom. I tumbled into the darkness as the slope of the canyon dropped toward the river. I was up and running again when I heard the voice.

"Father we are here," Topusana called to me from a thicket of brush and small saplings.

****

There were twelve children hidden within the brush, Sana tending them gently. She had made the run six times. On each trip back to the camp, she had carried two children to safety. Sana had returned again and again to the burning camp, rescuing the young children in her act of selfless bravery.

We rescued the remaining survivors throughout the night, moving each into the safety of the canyon. As the first light of the dawn appeared, we gathered our dead.

The unknown enemy had retreated to the south. Many of the enemy had fallen at the hands of our older men and young boys, their bodies scattered across the prairie. Strange lifeless humps, arrows protruding from their flesh, soulless death left behind by their cowardly leaders to rot and be consumed by animals and the scavenger birds of the air.

I crossed the prairie, observing the bodies of the fallen enemy. Mexican soldiers. I pieced together the evidence of the attack. The Mexican Army must have been pursuing the soldiers in the canyon. They had stumbled upon our camp accidentally, I was certain. As I had so many times been reminded and knew in my heart, we, the Comanche People, were simply in the way in a much larger struggle. Our camp was not a target. Would these people ever cease from their lust of the lands north of the river?

Once the survivors were settled and cared for, the funeral fires were prepared and struck. I had carefully constructed a soft bed of burned blankets and the few worldly possessions my woman so treasured. I then laid the body of my love, Kwanita (God is Gracious), into her makeshift grave. As the flames grew, my mind traveled to a different place and time. We walked hand in hand along the ancient trail that led into the high mountains. I felt the warmth of her hand in mine. I saw the light of love in her eyes. We turned and viewed our school from a vantage point along the ancient trail. We talked tenderly to one another, imagining together what our life, our future, might hold. Hope filled my heart for a moment. Then her spirit rose from the flames into the heavens. In my mind, I saw her turn to me as she rose. Her hand was held high, her palm open toward me.

There are places on this earth where the veil between the physical world we inhabit and the spirit world is but a thin undiscernible barrier, places where a soul can see and hear and possibly peer into the unseen spirit world. The Llano Estacado with its never-ending expanse of emerald grass and azure polished sky will forever, in my life experience, be one of those places. There are other such locations, I am certain, where the breadth of creation so calls out in a voice that is so gentle, filled with truth and undeniable to the creation it inhabits and the listeners who fear its wisdom, that the flowers of the field, the trees of the forest, and even the stones and waters bow in worship. The Voice of Truth I heard again this day as I laid my wife in a grave.

That same Voice I had heard along the banks of the Pecos River in the year 1808 contained only truth. I wished, I prayed, I pleaded…to never hear His voice again. The Voice of Truth was the only being in creation I truly feared. Fear of my Creator produced in me what was assuredly the beginning of wisdom, no matter the level of fear that attended its gentle whisper.

Chapter 55

Six Years later

For the first season in the history of our people, the annual buffalo hunt did not take place. Prairie Song, my granddaughter, sat at the feet of Topusana, playing her doll games.

I observed, attempting to place in my memory the scene before me. I wanted to forever remember this moment. It would give me strength to endure. For days now, I had attempted to do this very thing. Remember the good. The five years Kwanita and I had spent together on the high mountains. The discovering of our people along the Pecos. The birth of Topusana within the field of flowers. The victories over the army from across the sea. The run across the heat-soaked prairie with my friend One Horse. The peace-filled years we had spent along the banks of the San Saba. I placed these memories within the recesses of my mind so that I might carry them with me. I would be leaving tonight. Tosahwi's plan was good.

We were now hard pressed on every side. Thousands of whites had moved onto our lands from the east. Cavalry, Texas Rangers, and militia hunted our people continuously. We were at war. Our tribe had survived by moving into the most desolate places within our homeland. We lived along the cliffs and bluffs of the Big Bend. We spent our winters in the center of the Llano. The stronghold along the San Saba that we had wintered upon for centuries was also somewhat safe.

However, no location was completely safe. The whites had claimed our land at the defeat of Mexico. Strong men had established their own independent nation. The white man now referred to our Homeland as the Republic of Texas.

Buffalo Hump had attempted to negotiate a peace agreement with the leaders of this new nation. Their leader, a man I remembered from my history class, Sam Houston, had agreed and attempted to bring that peace agreement to the whites. The signed treaty had been rejected. We were hindering the progress of the white man and *The People* were in constant danger. The simple act of hunting or attempting to survive was becoming life threatening and impossible.

I sat in the circle within the council lodge. My words were few. I could not bear to reveal the truth of what my people, my daughter, my granddaughter, would face in the coming years. I thought inwardly, the time seemed to have swept by so quickly...like the blossoms of spring carried away by the prairie winds. Our way of life, our people, our culture I understood, as did Tosahwi, would not survive this ongoing invasion that was growing daily. Tosahwi's plan was good.

The People would escape.

Preparations were underway. I would enter the *Dream Time* one season ahead of the others. I would go to prepare the way for our tribe. I was a protector Warrior.

****

The ceremony was simple. The instructions in my grandfather's scroll were followed precisely by Tosahwi. The fire burned brightly, giving off a soft warmth within the cavern above the banks of the San Saba. I drank for the second time in my life from the sacred bowl. My eyes became heavy. I felt the soft sand beneath me. I was aware of the gentle breeze flowing throughout the cavern as it touched my skin. The sound of the burbling springs faded into silence. My body seemed to lighten and rise as the tunnel encircled me. The songs of Tosahwi blended into a tapestry of blessing, prophesy, and song. I was aware of his prayers, and the words he sang spoke within my spirit as I entered the *Dream Time.*

"*Daklugie, you must see that the light within you is not darkness. You must allow your light to shine forth so that others may see. The Creator has placed the light within the darkness...the darkness will never overcome that light.*"

Then I, Tenahpu (The Man), a Comanche Warrior, slept in *Dream Time.*

Kansas Territory 1838

Maguara lead *The People* along the frozen creek bank. They were starving. The wind stiffened; the cold burned within each breath. The light faded quickly as dusk fell across the land. He was grateful that Tabba had found the buffalo. Kota struck the lodge fire and began her songs.

Tabbananica knew his prayers had been answered. The animals had never sensed his presence. He and Neeko (One who Finds) had stalked near the huge beast and Tabba had driven his lance into the belly of the old bull. The animal had given its life easily. Tabba knew this was a blessing from the Great Spirit. The lodges were set up quickly. The lodge fires were lit. The smell of meat roasting wafted within the teepee lodges and along the frozen creek bank.

Tosahwi settled onto the buffalo robe within his lodge. Outside, the ice pelted the sides of the lodge. The wind whistled through the treetops. The wolves began their songs. He knew *The People* would need to enter the *Dream Time* soon. The scarcity of the buffalo herd was alarming. How could so many animals disappear from the earth?

Prairie Song, daughter of Tabbananica and Topusana, snuggled further into the warmth of the buffalo robe between her parents. The wind whispered in the treetops along the frozen creek bed as darkness settled across the prairie. For the first time in her young life, Prairie Song heard the voices in the wind. She saw that her parents would be leaving soon. She understood…she would not accompany them. The veil in this place was thin.

She knew her life journey on this earth would be cut short. Even so, she possessed a peace beyond understanding at the revelation the wind voices brought. Prairie Song determined she would never share her revelation and vision with her parents. They seemed so happy.

Chapter 56

I, Tenahpu (The Man), awakened abruptly in full awareness. There were no questions in my mind as to where I was and what had occurred. When, in what time, I had awakened was a question to which I would soon discover the answer.

My mind focused on the ceremony of my departure. What had Tosahwi prophesied over me? The darkness whispered. Protect, defend. What had he spoken over me? I sat in silence. My time of quiet would become my greatest tool.

****

I exited the cavern as the sun rested on the western horizon. The log shelter and barn below me, along with a double-cab ranch truck immediately gave away the time I now walked in. The truck was a late model. The year at least in the 2000s, possibly later. I had awakened in modern day Texas.

It was a shock to my senses. Even though I had lived in this time in my early life, I had become accustomed and attuned to living wild and free. I was a natural man fed by the bounty of the earth, unaccustomed to the noise and commotion of the modern world. My mind remembered the time and hurried activities of the twenty-first century. I had not thought the differences of the two worlds would be so severe. I heard a familiar sound. A semi-truck travelling east along the highway. The noise the vehicle generated was unbelievable. The sound of the wind being torn into, tires rumbling along pavement. The huge diesel engine churned out smoke and a noise level I had not experienced in—I paused doing the math problem in my mind—more than two hundred years. One semi-truck rolled across my vision, its headlights burning brightly, reflecting off the smooth surface of the asphalt. It was sickening and disturbing to my spirit as it sped across my field of vision and disappeared into the dusk. I longed already for the past.

I silently worked my way down the slope toward the rear of the massive ranch house. I peered into the window along the side of the structure. A woman was seated at a table, her man sat with his back toward me. He drank from a coffee cup as his woman rose and served him a slice of pie. My stomach grumbled as I observed the scene. My mind was filled with conflict as I moved away from the home and down the driveway entrance. I paused along the edge of the highway that ran through the center of our old home camp. The white man had won. I knew this fact from history, but the immediacy of the *Dream Time* travel was raw, there was no buffer between our attempt to survive, our struggle to prevail, and our failure to do so. I had been experiencing this obvious loss just yesterday…in a different time.

I crossed the highway lined with barbwire fencing on both sides. I found the little rise of land where I had walked just a few hours ago. There were no lodges, no ponies, no laughing families. There was nothing here that marked the centuries lived out along this quiet little river. I thought of the faces of my family and friends; I hoped some might survive and make the journey through the *Dream Time* and possibly attempt a new beginning. I considered how to best to prepare for their arrival, their survival. I moved back across the highway and skirted the ranch house, concealing my movement in the cover of brush. Silently I moved up the little canyon and entered the cavern that would become my home for the next few months, possibly longer, while I awaited their arrival. I was well supplied for now with a store of dried buffalo meat. The cavern would provide an excellent hiding place, shelter, and water. I needed to occasionally harvest deer or rabbit for sustenance. That process would not be difficult, the feeding of but one man. For now, I would simply wait. The waiting might be much more difficult than survival.

I arose the following morning after a full night of restful sleep. Breakfast consisted of dried buffalo and water from the springs within the cavern. The route out of the cavern was difficult with a long crawl in the area of the lowered ceiling, followed by a climb up a steep slope to the cavern entrance. I paused a few moments, listening as the sounds of a new world came to my ears. The noise of traffic as the occasional car or truck passed by below me. A light wind moved through the treetops above and just outside the entrance. I chanced a peek out. The enormous home below seemed quiet. The barn alongside had the doors on each end closed. The truck I had seen the previous evening was gone. It appeared no one was home. I exited the cavern and headed north up the remaining incline of the little canyon. I was familiar with the land, even intimate with its small canyons, creek beds, and valleys. I had lived here for many years. I knew its hiding places and where best to hunt or set snares, even where little secret springs flowed or dripped, providing hidden water sources. This was my Homeland, and I knew it by heart.

I traveled a mile or more and spotted the entrance to the larger cavern. The ground around it was undisturbed. I knew from our plans that many would enter the *Dream Time* and sleep in this cavern. I placed the sign, a large snake rattle near the entrance. If the tribe escaped, they would find the sign of my presence easily. Moving farther north, I topped the canyon upon a large rock surface that ran for one half of a mile or more. The open prairie lay before me. As far as my eye could see, there was nothing. Blue sky above with a whisp of horse tail clouds high in the atmosphere, deep green grass graced the surface of Mother Earth below. It had obviously been a good year for rain. I moved across the open prairie in awe. In this wide-open country away from the highway and automobiles it was now impossible to determine through what time I moved. This walk I was making appeared exactly as it had the last time I had walked here…almost two hundred years ago.

I walked most of the morning, exploring mainly to the north in the direction of the Llano. With the sun high overhead, I spotted them. They moved about slowly, undisturbed. Cattle, hundreds of them, watering along a small lake, grazing on the rich grass. I understood. Our homeland had become an immense cattle ranch. This was good news in many ways, the most significant was in how simple it would be to feed myself.

One Year Later

Patience is a thing that is only learned from experiencing the need for it. I had survived in isolation for a full year. I had become intimate with my neighbors who lived in the beautiful ranch house below my cavern in the Texas hills. Although, we had never met, never spoken, never shared a meal together, and they knew nothing of my presence. I knew them. I often sat in the brush outside the picture window that overlooked the San Saba and dined along with them. I listened in on their conversations in the warm summer months when the windows were open. I met some of their family and acquaintances, even occasionally read their mail from the box along the highway. Odd as it may have seemed, I admired Abby and David Ross. They seemed to be very kind and giving people. I knew intimate details of their life. I understood their struggle in the loss of their son. I felt a kinship to David Ross in particular. His loss brought to mind the loss of my friend One Horse. I knew what he was going through. I, however, was alone. I lived in concealment, awaiting the arrival of my family. It had been too long. I began to doubt. I did not see how they could have survived this long. I knew something had happened. I also knew I could not survive the aloneness. My family should have arrived by now. Sometimes I spent days without leaving the cavern. I spoke only within my mind. The occasional evenings I spent outside the quaint little breakfast nook within the Ross home deepened the longing for communication, touch, or the simple desire to look into the eyes of a friend. Isolation was a terrifying empty existence.

I finished my meal of fire-roasted calf liver and rose from the brush just outside the picture window of the Ross home. I said a somber goodbye to my friends that never knew of me. Tomorrow I would be leaving. I would return to check the caverns in the future. For now, I needed to build a new life. I would not survive living in isolation. Tomorrow I would start my walk back to New Mexico. A walk I had made several times in my life.

The following morning, I removed my skins. The beadwork and ornate detail of my clothing was a stark contrast to the denim jeans and western shirt I donned. My moccasins I kept and would wear for the walk. An old jacket I had taken from the barn would keep me warm. I had no money, yet was one of the wealthiest men on the planet. I thought of the gold deep in the recesses of the high mountains. I had sawed off a few corners of the ten-pound gold bar that I had carried with me to the riverbank near the Alamo, where my friend had lost his life. I tucked away in my front pocket the few ounces of gold and left the remainder of the bar hidden in the cavern. I dawned my bow and quiver; my grandfather's war club I tucked neatly into my belt. His long knife I looped onto the belt I had taken from the sleeping room in the barn. I was not a thief. I left two ounces of gold on the doorstep of the Ross home.

As I exited the cavern, I placed on my head the old cowboy hat I had found. I walked north up the canyon first, then once a mile or more from the Ross home, I descended toward the highway. Crossing the fence, I headed east. I had intended to head directly west toward New Mexico. A thought occurred to me. I would visit a sacred location before I moved west. I walked along the highway alone with my thoughts. What had happened to my people? I might never know. An emptiness ached within my soul as I thought of my beautiful daughter, Topusana. The light glimmered within my heart at the thought of her. What was it I had heard Tosahwi praying over me the night I had entered the *Dream Time*?

I heard the truck approaching from behind me as I walked along the road. I detected the slowing of the vehicle as it drew up alongside me and stopped. I turned to the open window of the vehicle and peered into the beautiful eyes of Abigail Ross. "Can I offer you a ride, friend?" she asked. Her voice was familiar and comfortable. I don't know if she recognized the look of longing, or the loneliness in my eyes, or possibly even my recognition of her that shone in my own eyes as I declined the offer.

"I think I will just enjoy the walk this morning, Abby. But thank you anyway." My words seemed awkward and echoed in my mind. Those few words were the first I had spoken aloud in over a year.

"Suit yourself, friend," she said in the same cheerful voice I had heard expressed many quiet evenings outside her window along the banks of the San Saba River…my former Homeland. She drove away with a questioning look I could see in her rearview mirror. I raised my hand in a slight wave, my palm open toward her. I attempted to repress the feelings of longing and closeness to Abby that felt wrong and out of place. She was a strikingly beautiful woman.

What had I done? My reply seemed natural and exactly as I had responded internally the many evenings I had listened in on conversations outside her window. Was the look in her rearview mirror one of a questioning "where have I met you before?" or one of concern, or even fear. I stopped and examined my moccasins, jeans, western shirt, even the cowboy hat. Then I noticed the bow string holding my grandfather's bow that was slung across my shoulders. The shadow of my long braids moved in the wind as the sun cast my silhouette across the pavement surface. I was certain I had made a mistake, albeit an innocent one.

I quickly took to the north side of the road. I crossed the fence and climbed the small hill, reaching its crest in just a few minutes. I traveled along the top of the ridge that overlooked the San Saba and the highway below. I was now completely concealed from anyone traveling the highway. I walked for over an hour before the ranch truck belonging to David Ross appeared. He was driving slowly, obviously scanning the terrain along and near the sides of the highway. I hid myself behind a large cedar until he was out of sight. I would be much more cautious in the future. I took to the open country traveling south and east. I would not approach the highway until I was near the river that flowed south from what I knew would now be San Antonio, Texas.

Chapter 57

I took me seven days to arrive along the banks of the river where the battle had been fought between the Casas and the Mexican army from the south. The field where over one thousand men had lost their lives was now a hayfield. A tractor worked along its edges, beginning a cutting.

The interstate highway streamed with an unbelievable movement of automobiles, trucks, busses, and even train tracks that followed its route through central Texas. My senses were on high alert, but somehow dulled by the constant drone of the traffic noise. The smell from the toxic exhaust gave me a dizzying feeling along with a rancid taste that lingered in my mouth and nose. I moved away from its noise and foul smell, climbing the hill I had walked on in the past.

I paused, remembering the run One Horse and I had made together up this very slope. The vision in my memory of cruel steel cutting into the flesh of my friend's wrists flashed across my mind. I closed my eyes, wishing, wondering what I might have done differently.

It was easy to locate the large boulder that overlooked the hurried activities along the San Antonio River below. Not much had changed about the slope I now stood on.

I remembered gazing across the soft Texas sky from this vantage point so many years ago. I remembered the flowers I had transplanted bowing before us in the gentle breeze. I began to sing again softly the songs of mourning.

The rock surface still displayed the cross of One Horse. Moss and lichens had evidently grown into the blood stains. The cross now was pale yellows and subtle green in color. However, its clear outlines were distinctly detectable along the surface of the boulder. It appeared the Cross of One Horse would grace this place for centuries. The flowers I had transplanted over his shallow grave had grown and spread down and across the slope. A huge meadow of color and flora now spread across the land below the cross.

I lowered myself to the ground and sat cross legged on the slope of flowers and remembered. "*You were my friend, Sumu Puku. I miss your smiling face. I am so glad you are not alone and Nadua has joined you.*" I sang with all that was within me. I sang for my friend. I sang for my wife. I sang for my daughter and my people.

Lastly, I sang for me. I sang through the veil of loneliness and loss. I sang until the sun lowered over my shoulder and the moon began to rise and rested on the eastern horizon.

The light that dwelt and flickered within my heart, the light that lived in the center of the darkness of my soul grew that night. Worship alone, I thought, has the ability to cause a reflection of the light within to take root and possibly grow. The prayer that Tosahwi had spoken over me as I entered the *Dream Time* came to me that night. I understood why I had come here.

I turned and headed west. The light from the full moon was just bright enough to light my steps one at a time. The light from within shined in the darkness, also directing my steps. I whispered a final farewell to my friend. This vision of the Cross of One Horse was burned into my mind. I would remember every detail. I had no idea this masterpiece would flow from my spirit and one day be replicated. I began my journey to the high mountains of New Mexico.

Chapter 58

Two months later

I stood along the edge of the caprock, observing the high mountains one hundred miles away. It was early summer but small patches of snow still gleamed on the distant peaks. I traveled along the wide-open country doing my best to avoid highways and even back roads. It was unbelievable to me the amount of barbwire that had been strung across the land. We had traveled this land as a people, wild and free in a time when there was none. Now I could scarcely travel an hour without crossing a fence. In places near towns or even cities it became impossible to travel swiftly as I spent more time crossing the wire fencing than I did walking. I had never really noticed the fencing in my younger days.

I slept on the open prairie. I hunted deer and antelope. I tanned a beautiful deer skin that I used to warm myself at night. I would sit by my small fire, nightly enjoying the sounds of creation. That had not changed, the rhythm of life here on the open prairie. Most evenings the distant sounds of traffic would subside, the night birds would begin their calling, the coyotes would commence their yelping and howling, the familiar stars would rise in the night sky. It was then I felt most at home within the familiarity of the wildness of creation. I enjoyed the journey immensely. Something within me knew I would never again travel on foot the vastness of what was formerly our homeland.

Two days later, I stood upon the ancient trail and observed my old high school. The parking lot was filled with trucks and cars. Young teens talked and laughed together in small groups. Many parents arrived, unloading families, coolers, hot dishes, and camp chairs. The small stands and football field were

198

decorated with flags and banners. The marching band began to assemble on one end of the field. Evidently, an event would be taking place today. I stashed my gear in a well concealed area of thick brush and casually made my way into the crowd.

The excitement level grew as parents and grandparents arrived and seated themselves in the bleachers. The band began to play our old fight song as I seated myself in an isolated corner of the stands. I was just another Native American relative here to observe the festivities. I drew my hat low over my brow as Kwanita's father approached the microphone set in the center of the elevated platform. Coach Tower, my basketball coach, stood from a row of seats at the rear of the platform and greeted him. Coach Tower stepped to the microphone and introduced David Runningdeer. Leader of our people.

Kwanita's father stepped to the microphone. "Let us begin this celebration of the graduating class of the year 2010 with a prayer." The entire stadium quieted, closed their eyes, and bowed their heads in reverence. I quickly and quietly stepped down the stairs and made a hasty exit while most heads were bowed. I heard his words through the loudspeaker system as I took my first few steps onto the ancient trail.

"We ask, Lord, that you allow your light to shine forth from our young people. In a world that is filled with much darkness, may your light shine through these young people like that of a city on a hill."

I began to run. Once well away from the school but still within hearing distance, I sat along the edge of the ancient trail and listened. The names I so easily recognized were called, and those names echoed across the mountains and in my heart. I pictured in my mind each student rising, shaking the hand of Chief Runningdeer, as the graduating class of 2010 received their diplomas. I turned and started toward the cavern in the high mountains. Now I knew the exact year in which I had awakened.

I knew I would not linger here for long. The life and world below were no longer mine. Perhaps our actions in a different place and time had allowed the ceremony that was occurring below me at the entrance to the ancient trail to take place.

It occurred to me as I ran the ancient trail that time and the aging effect it had on the human body, seemed to bend somewhat and benefit those who had slept in *Dream Time*. I was a father and a grandfather. I must have been at least in my mid-fifties age wise. However, my body had not seemed to age. I felt like I was maybe twenty-one years old. Perhaps it was the lifestyle of pure food, clean air, and water? I wondered if possibly others who had traveled through the *Dream Time* had experienced similar youth sustaining side effects?

I quickened my pace, running hard now up the trail that led to the cavern in the high mountains. The words of my grandfather I had not heard in years, but they came to my ears now. "Dak, you will continue to be and have been a blessing to all of our people."

Perhaps the price we had paid was worth what I had just witnessed. I was convinced Kwanita would agree. She certainly would willingly sacrifice her life for me, her siblings, her parents. I hard knot formed in my throat as I traveled the ancient trail, remembering the last time I had descended along this way, holding the hand of my expectant woman, Kwanita. I remembered how desperate we were, how the game had vanished. The tears within grew yet would not exit my soul. The darkness still had a stranglehold on my heart and mind.

So much loss, so many tragedies, overwhelming injustice. I ran along the ancient trail, the words of our leader David Runningdeer echoing in my ears. "May your light shine forth, like that of a city on a hill."

****

I slowed and recovered my wind quickly, then entered the concealed crevasse in the face of the granite rock. I waited several minutes for my eyesight to adjust, then moved well to the right of the cavern entrance until I felt the rock wall in my right hand. The flashlight I located on the rock shelf clicked on as I pushed the little button on its side. I silently made my way to the snowy river of calcite. I descended along the snowy river and entered the large rooms. Climbing the little steps to the sleeping room, our things were still there. The little camp stove, the bear rugs I had tanned from the night of the bear fight, my pack frame rested against the stone wall. I moved farther up the cavern and drank my fill from the spring. Moving another hundred yards into the depths of the cavern, the steaming hot spring appeared in my flashlight beam. I set the flashlight upright against a stone, removed my western clothing, moccasins, and my grandfather's weapons, then stepped into the warmth of the mineral-filled water. I thought of the walk across our homeland, picturing in my mind a modern-day map of Texas and New Mexico. I had, over a three-month period, just walked approximately one-thousand miles. I soaked my tired body for hours.

I was home.

Chapter 59

The following morning, I arose from our little sleeping room. I had tossed and turned through the night. Being here in this place where Kwanita and I had spent five years of our young life together magnified the loneliness within. So many evenings we had spent by our fire, talking quietly, loving away the time. I could still hear her voice. I longed for her touch. Her scent still graced the bear rugs. Being here brought the time of our past into perfect focus, and I knew I could not stay. Where could I possibly escape the memories and all that had occurred? How was I to begin life again? I had no answers.

I washed in the pool and made a decision to move on. But I needed supplies, and in this modern world I also needed something else. Money. I gathered my weapons and donned my pack frame I had left here years ago.

I traveled the descending trail and remembered precisely the location of the small side exit. Crawling through the switchback, then rising, I made my way along the trail as the cavern began to open into massive rooms. Half an hour later I stood at the base of the deep pit, my flashlight beam shining upward into the darkness. Ignoring the skeletons that surrounded me, I moved forward and located the small rock that protruded from the smooth surface of the stone wall. Remembering how the stone doorway closed once the handle was released, I located a nice size rock and wrestled the one-hundred-pound stone into position. Pressing the handle, the massive stone face slid open. I scooted the large stone into place and entered the hidden storehouse. The stone door began to close, but my one-hundred-pound doorstop did its intended job and jammed the stone door, preventing it from closing. Once inside I scanned the room with the small beam of light.

The neatly stacked rows of gold bricks appeared before me. I moved quickly, loading one of the forty-pound bars into my pack frame. Reversing my movements, I quickly exited the hidden storehouse. I removed the large stone from the doorway and the rock face closed gently into place. The small handle-shaped rock protruded from the rock wall as I turned and walked away from the bottom of the deep pit, a wealthy man.

In the year 2010, the price of gold, I would soon discover, was around $1,400 per ounce. I quickly deciphered the math equation sixteen ounces per pound times 1,400 just over $22,000 for a pound, times the factor of forty. I carried in my pack almost one million dollars' worth of pure gold. More than I needed. And much too difficult to carry. How to solve the problem of the shear bulk of this wealth was the question before me.

I moved through the cavern returning to the little sleeping room. I placed the gold bar in the sand of the floor. Taking my grandfather's long knife, I began to scrap the edges of the bar revealing the gleaming surface. The material was somewhat soft. It occurred to me I might simply chip away at its edges. Using my grandfather's long knife and a palm-sized stone, I struck the surface repeatedly using the stone as a hammer. I was surprised at how quickly along its edge I was able to work a small piece away from the surface. I continued the process and within an hour I had shaved and chiseled off what I thought was about two pounds of gold. The pieces I shaped into small irregular forms, that appeared natural, even perhaps like they had been dug from a vein within some hidden claim. I was confident I could occasionally sell an ounce or two when needed. I removed the end caps of my pack frame and filled the aluminum tubing with thirty-two ounces of pure gold. I gently tapped the tube covers into place. My pack frame handed down to me from my grandfather now carried almost fifty thousand dollars' worth of gold.

I took the remaining thirty-eight-pound gold bar and buried it in the soft sand of our little sleeping room. If I ever needed money, it would be here. Somehow, I felt dirty and unclean after spending the day retrieving the gold that so many had shed blood for and lost their lives over.

I returned to the hot spring in the cavern on the high mountains. I washed and soaked for hours…but the uncleanness remained. My quiet time that night was filled with visions of men being staked and chained to bedrock. The cries of the dying that fell on deaf ears for days or weeks, I heard through the night. The souls at the bottom of the dark pit had been disturbed from their resting. Whatever I did with this gold I would make certain to use it wisely, and I would forever recognize those to whom it truly belonged…my ancestors who had been enslaved by the Spaniards and whose bones now decayed at the bottom of the deep pit. This gold truly did belong to my people. I knew in my heart I would leave behind specific instructions as to the location of the treasure. I needed someone trustworthy to share the instructions and location with. The name came to my mind in an instant. I knew a man of integrity. I knew a man who would do his best for his people with what was located at the bottom of the deep pit.

I drafted my letter and map the following morning.

Chapter 60

I wandered the isles of the Tribal Store for an hour or more. The familiar smell of the wood stove, along with meat smoking and strong coffee brewing, brought my memories alive. It was a Sunday morning. Not a regular day for the Elders to gather here. An occasional customer would enter for the purchase of something ordinary. I made sure I was out of sight whenever someone entered. I made my way to the rear of the store. Here the coffee pot steamed, and the wood stove gave off its distinct warmth and scent. I poured myself a cup of the piping hot coffee and sat at the same table, in the same seat, as I had the last time I had been here with Mr. Natchi. My mind wandered into the days of the past. Good days. I heard the voice of my grandfather in my memories. I closed my eyes, enjoying the fond thoughts, reliving the closeness and love of my grandfather.

"Pie with your coffee, Dak?" She set the plate of apple pie topped with a scoop of vanilla ice cream in front of me. I was startled from my daydreaming into the reality of the moment.

"Yes, thank you, ma'am." The face was familiar, the eyes radiated a wisdom gained through a lifetime of experience.

"Your journey was a success?" she asked with a look of confidence and assurance on her face while nodding to my delayed response.

"Yes."

"Thank you for what you have done for *The People,* Daklugie." The old woman that I had known since I was just a boy turned and walked behind the counter and made herself busy with a few dishes. I must have missed the sound of the door opening during our conversation. I became aware of his presence an instant before he seated himself in the chair next to me.

Mr. Natchi sat in silence, peering into my eyes. "Dessert before your lunch, Dak?" he said, indicating the pie and coffee in front of me, a wry smile on his face.

We talked for hours. I relayed most of what had occurred as best I could. He seemed to listen intently. His eyes focused on my face, his expression one of knowing. I felt his compassion and heart as I shared what had happened with Kwanita. I saw in his eyes the tears as he learned of her death. I talked for most of the day, releasing all that I had held within my silence over the past year. It was, simply put, freeing.

The old grandmother listened intently, occasionally refilling our coffee cups. She would place her hand upon my shoulder each time my cup was filled. I felt the blessings she was silently speaking over me at each touch of her hand.

Late into the afternoon I ended my narration of all that had occurred in a time and place so far from where we now sat. Mr. Natchi rose from his seat. "I have a spare room. Looks like you could use a shower and a soft bed."

I nodded in agreement.

The old grandmother began to sing the song of victory as we exited the Tribal Store. I waved goodbye to her as her tune rose into the heavens along with the smoke from the old wood stove. She raised her hands to me, her palms open.

I sat in the passenger seat of the old Ford truck as Mr. Natchi fired up the engine, and we were off in a cloud of smoke. I observed again the Vietnam veteran's hat on the seat between us, the gun rack and ammunition boxes in the door panel. In that instant a seed was planted about my future as a soldier.

The following morning, we talked again, but this day the talk was of the survivors and what might have happened.

"Dak, in my experience it may be years before you hear from them or have complete knowledge of what might have occurred. I know from my quiet time there was in fact a battle along the San Saba. When you are ready you can possibly confirm what has happened."

"How?" I asked. "Who might know?"

"*You still have a long life journey ahead of you, Dak. The People of the Comanche Nation in Oklahoma will know what has happened. When you are ready you must travel there.*" He spoke his direction to me in our native tongue.

"*I understand,*" I replied.

I left New Mexico the following morning. The old faded blue Ford putting out a steady stream of light smoke in my rearview mirror. I had paid much more than she was worth, but Mr. Natchi had need of a newer truck. He was certain he could trade outright for the gold.

He tucked the map and instruction letter I had drawn neatly into his front pocket. I knew he had the wisdom to do exactly what was prudent and best... with hundreds of millions in gold.

I had no way of knowing what his plan might be. I drove in silence toward the summit, then down the valleys, winding my way along the foothills I had spent the last few days walking. I reached the Pecos River two hours later. I stopped along the side of the road and walked the banks of the river until dark. I slept that night on the open prairie very near where we had spent one of the most beautiful spring seasons of my life. Very near to the place my daughter, Topusana, had been born. I sat by my small fire, dining on a cottontail rabbit I had taken with a snare. I breathed deeply the scent of the open prairie.

****

That same evening Mr. Natchi, having never unfolded the map and letter revealing the location of hundreds of gold bars, lit the corners of the papers as he stood alongside his firepit outside his home beneath the high mountains. The map and letter flamed instantly, lighting the forest surrounding him and momentarily revealing the presence of the spirits watching. He dropped the papers into the flames of the firepit, their secrets rising into the heavens as a whisp of scented sacrifice.

His wisdom was beyond compare.

Chapter 61

The following morning, I took to the back roads of eastern New Mexico. In the first oil town of fair size, I entered and drove the main street of town, spotting the sign I was looking for. "We buy Gold and Silver" was displayed clearly on the dirty window front. I parked the old Ford pickup several doors down and made my way cautiously toward the store front, observing the vehicles and people who were busily going about their day. There was one truck with two men sitting in the front seat; they watched me enter the store front.

Reaching for the door entrance, my grip was met with the resistance of a locked door. In an instant I felt a slight buzz as the door clicked open from some unseen switch. I held the door a moment, glancing up at the cameras with the red dots recording my every move. I was thankful for the dark sunglasses and cowboy hat I wore. My long hair I had tucked inside my western coat. I wore long sleeves, covering my dark skin. I knew, however, my face would give away my Native American ancestry. I opened the door and stepped into basically what was a cage of steel wire and welded metal. The door clicked shut behind me, as my heart raced, I was locked in the small steel cage. In a moment, a man's voice came over the speaker mounted above and adjacent to yet another video camera.

"Just a moment," he said. I felt again the slight buzz as the door toward the shop clicked open in front of me. I took a deep breath of relief and entered the store.

"Welcome, friend," came a weak voice from behind the counter. The man was stooped and must have been in his nineties. He was small in stature, probably five foot three, and appeared to weigh less than one hundred pounds in my estimate. He looked up from his work and looked directly into my eyes. There was a wisdom about the old man I sensed. He offered his hand to me, introducing himself. "Abram Levi, and you are?" He spoke with a questioning look.

"Dak." I answered as I took his hand in the feeblest of grips. It was then I noticed the numbers tattooed on his forearm. It dawned on me what the name and numbers meant. Abram Levi, like me, was also a survivor of attempted genocide.

"You have traveled very far to come to this place," he said.

"Yes, I have." Pausing a moment, I added, "as have you."

"Indeed, it has been a blessed journey in many ways. But what is my past? Today it has brought me to a place where I might assist a fellow traveler." He spoke with wisdom glistening in his weak pale blue eyes. I reached into my front pocket and drew out what I thought was five or six ounces of gold and placed it on the scratched counter between us.

He raised one of the larger pieces, observing it with a small magnifying glass. "Humm, interesting." Abram turned and retrieved a small digital scale from the cluttered desk behind him. He held another piece of the gold up to the light, examining its surface. Without comment he placed it along with the remaining pieces into a small container and dropped it gently onto the scale. The digital readout quickly settled at "9.3 oz." The number flashed red on the display of the small scale. Abram peered upward, calculating the number in his mind. He then jotted it down on a piece of scrap paper.

"Spot price today is 1,385 per ounce. So that you know I have calculated the weight of the plastic container and adjusted the scale. Dak, demand is high. I can pay spot price less five percent. Let's see that's 12,880 less 644, how about we settle at 12,236 even."

I stood in wonder, attempting the math in my own mind. I was confident the figures were exact and precise. "Let's just make it 12,000 even," I replied, knowing the math was honest and correct. He gazed into my eyes again with a shrewd look and a wink. Abram then turned and walked to the rear of the store.

"I assume you may need some small bills?" he questioned.

"Yes, thank you," I said loudly.

He entered again, standing behind the little counter and said, "You don't have to yell. I can hear quite well." A curt smile appeared on his face. He rapidly counted out $12,000, making neat little rows of one thousand dollars each. Ten one-hundred-dollar bills peeled off with expert precision. Twelve rows of cash in perfect symmetry, the exception being the last five hundred dollars in twenties, neatly lining the scratched glass top. I was amazed at the swiftness and accuracy of the movement he had evidently performed thousands of times.

"You might want to count that…just to double check."

"I think that is probably not necessary," I said. He smiled.

"Suit yourself."

"Is it safe to leave here. I mean I'm not from here, but I am a cautious man," I questioned as I tucked the money into my jacket pocket.

"Yes, you will be safe, Dak. I will erase the video footage as soon as you leave, as far as I'm concerned you were never here." He spoke with a soft assuring voice.

"I wish I had time to hear your story, my friend. Perhaps another day," I said.

"And I, too, would love to know of your journey. I have a sense they might be similar. If you decide to hammer off a few more corners…please know you have a trusted friend in Abram Levi."

I nodded to him, no doubt with a surprised look on my face at his knowledge about the gold. The door behind me buzzed and I heard the lock click open. I moved into the cage as the door closed behind me. I waited a moment as the front door now buzzed again, its lock also clicking open. I stepped into the rain and walked down the street. I was convinced I was being watched as I fired up the old blue Ford. I drove but a block down the street, certain I was followed, but unable to identify any specific person or vehicle that might be doing so. I pulled into a large gas station and attempted to gas up the Ford. I was unsure about how to activate the pump. A voice came over a speaker saying I had to swipe my card. An uneasy feeling welled up as I replaced the pump handle and entered the front door of the station. "Card didn't work?" Came a woman's loud voice from behind the register.

"Um, I'll be paying cash," I said.

"Just leave me your ID and go fill up, then you can come back and pay." I panicked. I had no form of ID, no driver's license, no social security card, nothing. I turned and rapidly walked away. My breathing returned to normal once I reached the Ford. How was I to function in the present time? I could hunt and kill buffalo, deer, or antelope, I could lead men to victory against any enemy. I was certain I possessed skills few men could match…yet I did not know how to buy gasoline. Thinking through the problem, I drove down the street to the next gas station. I entered the station, paid forty dollars in cash to the clerk in advance, hoping the pump would come on when I lifted the handle.

I took a deep breath as the numbers clicked to zero and the fuel began to flow as I squeezed the pump handle. I added a quart of oil to the old Ford's engine from the supply behind the back seat and headed east on a small back road.

The sign along the road as I exited the town said Amarillo, Texas 285 miles. I had traveled only a few miles when I pulled the truck to the side of the road. I made a U-turn and headed back to the oil town.

Abram buzzed the locks for me as I entered his store front again. He stood stooped behind the counter, a welcoming look in his eyes.

"Welcome back, Dak, perhaps we can share a bit of our stories this evening. I was just closing up." He flipped a little switch behind the counter and the closed sign illuminated behind the smudge covered glass of the front window. "Follow me, friend, I hope you like lentils."

Chapter 62

Abram bowed his head and gave thanks for the day. He offered thanks for the sparing of his life, he asked for protection of his extended family, and the lives of his grandchildren and great grandchildren. In closing he asked for a blessing upon his people and their nation.

"That was a good prayer," I said. He simply gazed into my eyes with a look of brokenness. The soup was delicious. Lentil beans, celery, onions, flavored leaves of some kind. I ate sparingly, as did Abram. The little room in the rear of the storefront was also Abram's home. From where I sat at the small two-person table, I could see a little bedroom through the sheet draped across its doorway. In the kitchen where we dined was a small couch against one wall and a large radio rested atop an end table.

Abram observed me as I took in his humble living space. "Fit for a king, heh, Dak."

I smiled, thinking of where I had lived in my life. "I agree, Abram. I have lived in caves and on the open prairie and the high mountains…for decades. This is indeed one of the finest homes I have ever dined in." Again, he peered into my eyes with a curious look this time.

We talked for hours. His story was simply amazing. The man had survived due to his knowledge and ability in working with precious metals, gold, and silver. It was sickening to learn of his work. "Dak, many of the bodies had dental work performed. The gold would not be wasted in the grave. They kept me alive as long as I performed the work," he said, a faraway look in his eyes. "I kept a small amount each day in between my toes. After five years it was enough to bribe my keepers. I, too, have traveled the wild country, Dak. It took me three months to cross the Alps. I was afraid to leave the mountains; they offered much protection. After the war, I lived in Switzerland for forty-seven years. I was a wealthy man then, as I am now, as you can see." I laughed along with him. "My people benefit from my work daily, Dak."

"I understand," I said. I wondered how I might also use my giftings to benefit my people. Abram Levi was one of the finest men I have ever had the pleasure to meet in this world.

He turned his attention to the radio on the little end table. "It is morning in Israel," he said and moved across the room and turned a few knobs on the radio. The voice of the announcer came through, although there was much interference in the signal. Abram listened intently for an hour as news from his homeland filled his home in a language I had never heard.

I longed for a way to hear from my people.

The following morning Abram neatly printed out the name and address of the man I would meet at the synagogue in Amarillo, Texas. He also neatly tucked the five hundred dollars he had collected from me into an envelope and sealed it with a wax seal. "This will assure that you receive the identifications. Saul is particularly good at what he does. They will appear perfect to any who ask to see them. Joshua Daklugie…hum, your namesake was a great man, very brave."

"Yes, my grandmother picked the name. She was a woman of great faith, Abram."

He nodded. "Your story is one of survival and overcoming, Dak. I am proud of you."

The comfort of the words the man spoke over me had a profound effect. My loneliness seemed to disappear in the few hours I spent with him. Hope seemed to fill my soul. Seeing and hearing of what he had overcome gave me a new strength. As we moved into the front of his shop the following morning and said our goodbyes, he spoke aloud a blessing over me.

"May the Lord keep you and bless you, Dak, may His face shine upon you, may He be gracious unto you. May the Lord lift up his countenance upon you, And give you peace."

The light shined within as I drove along the backroads of what were the beginnings of the Llano Estacado. The sea of endless grass.

Chapter 63

The drive across the backroads of the Texas panhandle was a wonderous experience. I stopped often and wandered the edges of the highway. By midafternoon I was nearing the city of Amarillo. The small sign along the edge of the road indicated fifty-three miles to go. On a slight rise in the roadbed, I pulled the old Ford to the side of the road.

The wind whipped the grass into little waves of swirling movement. The sun shone down from the clear blue sky. I gazed across the prairie. The voices in the wind cried out softly. I had been here before...in another time. I saw in my mind the movement of *The People*. Hundreds moved across the plains, little ones, old grandfathers, Warriors, silently gliding across Mother Earth, leaving nothing but tracks in our wake. I welcomed the memories into my soul.

I stepped across the barbwire fence and climbed the small hill. I stared in wonder at what appeared on the other side of the small rise of land.

Huge wind machines cut into the wind in the distance as they churned silently. Hundreds of them lined the skyline to the east. Enormous blades spun within the heavens. Giant other worldly creatures so out of place on the prairie their appearance was lewd and sickening. "What have you done to the prairie?" I spoke aloud. I could not imagine how a buffalo herd might react to the appearance of these alien monsters that had been strewn across the land. How might the birds of the air possibly navigate the gauntlet of spinning blades? The voices of the wind faded from my hearing.

How could mankind invite this crudeness into this special place? I had much to learn about the modern world. I knew my learning would be forever filled with a different perspective, that of a natural man who had lived upon and alongside Mother Earth.

****

I walked the small hills back to the Ford. As I approached the truck another vehicle passed by slowly. The men I had seen outside Abram's storefront I recognized in an instant. They observed me as they drove by. The truck they traveled in was loaded with equipment and tools. Perhaps they were just headed to their work site in the oil fields. But I was a Warrior, and I knew better.

I opened the passenger side door of the Ford and removed my bow. I slung it across my shoulder, just as I had seen my grandfather do so many times. I removed a few arrows from my quiver. I stood in the wind of the prairie, checking their edge, making sure they were razor sharp, although I knew they were perfect. It had become a ritual I always practiced prior to any possible battle. These men had no idea who they were contemplating an encounter with.

Tenahpu (The Man) was the fiercest of all Comanche Warriors.

The men had picked a poor location for their plan. I saw the truck parked along the side of the road one mile ahead of the rise I had just crossed. To them the place must have seemed obscured from view. The little draw filled with young cottonwoods would give me easy cover as the hunters became the hunted. I slowed but continued until within about two hundred yards of the draw. I stopped the Ford. I gathered my war club and long knife. I locked the doors to the truck and ran south across the prairie. Behind a slight hill I turned, running toward the creek bottom. Within a minute of my leaving the Ford, I was concealed in the trees and brush along the small creek. I silently stalked closer to the highway until within earshot of the men.

"Where did he go?" the first man questioned.

"Hell, I don't know. He's some kind of chicken shit, taking off running like that. Let's just go bust out the windows and take the money. You know damn well he sold something back there."

I moved even closer, observing the men. They were both armed, pistols tucked into their belts. I would need to be extremely cautious.

When to act? All Warriors know surprise is the greatest advantage in any conflict. My bow was drawn, yet I hesitated. I could easily kill these men; their intentions were clearly set on evil. Was there another way? Might these men be persuaded to abandon their plan for evil without it costing them their lives? I was uncertain. I prayed a silent prayer for wisdom. Immediately I saw the scales tip in my favor.

I stepped into the open, giving my location away, my bow at full draw.

"Do you men wish to die a good death this fine afternoon?"

"What the?" the first man blurted out as he reached for his weapon. I loosed the arrow, intentionally sighting the arm that held the gun. The arrow met its mark, tearing through the muscle and tendons of his huge bicep. The gun clattered to the surface of the highway as he screamed out in pain. The second man likewise reached for his weapon...a mistake on his part.

The arrow met its mark lower on the forearm of his weapon hand. Blood sprayed across his vehicle window; an artery had obviously been hit. He fell to the surface of the highway as he attempted to escape. I walked calmly up the slope of the little draw.

Both men had fallen to the ground, writhing in pain. I quickly kicked the guns away from their reach. They sat terrified as I addressed them.

"Choose now. Your life is in your own hands. The next arrow will pierce your hearts," I said calmly. I nocked an arrow and drew my bow, awaiting their response. "Choose now...life or death?" I said again. "If it helps your decision, I sold nothing. I actually bought something from Abram."

"I choose life," the first man said. I trained my arrow on the second man. He was losing much blood.

"Life." He spoke in a weak voice. I released the tension on my bow and moved toward him. Working quickly, I removed his belt and tied it securely around his upper arm. The blood flow stopped immediately. The other man sat upright, holding his right arm.

"You better get him to a doctor soon," I said. He nodded, indicating the arrow protruding from his arm. I walked near him, reached down and snapped the arrow in half. I gave the man the half arrow I had just broken and said, "Bite down hard." He did so as I pushed the remaining arrow through the flesh in the back side of his arm. To his credit, he did not cry out. I took the broken arrow, then walked calmly to the roadside and located the other arrow I had fired, placing them both within my quiver.

I moved away from the men and gathered their guns. I tucked them neatly into my belt.

"You cain't take our guns!" the man with the tourniquet protested.

"I can loosen that for you if you are not agreeable with our arrangement," I stated. "You might consider in the future the cost of planning evil, especially against a Native American Warrior." The two seemed to shudder at my words.

I walked into the brush along the little creek bottom and disappeared from their sight. From my hidden location, I watched the men load themselves into the work truck and drive away.

Chapter 64

Saul Lowenstein was a man of wisdom. I looked him directly in the eyes. Eyes are the window to the soul, and I had learned much about men and who they were by simply, deliberately, looking into their souls. Saul was a good and honest man. Another servant of his people, and any in need for that matter. I had presented the sealed envelope from Abram and he had dropped whatever he had been doing and went to work. He took several photographs of me, which he scanned into his computer.

"Joshua, this will take me a few hours to complete. Go next door to the soup kitchen, tell them I sent you. They will feed you well, my friend."

I said thank you and climbed the stairs, lifting the heavy oak boards that concealed the entrance to his hidden workspace below the sanctuary.

Stepping into the sunshine outside the synagogue, I instantly tasted the exhaust-filled air as automobiles of all shapes and sizes sped by in a never-ending stream of hurry. I had never been so uncertain about what mankind had become. The hurried pace and constant noise of the city gave me a feeling of uneasiness. I did not belong here. Questions floated across my mind. How would my people survive in this world, if, and when, any arrived here from *Dream Time*? Had they survived the attack on the San Saba? How long would it be before I received word? I needed to hear of my *People*. I needed to get to Oklahoma, and soon.

I watched from my little corner table as people streamed in and out of the soup line. Dirty people. Loud people who spoke to unseen images within their minds. Sad people with eyes downcast, small children at their sides, dirty and unkempt. I was taken aback at the lives that walked before me. Broken lives with broken hearts paraded through the soup line. What kind of world was

I now walking in? I was certain from my observations these people would go hungry if not for the generosity of Saul Lowenstein and his parishioners.

A few hours later Saul seated himself next to me. The table was away from the commotion of the room. He spoke in a hushed voice.

"Joshua, the work is perfect. You should have no trouble as far as identification is concerned. The plight of your people is another matter." Wisdom radiated from the man's face. He was keenly aware Native Americans had walked a difficult and similar path to that of his own people. "I will pray for you, Joshua."

The light within my heart swelled at his words, like an unseen wave of emotion. I reached into my jacket and placed an envelope containing $5000 in cash and slid it across the table.

"I want to help. The soup is a great tool in helping the people of this city; I can see that. Thank you for feeding the hungry, Saul."

The man rose from the table with a nod of his head and a whispered thank you. I could see in his eyes he was also moved by my small act of generosity.

****

The drive through the city was terrifying. The open roads where I had driven were easy to navigate with one or two cars or trucks occasionally passing by. This drive, however, was not for the beginner. Cars honked. Drivers cursed. Faces contorted behind steering wheels and angry hands made lude motions toward one another. The people seemed crazed to me. Driving in a city was a difficult task and one I would not soon repeat. After thirty minutes of intense stress, the traffic began to thin. I relaxed my grip on the steering wheel of the old Ford and exited onto a smaller highway heading east and south.

The grass of the Llano was burned and brown. I had seen the prairie appear this dry only one other time in my life. The year I had made the run to Mescalero Springs with my friend One Horse. Drought effects the mind of the natural man. I prayed for the animals; I understood how much they were suffering. I had experienced their struggle.

Within an hour the canyon country began to reveal itself. I was traveling along the northern edge of the Llano. It was here I had lost my wife. I slowed but did not stop. Our future, my future lay ahead.

The sign along the edge of the highway indicated 190 miles to Lawton, Oklahoma. I traveled another half an hour toward the south and east and spotted yet another sign: Historic Marker One Mile.

I stopped along the side of the road and parked the old Ford. The place offered a beautiful view of the canyons below. I stood in front of the marker and read repeatedly the raised letters that had somehow been pressed into the steel monument.

"September 28, 1874. One of the last free bands of Comanche led by Chief Poor Buffalo, along with Kiowa Bands led by Chief Lone Wolf, were defeated by Colonel Mackenzie and the United States Fourth Cavalry, along the base of Palo Duro Canyon below. The villages located along the bottom of the canyon were demolished, along with the entire winter food supply. More than 1,400 horses belonging to the Comanche Bands were rounded up and destroyed by the Cavalry soldiers. Many of the Warriors took to the prairie on foot, escaping. By the end of this eventful day Colonel Mackenzie declared victory as most of the Native Americans were captured. The surviving Indian Nations were eventually moved to Fort Sill area of Oklahoma Indian Territory. This battle represents the last effort at military resistance by the southern Plains Indians against the advancing white settlers."

I stood along the edge of the canyon. I wondered how many escaped, and where they might flee. I wondered what it meant to destroy 1,400 horses. Shooting the ponies one by one would have been the only way. I thought of how much work was involved in preparing and storing a winter food supply for a Comanche band. I imagined the struggle against the wagon guns, the terror as mothers and children fled. I stood on the edge of the canyon and my tears at last opened. The floodgates of my soul poured onto the ground along the edge of what was now called Palo Duro Canyon, a place on the outskirts of the Llano that was evidently the last stronghold of my people.

A van filled with a family stopped. The children exited followed by their parents. The children laughed and played along the roadside as their parents read the words on the marker. I stood to the side, turning my face away from them, suddenly embarrassed at my tears. My long hair blew across my shoulders in the wind. I sensed the presence of the two as they approached me.

"Pretty amazing story, don't you think."

I was surprised at the comment and their willingness to approach me.

"Yes," I replied. "Although amazing might not be the correct term." I turned and looked at the man. His wife saw the tears on my face and reached for her children.

"They shot the war ponies, all of them…one by one. The ponies must have panicked at the smell of so much blood." I spoke with my eyes closed, imagining the scene. "I'm sure they ran swifter than ever before in their lives. I'm certain the stallions attempted to protect the mares." I glanced at the man's wife as she gathered and called to her children. I added, "It is what they do...protect. It must have taken days to kill so many."

The man extended his arm toward me, touching my shoulder.

"I am sorry, my friend. Amazing is not the correct word," he said.

I turned and walked to the old Ford with a sickening feeling in my gut. As I drove along the highway descending into the canyon, I softly sang the songs of sorrow and loss. The songs my grandfather had taught me.

****

The remainder of the drive to Oklahoma was filled with panoramic views of a land I had crossed on foot for many seasons. I knew *The People* moved and lived within these canyons and prairie lands for centuries. It suddenly occurred to me what was most different about this place now: the lack of buffalo. There were none.

In a different time, there were hundreds of thousands, perhaps millions of these creatures wandering the plains. They provided food, clothing, even tepee lodges for our people. Their presence also brought about the balance of life on the prairie. They consumed native grasses, tilled the soil, fertilized the ground, even fed the wolves as the weaker ones were eliminated. Those carcasses left by the wolves would then feed the birds of the air. The spring grasses that blossomed within the bones of the buffalo grew and fed the rabbit, which in turn fed the coyote, who also fed on the mice and prairie dogs, which fed on the flowers, plants, and trees. Those trees in turn generated pure oxygen, giving life breath to all. It was the cycle of life so perfectly created, complex, and balanced that it would so move the spirit of mankind living within and upon this sacred land...that he created song. Songs that glorified the Creator. Inspiration from the human soul so deep that the songs would be sung for generations.

I knew the elimination of the buffalo from the prairie must have had an immense impact on Mother Earth and all the creatures in the circle of life on the prairie, including the natural man that had once lived here.

As I drove along slowly, I entered a field of massive wind generators. The highway followed near their spinning blades for miles. I could sense the bodies and spirits of the birds as they lay dead in the grass below the massive machines. "What have you done to the prairie?" I said aloud...again and again.

Chapter 65

Lawton, Oklahoma

I drove through and around the town repeatedly. I had no idea what I was looking for. Having focused on simply getting here, once I arrived, I had no plan of whom to contact, or what I might even say. A little river flowed along the outskirts of town near a sign that said, "Entering the homelands of the Comanche Nation." I eased the Ford down a rutted road near the edge of the riverbank and parked. Enormous oak tress created a canopy of leaves above as a cool breeze drifted along the water. I could taste the moisture-laden clean air. The evening sky was darkening as the sun sank below the horizon. I made a small camp and struck a fire. I was hungry. Spotting the ducks working along the slow-moving river, I quickly, expertly laid two snares. The night sky faded into darkness. I inched closer to the fire as the sounds of the city echoed along the river. I dozed off into a restless sleep.

I awakened a few hours later to a familiar sound. A fat duck wrestled in the snare, quacking loudly. I expertly removed its head with a pop of my wrist and held its warm body as the life blood drained from the animal. I knelt and gave thanks for the bounty of the earth. The stars to the east showed it was now past midnight as I kindled the fire and ran a spit of green branch through the duck. The fire sizzled and popped as the fat of the roasting duck dripped into the open flame. I rotated the duck every few moments. The aroma of fire grilled meat drifted along the riverbank. My stomach grumbled. An hour later I consumed the entire animal. The meat was delicious. I cleaned myself along the edge of the water, settled again by the fire, and fell fast asleep.

I was awakened again, this time by an unfamiliar sound. Crunching twigs and grass, rocks overturning. I looked in the direction of the sound as a large pick-up truck made its way along the rutted road toward me. Bright red lights began to flash along the top of the truck. The sound of a radio with much static in the background crackled loudly. I rose from my little camp and placed my hand on my grandfather's war club tucked neatly into my belt. The man approached me cautiously with a loud greeting. "Hello, the camp. I need to see your hands in the air."

How to respond, I thought.

"*My Name is Tenahpu. I am a Comanche Warrior. I have come here in peace. Why do you ask such a strange question? The Comanche Warrior does not show his hands to any man.*"

I saw the man remove his hand from the weapon by his side and reach for a microphone attached to his shoulder. "Unit seven, all clear. He's Tribal." Then I heard the reply come over a speaker mounted outside the truck.

"Understood, unit seven, all clear."

"*We will talk a moment, Tenahpu,*" he replied in our native tongue. "*My name is Joseph Red Cloud.*" I removed my hand from the war club and moved toward the fire. I stoked it, adding a few sticks, then some larger logs. The flame rose, radiating a soft warmth into the early morning chill. I recognized the name...from another time.

The man, who was obviously Native, walked to the edge of the fire and seated himself upwind of the smoke as it drifted along the edge of the river. Another duck began the loud squawking as it became entangled in the second snare. I quickly cleaned and prepared the roasted duck as he looked on in amazement. I could sense the admiration in the man's eyes.

I knew I had made a new friend.

I offered the roasted duck to Officer Red Cloud and he rended the duck in half, passing the other half back to me. I sat by the fire and we enjoyed the savory meat.

"*Many of The People no longer possess the skills of the snare and war club,*" he said, indicating my weapon.

"*In my travels both have been invaluable,*" I replied. We sat in silence, enjoying the sunrise, the meal, and even the quietness of company. I could see wisdom in the eyes of Joseph Red Cloud. For now, too many words were not needed. After our meal we both washed along the riverbank and returned to the fireside.

"*You have traveled far, Tenahpu?*" he asked, a questioning look on his face.

"Yes," I replied.

"*How might I assist you, my friend?*"

I decided this was a man I could trust.

"*I seek information of what has happened to our* People. *My family. I am a protector Warrior. It is why I have come to this time and place.*"

Joseph Red Cloud nodded in understanding.

"*There is a woman. She is referred to as Old Grandmother by most. Her proper name is Hantaywee (Faithful One). She is gifted in healing and visions. Hantaywee has much wisdom concerning the story and history of* The People. *She may know the answers you seek, Tenahpu.*"

I nodded in agreement.

"*We will go to her now,*" he said.

Again, I nodded in agreement. I gathered the few items from my camp and loaded them into the old Ford while Joseph Red Cloud doused the fire with river water. I followed along in the Ford as we took to the back roads of the reservation.

It took an hour of driving along muddy rutted roads to reach the little home overlooking the expanse of beautiful prairie. Again, it was evident from my viewpoint, that I had traveled here in the past. The view of the plain before us as we walked through the sparse brush toward the Hantaywee home was unbroken and stunning. There were, however, no buffalo in sight.

****

The old woman arose from a rocking chair on the front porch of her small home. She peered our direction as we approached the quaint little house, straining to see.

"*Welcome, Tenahpu. Welcome, Joseph.*" She took a few feeble steps in our direction and greeted us with a warm smile.

"*Old Grandmother, Tenahpu has traveled far. He will meet with you now,*" Joseph said.

"*Please come inside, my children. I have been awaiting your arrival. Our food is almost ready. The* Dream Time *leaves a soul and body hungry for many days.*"

She turned and entered the lodge shaped home. Her singing drifted across the prairie outside her home. The songs were familiar. Songs of rejoicing filled the atmosphere of the little home…and my heart. I joined in the song, as did Joseph Red Cloud as I took my seat on the huge buffalo hide.

Chapter 66

The aroma of meat cooking and oak wood greeted our senses as we seated ourselves on the buffalo hide in the tradition of our people. Old Grandmother moved across the room slowly to the wood stove, lifted the lid of the iron pot, and stirred. The scent from the cooking pot, as only familiar smells can do, brought my mind to a different time. Buffalo stew, dim firelight, my wife, Kwanita, my daughter, Topusana, my friends. I closed my eyes, allowing the memories, welcoming them into my mind.

She began the song of thanksgiving. I joined in the song; my eyes still closed. My heart filled at the presence of the Spirit, the light within the darkness glowed brightly. I had only been here for a few moments, yet I knew after more than a year of wandering and waiting…I felt as if I were home.

"*Let us eat first, my sons, then we will talk.*"

We both nodded in agreement and respect.

The stew was delicious and prepared exactly as it had been for centuries. Wild onion and garlic, crisp cattail stalks, a hint of wild herb. We ate loudly. Joseph finished his serving first, quickly asking for seconds. Old Grandmother smiled, moved across the room, and filled his bowl to overflowing. I rose and offered my wood carved bowl to her. Smiling again, she filled my bowl to overflowing with the piping hot stew steaming into the atmosphere of the little home. It seemed the vapors of the buffalo stew mingled and rose with gratefulness of the three souls that feasted on the goodness and bounty of the earth.

We ate in silence. Too many words were not needed in this sacred moment. Later after we had eaten our fill, Old Grandmother spoke.

"*I have forgotten what it is to have hungry Warriors gracing my lodge.*" Her eyes, faded and pale, cast a remembering gaze as if she were looking very far into the distance or, perhaps the past.

"*I am grateful for the meal, Old Grandmother. This brings my heart and mind to the reason for my travel. My Tribe. Our people. I have waited more than a year. Might you have insight into what has happened*?" I asked.

She rose again, collecting our empty bowls. Then she added a few logs to the wood burning stove, the smoke of the wood rising and surrounding her as she turned to me with a knowing look.

"*Patience, Tenahpu, is a thing that is only gained by its need in a person's life.*" She seated herself again upon the buffalo robe. "*You will need much patience for what you will soon learn of.*" Looking toward Joseph, she added. "*This word is for both of you, sons.*"

I nodded as did Joseph. We sat in silence, awaiting her next words.

"*Let us smoke and rest awhile. The past night was restless for all of us.*" She removed the sacred pipe from a nearby shelf. Lighting it, she drew deeply of its distinct flavor, blowing out the deep blue smoke across the lodge. Old Grandmother passed the pipe to me and reached into her medicine bag. She tossed the fine dust into the air and it seemed to mingle in the cloud of blue smoke that hung around us. I smoked, as I had in so many other lodges and sacred councils, across so many miles, and so many years. The cloud of blue smoke swirled before us.

I passed the pipe to Joseph. He, too, drew a deep breath of the pipe. The smoke seemed intoxicating. It had been many moons since I had experienced the comfort and security of family, friends, and the sacred pipe.

I yawned deeply and leaned against the soft hide-covered wall of the lodge. My eyes became heavy as my mind wandered. I tried to fight off the sleepy feeling, forcing myself back into awareness a few times. Eventually my chin dropped to my chest and I drifted into a deep sleep.

****

I knew I was dreaming. But what was happening before me I could feel, taste, see, and even hear. The battle raged. There were many, many soldiers. My people fell along the banks of the San Saba, our once quiet little safe haven.

Bullets whipped through the wind. I saw their smoke trails in slow motion. Some bullets landed in the dust along the riverbank with a quiet puff. Some penetrated the skins of the teepee lodges. Others tore flesh and bone, indiscriminately. Children fell. Old ones bled. It was then I saw her as she ran toward the camp.

Topusana, yelling her war cry. Prairie Song, my granddaughter exited the lodge, gazing toward her mother with a look that seemed to be something like acceptance.

The bullet exited the muzzle of the rifle. Topusana raced toward her daughter then fell as the bullet entered her side. Blood flowed freely as she fell to the ground. She did not rise. Prairie Song was wrestled to the ground and tied with ropes. The soldiers moved her away from the battle, tearing her clothing away. I reached for my bow; it was not there in its comfortable place across my shoulder. I grasped for my war club; it was not in my belt. In my dream I was only an observer. I watched in horror as my tribe was decimated. Prairie Song attacked the soldier in the midst of cruel violation. She attempted to escape. The bullet took her life and her spirit rose from the burning camp. I could see Topusana observing, witnessing the murder of her child. She collapsed into the dust of Mother Earth. In my dream the dark cloud grew to a level I had never felt or imagined.

I drifted above the scene. Spirits of friends and family rose into His presence. I observed a few children and old women escape.

Hours later in the darkness, I observed Tabbananica silently working his way across the camp. Tabba was a Warrior. I felt deep satisfaction as he killed many soldiers with his long knife.

Twenty-one.

The number floated in the sky across the bloody scene.

21

There were twenty-one. Twenty-one members of my tribe escaped into the caverns. Nineteen of those survivors now slept in *Dream Time*; the other two slept in the little lodge home on the outskirts of the reservation in Lawton, Oklahoma.

I would not awaken for hours.

****

The fire crackled as Old Grandmother added a large piece of oak wood. The door made a little screeching sound as she closed the latch. I sat upright, the memories of my dream rushing into the forefront of my mind. I felt sick. I felt helpless. I had but one remaining question, but Old Grandmother knew the question. When? When would they arrive? She would reveal to me the answer when the time was right. For now, I would be patient.

I spied Joseph across the small room. He was still asleep lying on the buffalo robe. He called out occasionally, struggling against some unseen enemy. I somehow knew it was the same army of militia and Rangers that had attacked our home camp that he wrestled within his dream. I stood on weak knees and stumbled across the room to the doorway.

I seated myself on one of the chairs that overlooked the prairie outside Old Grandmother's lodge. The wind whistled through the brush and tall grass. The sun shone bright in the early summer sky; the blue sky was soft and clear. The birds sang as they worked along a little creek adjacent to the lodge home. It seemed all was well with creation. However, the storm within my own soul was raging. How could these men be so ruthless?

She was just a child.

Chapter 67

A few hours later, Joseph Red Cloud exited the lodge and seated himself next to me. The sun was low in the western sky and the rolling hills across the plain were aglow with a thousand hues of gold and yellow.

"*I saw my grandfathers fall, along with their children,*" he said as he peered into the distance. I gazed into his eyes and saw the dark cloud I so easily recognized. Old Grandmother feebly exited the home and seated herself in her rocking chair.

"*If I only had some antelope meat, I could prepare my favorite meal for our dinner this day,*" she said with a sly look on her face. It took just a few moments for me to gather my weapons. Joseph likewise gathered a bag from his truck, went inside and changed out of his uniform into his modern-day hunting gear.

"You have no bow?" I questioned.

"You will be the shooter," he replied. Words that would, in the future, be quite prophetic. I turned and began to run across the prairie. I heard Joseph following close behind, keeping the pace in perfect stride with me.

The pace was easy for the first mile or so. I decided to test him. I accelerated to the point that I was struggling. Behind me I could hear only footfalls, no labored breaths. I was impressed. The dark cloud within our souls dissipated. Joseph drew up alongside me as we ran. I was just thinking of slowing for some recovery time.

"*Are you warmed up now, Tenahpu?*" He accelerated and ran away from me, gaining ground with every stride. After a few minutes, he was over the small hills ahead of me. It was all I could do to follow in his tracks. I had never seen a Warrior run as Joseph Red Cloud could run. I caught myself in thought and memories. Perhaps there was one other that might equal his pace. Sumu

Puku. One Horse might have been as strong and swift. I spotted Joseph as he stopped on the side of a hill two hundred yards ahead. From this distance he even looked a bit like One Horse, tall and thin, his long hair flowing across his shoulders. I slowed and by the time I arrived I had recovered somewhat.

"*I think you are a good runner,*" he said. I sat on the little hillside in wonder. Those were the exact words of my old friend One Horse.

"*I love to run,*" was all I could say, as I choked back my emotions.

"*They are just over the next rise of land. I will raise the flag. There is good cover there to the east.*" He indicated the small trees and brush just forty yards away. "*It should be an easy shot for a Warrior of your ability.*"

I nodded in agreement and rose, moving into the cover. Joseph tied the bright red flag onto a plastic expandable pole and planted it on the little hilltop. He then ran toward the west, opposite my direction. I knew he was showing himself to the antelope. They would consider the danger to have departed.

One hour later, the buck climbed the little hill, staring at the flag. My bow shot was perfect. The animal fell. The others escaped as they scattered along the prairie. I heard Joseph's voice from what seemed like a mile away to the west.

"Good shot, Dak." Had I heard correctly? I knelt in prayer, giving thanks for the life of the beautiful animal.

On our return we carried the dressed antelope between us on a long pole we had shaped from a cottonwood tree.

We talked the entire three-hour trip back to Old Grandmother's. Joseph told me of his time spent in a world I had never imagined. Time in a place half a world away, in Iraq. Joseph held back some of what had happened in his life story. But I knew he was a hero, a highly decorated war veteran. He had served his *People* and his country well. He talked of the battlefield, his friends who had made the ultimate sacrifice. He spoke of their bravery and their unwavering selflessness. I sensed his brokenness at the loss of his friends to the battlefield in a place far away. I understood completely his loss.

That day a new friendship was formed and molded out of the hard steel of shared loss and shared victory. Two Warriors carried together the bounty of the earth; we also carried the wounds and scars of war. I shared with him the loss of my friend One Horse, even the location of his cross. I had never spoken of his death to any person. Joseph, in kind also understood. He nodded repeatedly as we carried the body of the antelope across the plain. He remained quiet as I spoke. Joseph was a good listener.

As he had done in a different time, God knit two hearts together that day on the prairie lands of Oklahoma. In His wisdom, it is what was most needed for two darkened, wounded souls. I would be forever grateful to the Creator for placing the two of us together across the years of time and space neither of us could comprehend.

"*You called me, Dak,*" I said in a questioning voice as we neared the lodge.

"*I saw many things within my dream in Old Grandmother's lodge. Kwanita was a beautiful woman and mother. You have been a blessed man, Daklugie.*"

"*It is a rare friend who can remind one of his blessings and bring attention to the good in a man's life,*" I said. We continued toward the front of Old Grandmother's lodge. He lowered the tail gate of his truck and we set the carcass of the antelope on it.

"*In my life I have found many that have the ability to bring out the negative or remind us of our setbacks or even our failures. I have made it a point in my walk to intentionally do the opposite. You and I, my friend, are very blessed men, in spite of the difficulties we have faced.*"

I nodded in agreement as we began the butchering of the antelope. The difficult task was enjoyable and easy with two men working together. I cut branches and set them near the front of the lodge, then gathered both dry and green wood for the smoking process. I then fashioned the legs of the meat racks, tying the ends and tops together with strips cut from the antelope hide. All the while, Joseph, after setting aside a few large roasts, cut the remaining meat into strips. Within an hour the meat racks were full. As the smoke rose along the racks, the scent of slow roasting meat drifted in the air. We continued to work the carcass, removing every usable piece of meat. These small pieces we gathered into a large bowl, and I set it aside for Old Grandmother's stew. We washed in the creek alongside the lodge, then spent the remainder of the afternoon tending the smoke fires and lounging in the warmth of the afternoon sun. Our conversation waned, and we were both comfortable in the silence.

The view across the prairie, the sounds of the little creek tumbling alongside the lodge, combined with songs of the birds, the crackling of the fire, and the scent of meat and woodsmoke, nurtured and brought a comfort to my soul.

Old Grandmother observed our work and progress from her chair on the front porch with a look of satisfaction, or was it peace that reflected from her wrinkled face.

That evening we dined on fresh antelope stew. Our conversation was graced with goodness and the stories of our people from Old Grandmother. We sang the songs of old. Songs of the hunt, songs of creation, songs of bounty and plenty. My eyes became heavy again. I gazed across the room at Joseph, noticing he was already sleeping soundly. I stretched out and said my goodnight to Old Grandmother as she moved to her little bed along the side of the lodge.

"Ten years, Tenahpu. It will be another ten years before they arrive."

Chapter 68

Two years later

Iraq

It always created a rush of adrenaline when the fifty-caliber sniper rifle exploded at the gentle near undetectable squeeze of my trigger finger. The soft but firm grip of my hands assured there was no movement of the weapon at the firing. The bullet sped through the atmosphere at an incredible velocity, breaking the sound barrier instantly. The target fell two full seconds later as the bullet entered the man's head.

"Kill…Time to move, Dak," Joseph said as we rolled a few meters to our left. Those words he had called out and spoken to me repeatedly on many missions. We were experts at what we did, and deadly.

I learned much in the training I had received from the white man's army. They had recognized my gifting very early. I could shoot any weapon handed me with a precision unmatched, and so, they trained me to kill. A skill set I already possessed with many other types of weapons.

I was trained and studied ballistics, muzzle velocities, the effects of wind and temperature, even the effect that humidity had on trajectories. I had learned of caliber advantages and disadvantages, rifles, handguns, which materials made the best rifles, which failed. I had been instructed in loading ammunition, handling gunpowder, what metals made the best bullets for any given environment. I had learned the tactics of modern warfare. All tools the men over me wished for me to use against their enemies. I would comply for now. I had ten years to wait. It was a good decision Joseph had made. We were

Warriors. Our ability as a team was unmatched. We were accommodated in a slightly different fashion and treated with an honor and respect different from most, due to our success. The places we traveled and lived were, I suppose, in some ways the worst places on the planet. We traveled within expansive deserts filled with trash; we traversed remote desolate mountains where the trees had been stripped from the earth; and we walked through open mining scars that had been ripped into the land along the broken mountains. The oceans were filled with grease and oil that coated all it touched. I hated these places that had been so misused and disrespected. For these reasons, more than any agenda our keepers offered, I was motivated. I had no problem killing those who had so wounded Mother Earth.

Three tours of duty, and four years later, I had seen my fill of inefficient decision making and political posturing. I could no longer obey those in power who made so many foolish decisions, decisions that ultimately resulted in the unnecessary loss of life and treasure. The war we fought and many died in could have been ended in a matter of days or weeks. It became apparent to me and many who were there, the men who made the decisions had other interests at heart. As a Warrior, I could have never imagined using young men and women for some protracted political purpose. It takes time to learn of motive. But time, in particular quiet time, does eventually reveal truth to those who seek it out.

Joseph and I were awarded many medals and honors at the completion of our obligation. We were also offered attractive bonuses and benefits if we would re-up. I had no intention of doing so. I placed my medals, ribbons, award letters, and uniforms in a box in the little closet of my one-bedroom trailer on the Rez in Lawton, Oklahoma. They meant nothing to me. I would use the skills I had gained in the white man's army to my advantage, when and if the time ever came. For now, I would simply survive. I had six more years to wait. How to spend them? How to best prepare? What actions could I take to protect my people once they exited the *Dream Time?*

I would return to Texas in time to supply the caverns with food, equipment, tools, and whatever else might aid in their survival.

After our time in the army together, Joseph had returned to his work as a Tribal Officer. Our friendship had grown in the trials we had endured together. We talked most days. He seemed to fit easily back into the routine of daily modern life on the reservation. I did not.

My life in the past haunted me. I was unable to duplicate the years I had spent living as a natural man with my people. For me, the modern world was disturbing and confusing. I had a plan; I knew of a place I might go and live out the time in the old ways. A place far from civilization as we know it. A place my skills would be needed on a daily basis. I loaded the old Ford and studied the map. I would leave the reservation, knowing it was two days drive to the Big Bend National Park in Texas. There existed locations along the river and canyon country where a man could survive and be unseen. I had hunted and lived there for years. It was a good plan.

I spent my last night on the reservation enjoying a quiet evening with my friends Joseph and Old Grandmother. But it was more than friendship. These two were family to me, the only family I had. Both sat in silence most of the evening, troubled. They understood my need to prepare. They also knew me well enough to know I was struggling, unable to adapt to this modern world. They understood I needed to leave, to live in a different way.

"*Sometimes the tourists travel the river, Tenahpu. You will need to stay hidden many days,*" Joseph said. I nodded. Old Grandmother listened quietly with a knowing.

I waited the entire evening for her to speak some wisdom or reveal what she might have seen of my future. As the fire gently crackling in the little wood stove died down, she began her songs. Songs of blessing. Songs of strength and endurance. There was a message in the songs she sang. A message I would not understand for a time.

****

I camped the first night along the highway somewhere in central Texas. The weather was clear and quite cold for November in Texas. The stars glimmered brightly in the night sky. A rabbit sizzled on a spit over the little fire, and the smoke drifted up in odd little swirls. My quiet time was troubled, just as the prior evening meal had been with my friends. I knew the Spirit was speaking. The only thing I felt or heard was that I should be extremely cautious. Of what it was not clear.

The following morning, I made my way south and west. The small towns grew farther apart and less populated as I traveled along in the old Ford. I began to recognize features in the topography of the earth. The mountains in the distance were familiar. I had crossed this land on foot several times in my life. I had grown comfortable with travel in the old Ford. However, I knew at some point very soon, I would leave her behind.

Two hours later I paid the man at the storage yard for one year of storage. I gathered my gear: my grandfather's bow, war club, long knife, and quiver. I donned my moccasins as the man looked on in wonder. I would make skins soon enough, for now I wore my western jeans and shirt. I shouldered my pack frame onto my back and adjusted the straps. No one would ever know it contained the treasure of gold in its frame. I had broken down my sniper rifle into its various parts so that it fit neatly into the pack along with several boxes of ammunition. I posted a letter to Joseph with instructions for annual payment of the storage fees for the old Ford. I walked through the little town that had grown into a minor tourist destination. A sign announced the new name of the ancient Springs of Mescalero. This place was now called Balmorhea State Park.

I walked along the side of the road toward the springs in wonder, recalling the run One Horse and I had made. The run to save our people. The little campground around the spring was deserted. Too late in the year for families to enjoy the little lakes and ponds. I sat in the green grass along the edge of the main lake, remembering.

More than anything I recalled Kwanita's touch. I closed my eyes in longing, remembering the day we spoke of our wedding in her parent's home. I sensed her voice as a gentle whisper in the wind. Her whisper brought a comfort to my soul for a moment. I breathed in a deep breath, the words within my sigh as I exhaled rose to her in the unseen spirit world.

"*I will never love another as I loved you, Kwanita,*" I spoke softly into the heavens. I sat listening for an hour or more, in quiet time.

I filled my canteen and moved across the wide prairie toward the great bend in the river the Mexicans had named Rio Grande. The Big Bend country of Texas lay before me. This land was wide and vast and unpopulated, and it was my former home.

Chapter 69

One Year Later

I watched from the bluff overlooking the river as the caravan of SUVs and four-wheel drive trucks plowed through the shallow water. My skins were the same color tint as the surrounding boulders and hid my presence from the group of men as they crossed the river below.

The year I had lived here along the river had been exhilarating in many ways. Mother Earth had provided all I needed for survival. I fed myself with fresh deer meat, rabbit, and quail and dove, even the javelina were a plentiful food supply. I made new skins from the deer hides. I used several cavern sites along the river for protection from the occasional storm, but the shallow caves primarily provided protection from the blistering heat and chilling cold winter wind of this remote harsh environment.

The tourists that occasionally traveled the river by raft rarely moved more than a few feet from the riverbank. The ranchers to the north and south of the border had no idea of my presence. I knew their routines. I recognized their vehicles and even the men who worked the ranches along both sides of the river. The men below me this morning, however, were unpredictable and dangerous. I had witnessed several guns battles between the groups of men on the south side of the river, and between them and both Mexican and American authorities.

The presence of these men and their activities was the greatest threat to my life of seclusion. I had no idea what they did, but I was learning in my observations of them. Some days they would drop truckloads of people off along the shallow rapids in the river. These groups then made their way north following one or two of the leaders who seemed to be guiding them across the difficult terrain. Other times they would meet with several trucks from the north and receive bulky duffle bags filled with what, I had no idea. I suspected it was money. I had no interest whatsoever in what these ruthless men were involved in and I did my best to steer clear of them. I understood I needed to live very cautiously. Old Grandmother's songs of protection began to take on clear meaning.

I had traveled north and east from here on several occasions. It was just a few days walk to the Ross ranch. I spent several evenings outside their window. It was good to hear their familiar voices, to learn of the healing that had taken place. I understood now more than ever, the loss of their son Jonathan to the war I had taken part in. I had left friends behind in that terrible place also.

They talked of David's friend and attorney William Travis. The man had evidently represented Jonathan Ross and his fellow soldiers. I listened intently outside the window one dark night as I learned of those brave soldiers and their recommendation for the Medal of Honor. Something within my heart sank as I learned of the failure of the effort to award them the medal. Somehow, I felt a closeness to David and especially to Abby, a kindred spirit of loss. Losing a son, or in my case, a wife, a friend, a granddaughter, to war, was an unthinkable emotional wound. Those who have suffered that kind of tragedy would forever carry the loss, and only those who knew that darkness the loss created could ever relate or understand.

I understood.

I had supplied the cavern with more firewood, and even some clothing. I had just over four more years to wait. With a possible date in sight, an approximate time frame that the waiting would end, the loneliness became bearable.

This day would bring about a change in my plans. I observed the scene below in the bright morning sunlight. I watched the vehicles stop along the north side of the river. The rear doors opened and a young woman and her two small children were led along the riverbank, blindfolded. The report of the three pistol shots echoed along the canyon walls as the three fell in the dust of the riverbank.

I had attempted to remain uninvolved. But this act of cowardice no true Warrior could overlook. I quickly assembled my sniper rifle and spied the men through the high-powered scope, noting facial features, vehicle descriptions, even license tag numbers. I knew I could not kill all of them now.

Observing the wind and making a minor adjustment, I took in a deep breath and then slowly let it out. Then momentarily held my breath while I indiscernibly squeezed the trigger. The chest cavity of the man who had executed the women and children exploded in a spray of red mist. Several of the others ducked behind their vehicles as I chambered a new round. I took aim at the apparent leader of the group. I was eight hundred meters away. I spoke softly to myself as the headwind died. "Just an inch lower," I exhaled slowly and then held my breath…then the soft movement of my trigger finger again. The man's head exploded, spraying blood across the hood of the truck. Several men began to fire indiscriminately in all directions. They had no idea where the rifle shots originated. I had already moved from my concealed position.

From my new position I again tested the wind, chambered a third round, and fired at an escaping SUV. The front windshield shattered as the driver side window was coated instantly in blood. The vehicle swerved hard toward the river and came to a stop as its front wheels sank into the shallow water. Several men jumped from the SUV and ran across the water to the south. It was then I noticed the dust cloud to the north. Vehicles from the north side of the river began to depart the scene. I watched as the distinct white and green striped trucks of the Border Patrol drove away at high speed. They had been watching. They also had taken no action to defend the woman and her young children. What was happening here? Why would they have not intervened?

As I silently moved along the boulders, moving away from the scene, I knew the men on the north side of the border were just as dangerous and possibly even complicit in what had occurred this day. If this was true, perhaps they were complicit in much of what was happening with the dangerous groups of men from the south side of the river. Most concerning was, had the observing Border Patrol agents detected my position, or worse, had they seen me? My military training and reconnaissance skills would prove invaluable over the next few weeks.

For now, I would disappear into the vastness of the Big Bend country. I had been a ghost Warrior in my past…it was now necessary for me to become one again. Within a few days, I determined the men from north of the border were actually searching for me.

****

I sat by my little fire as the shadows danced along the walls of the cavern. The river just outside the shallow cave reflected the glow of the full moon as it rose above the eastern horizon. The night air was warm; the smell of the air along the canyon had a distinct scent of moisture. The night birds called. The coyotes yipped, giving away their locations to one another. All was well with creation.

I ate slowly, savoring the delicious meat of the quail. Just this evening, I had moved, completely concealed, to within earshot of the Border Patrol men as they scanned the canyon below them with their high-powered binoculars.

"It could just be a rancher…Taking the law into his own hands." The man's voice reached my ears easily.

"I'm not sure who we're dealing with. Not many have the skill to make those shots. The bullets recovered were military grade. Someone's onto us," the second man said as he scanned the canyon.

I silently moved away from the men. I wanted to kill them. It was clear they were involved in the death of the woman and her children. I knew doing so would only bring more men to hunt me.

I must not lose sight of my primary goal: assisting, protecting, preparing for my family and their arrival. I lay back down into the soft sand, knowing I must move on from here and again disappear from this place, these men, and their evil schemes. Tomorrow night I would begin my trek north. The old Ford would be waiting.

****

Ten days later I arrived at the storage lot. After installing a new battery, changing the oil, and flushing the gas tank and filling her with new fuel, we were off in the little cloud of blue smoke. I waved goodbye to the lot owner who had assisted me with the work on the Ford. I had paid the man $200 in cash.

"Sometimes a nice tip buys a man some confidentiality as to his movements," I said as I handed the man the cash.

"It always does in my world. And may I say thank you for your service," he said, indicating the dog tags hanging from the rearview mirror.

"It was an honor," I replied. As I drove away, I looked at myself in the rearview mirror. My skin was dark from the days spent in the sun. My hair was long and shining with a few streaks of grey. Little wrinkles appeared in my skin along my forehead and the corners of my eyes. For the first time in my life, I looked old. The clothing I had taken from a clothesline on the outskirts of town did not fit too well, but I would replace them at the next secondhand store I came to. I had replaced the clothing I had taken from the line with two perfectly tanned deer hides, knowing the owner would be agreeable with the trade.

I drove for hours, thinking of what this land had become and how our little tribe might possibly survive.

Chapter 70

The sign said Austin, Texas 87 miles. Traffic was already beginning to pick up as I neared the city. Deciding to stay on a route less traveled, I turned north onto a small farm-to-market road. It was nearing sunset. I decided to find a secluded spot along a side road to make camp and spend the night. The little gas station and liquor store sign appeared in the distance. I decided it might be a good idea to fill up before morning. These little decisions we make that seem to have no consequences to our daily lives can, in fact, change the course of our futures. I have thought many days and nights if I had only continued on and refueled elsewhere. The Spirit has purpose in all these seemingly random decisions. For me, the consequences of the decision would be severe. For another, life or death was in the balance.

I stood at the counter paying for my gasoline. The man entered the store, his hands hidden beneath a jacket. I sensed instantly something was wrong. He moved quickly, placing the handgun at the temple of the woman behind the register and demanding the drawer be opened. She began to scream as the few other customers ducked behind isles of groceries.

I acted quickly, without hesitation; I punched the gun hand while simultaneously striking a wicked blow. My war club met its mark. The man fell in a shower of blood, his skull caving at the force of my grandfather's weapon. The woman screamed at me. "What have you done?" She reached for the man, calling him by name. "Charlie, Charlie…don't die. Oh, Charlie?"

I was confused for a moment, the woman dialed 911, screaming into the phone, "He killed him. It wasn't supposed to happen this way. The Indian killed Charlie!"

I ran.

I was out the door in an instant. I started the Ford and sped down the little side road. The sheriff deputies passed me going the opposite direction, lights flashing, sirens wailing. What had just happened. I was a Warrior. It was in my being to protect. I could never imagine that a person would fake a robbery. But that is exactly, I would discover in the near future, what had just occurred. I was on the video, killing the man. My truck was also captured on the video cameras as I drove away.

I drove a few miles, sorting out the scene in my mind. Would they consider me as having committed a crime? Should I simply turn myself in and tell my story? I thought of Officer Victorio and my only experience with police and simply telling the truth. I thought of my friend Joseph and what he would advise. For the first time in my life, I was afraid, and I did not know what to do or where to turn.

I pulled off the side road into the grass. Making my way down a ravine and into the seclusion of the trees and brush. I parked the old Ford, loaded my equipment in my pack frame, and began to run. I ran to the east, knowing that was the direction of Austin. I needed help. I stopped. Should I run to the city eighty-seven miles to the east? Or to the cavern approximately sixty miles to the west, where I could disappear for years if necessary? Another decision with severe consequences. I knew the authorities would identify me on the video. I made my decision and started my run…east toward the city.

****

The following morning the helicopter flew in a search grid. I had seen the technique employed many times in Iraq. Thankfully, it was at least eight miles behind me and staying in a grid pattern near my old Ford. They had no idea how well I could run and how much ground I could cover. I would move another twenty or thirty miles today. This would be well outside any possible search area. I had intentionally left tracks moving toward the west, then backtracked erasing my trail and any sign that I had traveled east. I made the tracks clear and obvious; the authorities would know I was on foot and they would be searching in the wrong direction. Within another hour I could no longer hear the helicopter.

Around noon, the following day I stopped in a shallow little canyon with good tree cover. I bathed in the little creek bottom and settled in for a meal of dried venison. I would not move again until nightfall. I had time to rest and think. Where to go? Who to contact, and what method to use to communicate? I had more questions than answers. I had learned a great deal concerning "man hunting" during my tours of duty in Iraq. I would not be found.

I entered my "time of quiet" under the canopy of oak trees in my little hiding place. My mind drifted to the conversations I had eavesdropped on outside the window of the Ross's ranch house.

There was a name I had heard repeatedly. The man was a friend. He had attempted to assist Abby and David. What was the name? It would not come to my mind. I went through the alphabet in my mind going through the list of names that begin with each letter. He was an attorney. He had served in the navy. He lived in Austin. I drifted off to sleep. My body needed the rest. I slept soundly through the remainder of the day.

I awakened after the sun had set. The western sky was aglow with the fading edge of sunset, twilight growing steadily in the eastern sky. I gathered my pack and started in a slow jog to the east. I knew I had traveled this land in the past. The countryside was familiar. One Horse and I had traveled here on our journey to intercept the Mexican Army from the south. I thought of the battle I had witnessed, and the day that more than one thousand men from the north had fallen. Those men had traveled from San Antonio toward the south to intercept the Mexican Army. As I ran, the thought occurred to me those men would have had a much better chance at defending the land north of the river if they had simply stayed put and defended the Alamo from within its secure walls.

It was then the name came to me. The name of the friend and attorney of David and Abby Ross. The man whose practice specialized in representing war veterans.

William Travis.

Chapter 71

Two Days Later

I waited outside the office located along Fifth Street, observing from across the busy avenue. The man carried himself as a soldier. It was clearly evident William Travis was a disciplined military man. He arrived twenty minutes prior to the posted open hours on the door. William Travis entered the office and promptly locked the door behind him.

I crossed the busy street. I had tucked my long hair into my shirt and wore my cowboy hat low across my eyes. My moccasins were the only unusual feature a stranger might notice. But this was Austin, Texas, a weird city by all accounts. I had spent the previous day finding my way through the streets and the strangest people I had ever encountered. Men dressed in what I considered working cowboy apparel, sipped from Starbucks drink containers, and talked or texted on cell phones, completely unaware of their surroundings. Women, from the scantily dressed, to the professional looking, to the obvious women of the night, filled the walkways and little parks dotting the downtown area of Austin. The more I observed, the more I felt I was probably unnoticeable.

I knocked on the door of one William Travis, Esquire.

The lock turned from behind a metal shade. I peered into the eyes of the man. There seemed to be an understanding look on his face. I'm sure he'd had many encounters with veterans just like the one he would have this fine morning with Joshua Daklugie.

"How can I help you?" he said as he opened the door wide, welcoming me in.

****

William Travis listened with fascination as I told him some, but not all…of my story.

The following day, on the advice of my attorney, I surrendered myself to the court and was promptly placed under arrest by the Travis County Sheriff's Department.

The prosecutor from the adjoining county where the alleged crime had occurred, one JD Sneed, initially felt I should be prosecuted to the full extent of the law. However, according to William Travis, I had not violated any law in the state of Texas. At the first meeting between myself, William Travis, and the prosecutor JD Sneed, I read the man. His eyes were dark and flitted about the room, never really making contact with mine. I sensed in my spirit JD Sneed was a liar and a thief. I shared my insights with William Travis who agreed with my thoughts. He was able to obtain a change of venue.

In Texas, there was a law that required a citizen to assist when, and if, a crime being committed might result in great bodily harm to a victim. I felt good about my chances of simply telling my story before the court, as did William Travis. I was certain the truth would set me free. The man I killed had held a loaded gun to the woman's head.

****

I was released from jail the following day having posted the $100,000 bail (ten percent allowed) from the sale of a few ounces of gold that my pack frame held. I mailed the package with the assistance of William Travis to Abram Levi. He in turn wired the money to William Travis's account.

The trial process was surprisingly quick. A few weeks later, Joseph Red Cloud traveled to Texas to testify on my behalf. The testimony he gave of my highly decorated past, fighting for our nation in a far-away place, seemed to fall on deaf ears. The judge was not impressed.

William Travis had attempted repeatedly to be assigned a different judge once he discovered this judge's anti-war activism and anti-war protest history. I could read the judge also. I knew he was not fully a man somehow. That concept was foreign to me. The man displayed feminine mannerisms I had only seen displayed in women. I did not understand. The judge's personal lifestyle mattered not to me. I supposed that was his business. His decision-making process is what I would soon have a serious issue with. I was astounded at my predicament. In a world where I had come to the defense of a defenseless woman, I was considered a criminal. For a completely different reason than his being a character witness, I was relieved Joseph Red Cloud had traveled to Texas.

I needed him to safely and securely locate and remove my weapons from the hidden location along a riverbank west of Austin. Using the map I drew, he was able to find my hidden cache. He would later relocate the items to Lawton where he would replace the barrel of my rifle and destroy the original.

I was much more concerned with the possible ballistic testing of my sniper rifle if it were ever to be discovered. There were other evil men that were of much more concern to me than the effeminate judge I stood trial before.

Three weeks later before one of the most liberal judges in the state of Texas, I was convicted of manslaughter and sentenced to five years in the Texas State Penitentiary. The appeals would start immediately, but it could be several years before I might possibly be released. The time frame did not work well for being in or living near the cavern when according to Old Grandmother, my remaining family would arrive. My heart felt sick. The darkness within began to grow again.

Being a Warrior, and a man who had spent his entire life correcting injustices, I took note of the judge's full name. With the assistance of Joseph, I was able to discover his physical address. Joseph was even able to determine his work schedule, and the places he frequented socially. I was certain I would meet with this person in the future to correct a grievous injustice meted out by his flawed decision making.

****

I spent four years in the Texas State Penitentiary. I counted the days, and each day the cloud that injustice brought to my life grew. I spent much time in prayer. I also quickly discovered the necessity of joining a new tribe of men. I was a member of two Native American Tribal Nations, the Apache and the Comanche, and I held the title of Warrior in both tribes. I was also now officially a Warrior within a tribe of men who rode motorcycles, participated in organized crime, and fought their battles in the "old way." I was an expert with the long knife. My skills earned much respect within this new tribe.

Not a soul dared lay a hand upon "The Man," Tenahpu, during the days I spent in the white man's prison. As Tosahwi would say, "I was the fiercest of all Warriors." But that is a tale for another time.

After four years, I was released on parole. William Travis awaited my arrival outside the gates of the huge prison in my old Ford pickup. He had fought tirelessly on my appeal process yet was unsuccessful.

"It is good to see you, Dak. You look well," he said.

"Hello, Will, you look great also. I am well." I peered directly into his eyes. "Will, it was not your fault we drew the unjust judge." He nodded with an understanding look.

"Let's get out of here. You have a long trip ahead of you."

He had no idea the list of places I needed to visit and people I needed to see. He had no idea how desperate I was to discover the news of my family. Had I been released in time?

****

One week later the death of an Austin judge and his lover made all the local newspapers. William Travis sat at his desk, reading the gruesome account. He knew Dak was in Oklahoma the night of the murder. He had talked to him personally from his home on the reservation, on a land line. Yes, he was certain the voice was that of Dak. The sheriff's investigators who questioned both William and Joshua Daklugie immediately removed Joshua Daklugie from their suspect list. The Elder from the reservation also corroborated Daklugie's whereabouts at the time of the murder. His alibi was completely intact.

Still, William Travis took pause at the timing of the murder. The case would go cold after a few months. It would never be solved.

Chapter 72

Lawton, Oklahoma

I had only been in town for one day. I had been released from prison just yesterday and driven through the night to reach Lawton. Old Grandmother's lodge was empty. It was obvious no one had lived there for an extended time.

The following morning after visiting the Tribal Police, I discovered Old Grandmother along with Joseph and his woman, Chepi (Fairy), and his family, and many others from the tribe had traveled to Texas for the trial of Tabbananica. Locked away in a prison cell, I had missed the arrival of my family. If only. Perhaps I could have protected…or prevented the trouble for Tabba. I would not fail to protect in the future. I sat in the emptiness of my trailer on the Rez in Lawton, Oklahoma. I watched in wonder at the coverage on the little television set. I was dumbfounded; William Travis was representing Tabba.

I began to load my truck for the trip back to Texas. How could a man say such cruel and untrue things about my people, my family? I would visit the Tribal Store first thing tomorrow morning. The details of my hunting trip would be shared with the other hunting guides, the Warriors, and the Elder. My alibi would be complete and irrefutable. I had spent enough time in the white man's prison. I visited the tribal library the following morning prior to my meeting at the Tribal Store. I learned a great deal online about the man, the jury foreman, who had spoken ill and evil of my family. Jim Bob Skaggs of Little Grove, Texas.

The trip to Texas was uneventful. I parked on a side street away from the town square, knowing there would be cameras in various places along the storefronts and courthouse. Before exiting my truck, I checked the map again.

Skaggs' funeral home was just one hundred yards ahead. I entered the town square on foot and casually made several trips around the courthouse park. Most businesses were closed, but there were several groups of Native American families coming and going from the few breakfast places along the square that were open at this early hour. I was not out of place.

I walked back to the old Ford, passing the funeral home and the obvious processing room to the rear of the main building. There was an old hearse backed up to the garage door of the processing building. I could hear the muted sound of equipment running. Someone was working in the building.

I returned to my truck, scanning the homes along the side street for cameras. I saw none.

I checked my equipment. The arrows were modern fiberglass with razor sharp broadhead tips, sharper than anything I could ever fashion from stone. I shouldered my grandfather's bow and again casually walked the one hundred yards toward the funeral home.

I heard the door swing open. I recognized Jim Bob Skags who turned and locked the door securely behind him. Without looking my direction, he strode toward the town square like a man without a worry in this world.

I breathed deeply and exhaled slowly, then drew my bow. For an instant I held my breath as the words of my grandfather spoke to me again…as they had many times, across many battlefields, across the chasms of time. "See the arrow hit its mark, Dak. In your mind see only the kill zone. Place the arrow perfectly, in your mind first…then allow your body to obey what your mind has already seen."

"You there," I called out. The man turned toward the sound of my voice…I released the arrow. Jim Bob Skaggs fell to the sidewalk. I turned and walked the one hundred yards to my truck.

As I drove away, I began to sing the song of victory over one's enemy. The voice of evil had been silenced. Perhaps others would take note.

****

I needed to return to the Reservation for my scheduled meeting with the Warriors and the Elder. The drive across what was formerly the Llano Estacada was filled with rejoicing and song. I had found my surviving family. I listened to the news coverage on the AM radio in the old Ford. Tabbananica, my son-in-law, had been released. A mistrial had been declared. I heard a familiar voice emanating from the little speaker on the dash of the old Ford.

William Travis spoke to the interviewer. "This case should have never been brought to trial. Tampering with evidence when a man's life is in the balance, as JD Sneed has done, is frankly inexcusable. We clearly had the wrong man on trial in that courtroom."

"And do you expect new charges to be filed? Or possibly a new trial?" the interviewer asked.

"No, I do not," William Travis answered quickly. "Self-defense is allowed in this country, even if a person is defending themselves against law enforcement."

****

The pungent smell of wood smoke and coffee brewing filled the room. The sound of the wind whistled through the cracked windowpanes of the Tribal Store.

"*Your hunt was a success, Tenahpu?*" my Elder questioned.

"*Yes, Grandfather,*" I said.

Steam rose in little clouds of vapor from the coffee cups around the table.

"*It is a good thing when the voice of evil is silenced,*" the Elder said. The other Warriors seated around the table all nodded in agreement.

Chapter 73

One week later

I stopped at the end of the dirt road that led to Old Grandmother's home. The view across the open prairie from this vantage would forever transport me to a different place and time. A place where we had lived as a free and natural people. Joseph exited the little lodge-shaped home and greeted me with the raised hand and open palm.

"Are you certain you will not join me, my friend?" I asked. But I knew the answer to the question.

His woman exited the door, her belly showing the growth within her womb. Chepi (Fairy) was one of the most attractive women I had ever met. Her skin was perfect, with a dark red hue unusual even for our people. Her hair was jet black, her cheek bones were high, and her figure was graceful. She carried herself as a proud Native woman, confident, assertive, and stunningly beautiful. She reminded me very much of Nadua, wife of One Horse.

"Do not tempt my man with some tale of adventure, Tenahpu. He has enough adventure within his own lodge and upon his own sleeping mat." She smiled at Joseph with a wink of her deep blue eyes.

"I am here only to say goodbye to my friend. He would be a fool to ever leave this place," I said, gazing across the plain. *"Or his woman,"* I added with a smile.

****

The little caverns above and only one mile to the north of the hunting lodge on David Ross's ranch proved to be a perfect place to remain concealed yet close to my family. I kept a constant vigil over my little tribe as there were many threats to their existence.

It was during this time that for the first time in my life I began to write. The long days I spent in the cavern provided the hours needed for the journaling that I continue to this day. On my nighttime forays I would occasionally restock my notebooks and pens when I had made the long trek to Little Grove and back. I suppose to date, I have written one thousand tales concerning the story of my people. I knew in my spirit…one day I would become a teller of tales.

I patrolled constantly, keeping watch in the night. Spending most daylight hours hidden in the cavern; however, I had several vantage points where I could observe most of my family during the day with little movement and no chance of detection.

It was also during this time that I would have another first. On my departure from the Rez in Oklahoma, I stopped and purchased a no contract cell phone. The technology was important and vital to the reconnaissance it provided. Joseph Red Cloud kept abreast of all the latest news and often forwarded news articles, pictures, and video files concerning the activities of both the State of Texas, and any progress or developments concerning my little tribe. I disposed of and replaced the phone regularly.

This was how I learned of the trip north to Lawton that Sana and Tabba, along with Tosahwi and Old Grandmother, planned to make. I arrived in Lawton the day before my family would arrive. The Warriors would assist in the process. I was grateful for Joseph and his position in Tribal law enforcement. He knew of the scheduled procedure weeks in advance.

We waited among the sparse trees that lined the edge of the old burial ground. The storms along the western skyline rumbled with thunder that shook the earth. Distant lightning danced across the storms in a display of brilliant blinding flashes. A curtain of heavy rain completely blacked out the western sky for an hour or more. We sat in silence, pondering the task before us as the storms moved away to the north. The sun dipped beneath the veil of clouds in the west, streaming sunbeams across the open sky as the van pulled to a stop in the center of the burial ground.

My beautiful daughter exited and wandered among the little stone markers. I heard her sobs, as she recognized the names of friends and family that had passed on to the great land. I drew my hat low over my brow. The bandana and dark sunglasses concealed my identity to most. Tosahwi, however, clearly recognized me in the indiscernible nod he gave in my direction as we began to dig.

I am certain that for a father there is nothing more painful than watching a child suffer. Perhaps even more so when the child is a daughter as it is our duty as fathers to protect them. Whether that suffering is physical, emotional, mental, or spiritual, it matters not. My tears rolled down my face under the bandana. I wanted to comfort, console, or simply hold my daughter, Topusana. I felt helpless. I was much relieved when Tabba took her hand and spoke to her gently. He whispered softly in her ear. I was never prouder of him than in that moment.

The two turned and moved toward us. The Warriors had struck the wooden casket.

I gently swept away the loose dirt and dust, then stepped aside with my fellow Warriors as Tosahwi and Old Grandmother began their prayers.

We Warriors moved away from the group and sat in the shade of the trees along the edge of the burial ground. In the wind I could hear the voices of my people singing. I joined in silently as the DNA sampling procedure was performed.

My friends and family made their way to the van and loaded up for the drive back to Lawton. As the group drove away, I held my hand high along with the Warriors, our palms open to our friends and loved ones.

We worked in silence as we covered our Grandfather Buffalo Hump with the dust of the earth for the last time. As we completed our task, we began the songs of old. The voices of our people accompanied us; their songs whispered within the wind that floated across the prairie.

****

The next morning, I greeted Tosahwi in the Tribal Store in Lawton. It had been a long ten years for me since I had last seen him. The time from my perspective had been difficult. A year in isolation, waiting in the cavern. Four years in a faraway place across the world, four years within the walls of a prison, another year in the wilderness of the Big Bend. Those years had aged me and changed me in many ways. Seeing my friend brought into focus my purpose, my reason for departing ahead of the others. My life as a Warrior once in the presence of my friend at long last filled me with resolve. Tosahwi looked younger than he had the last time I had seen him. From his perspective, we had been with one another...just a few days ago.

"It is good to be with you again, Tenahpu," Tosahwi said. He embraced me and held me a moment. "I know the years in this new time have been difficult for

251

you. But now you are free from the white man's prison. Free to be a Warrior. Free to be a protector and defender of The People."

"*This thing you say is true, Tosahwi. Freedom is a good thing,*" I replied. The others listened quietly, nodding in agreement at the truth of what was said.

The Elder spoke. "*There are others who will soon rise up against our people, Tenahpu. I fear your actions have not yet convinced many of the white leaders. I have seen this clearly. Your protection will be needed for a time. We must be vigilant. You must be fierce. It is a thing the whites will soon take note of and understand. It is exactly how the whites behaved toward our people when they were building their nation.*"

I turned and addressed the other men and Warriors present.

"*These few survivors are all that is left of my family. I will defend them until the day I breathe my last. It is why I have come to this time. Tosahwi's plan is good. He alone had the knowledge to send me into the* Dream Time *ahead of the others. His wisdom will indeed be seen forever as an incredibly good thing. I have been told of my grandsons. They will enter the world soon. Perhaps one day I will meet them.*"

"*It is best for now that you remain hidden,*" Tosahwi replied. "*The whites have no idea that the survivors have a protector. You, Tenahpu, were the fiercest of all Warriors. You must use your skills to defend the defenseless.*"

"*I understand,*" I said. "*If I must remain hidden for all my days, it is a thing I can do. I learned much in the training I received in the white man's army. Ranger school focused much on tactics. It is the best strategic factor to possess against an enemy, the element of surprise. The whites have no idea that I even exist. It will remain this way. I will remain hidden. It is also a thing that brings me deep satisfaction as a Comanche Warrior. Protecting our family, my brothers, is the purpose of my very existence.*"

The brothers and Warriors again nodded in agreement. The men sat in silence for a few minutes. The wind whistled through the thin cracked panes of the windows, and the smoke occasionally rose from the stove. A knowing, an awareness, a wisdom, and a purpose permeated the silence. I drank slowly from the steaming coffee cup, enjoying the quiet reflection. The soft, scarcely discernable, yet distinct sound of drumbeats could be heard in the wind.

Chapter 74

The sun was beginning to lighten the eastern sky. I was always amazed at the birth of a new day, how the light reflected from the sky slowly begins to reveal trees, boulders, the little rises and falls in the land. It takes several minutes for peering eyes to distinguish land from water. As slow and unhurried as the process is, suddenly a man can see an animal moving or details of the fallen leaves and the rocks along his path. The birds begin to sing in the semi light of pre-dawn. The stars fade slowly, their lights are there at a glance and then gone in the twinkling of an eye. As the sun breaks upon the horizon, the human eye can look directly at it for several minutes until its beams arrive from their journey across the heavens. It was a fine morning as I moved toward my hidden overlook and then sat watch for another two hours. I was just about to enter the cavern for the day when I heard them coming. Then I spotted Topusana, Grace, Nita, and Abby touring the construction site.

At least a dozen men in uniform moved noisily through the brush below the hunting lodge.

I quickly unshouldered my sniper rifle. I needed a better position. I moved quickly, silently toward the rear of the group of men. Why were they here? I paused on a small rise of land. A perfect firing position.

Topusana let out her war cry. I had seen a similar scene in my dream within Old Grandmother's lodge. How could this be happening again? Nita was wrestled to the ground and handcuffed. My daughter was the first to fall, as she was knocked violently to the ground. I pulled the trigger a moment to late as the butt of the rifle opened a gaping wound in her forehead. The man fell dead into the brush. I changed barrels.

Abby was next. She too was wrestled to the ground and handcuffed. My blood came to a boil in emotion I had never felt as I observed the soldier kick her in the side. She fell from her knees writhing in pain. I had no clear shot. I moved swiftly to the next small rise of land. Grace attempted to assist her mother, Abby. She too was handcuffed. The men began testing the doors of the hunting lodge. That is when I spotted Neeko and Tosa, their bows at the ready. I moved closer as I heard the sound of a helicopter approaching. I kept my eyes trained on the man who had injured Topusana and Abby.

For a moment nothing happened. Time seemed to stand still while the chopper landed and David Ross exited. The leader of the soldiers spoke to his men, directing them to hold their ground. David Ross, in an act of incredible bravery, ignored the leader's command and walked directly toward him. His soldier held a gun to David Ross's head. The arrow pierced the soldier's body as he fell dead at the feet of his leader. This was the soldier who had attacked Topusana and Abby. I breathed deeply.

At the command of David Ross, the soldiers lowered their weapons. He warned them that any who did not comply would die now. The men dropped their weapons to the ground. David Ross stepped forward and struck the apparent leader in the face with a mighty blow. The man fell, unconscious. I saw the nearest soldier reach for his weapon. I fired. The soldier fell to the ground, dead before reaching it. I quickly changed barrels again.

Tabba arrived on his mount. Racing to Topusana, he lifted her from the ground and carried her to the helicopter. David Ross moved to Abby, and then he, too, carried his wife to the chopper and loaded her in the rear seat. The pilot started the chopper. As Tabba attempted to lift Sana gently into the rear of the helicopter, I heard the report of a gunshot. Blood sprayed across the side of the chopper. The blood of my only daughter. I quickly spotted the soldier with the pistol. My shot penetrated his body armor and killed him instantly. The death of the man, who had just severely wounded my daughter, was much too easy.

I heard sirens as the chopper lifted into the heavens. The sheriff's deputies arrived. The remaining soldiers were ordered to the ground. I observed Tosa and Neeko make a stealthy departure to the west. I moved north toward my hidden cavern.

I peered into the sky as the helicopter departed the scene. I saw the spirit of my beautiful daughter, Topusana, Prairie Flower, floating into the heavens, moving away from the helicopter. My heart broke at the sight.

I had failed.

****

I watched the video clip Joseph had sent me on the cell phone in the darkness of my little cavern. I journaled one page in my notebook that night. Badge numbers, name tags, facial details. I played the video again and again. CL Reuter Sr., his name tag said, was shown spitting toward the women handcuffed on the ground. The darkness whispered within. I would, with all that was in me, make certain that none of these cowards would have many days left on this earth.

Chapter 75

I followed CL Reuter for the third straight morning. His routine was the same each day. He pulled onto the side road, exited his game department truck, and unlocked the gate, swinging it wide open. He then drove through the gate, carelessly leaving it open behind him. A few moments later, I followed on foot, hidden in the underbrush.

It was unbelievable to me how the man hunted. I considered his activity more of a shooting; it was not a hunt whatsoever. He exited his truck and climbed the little ladder to his heated deer blind. Once inside, CL Reuter simply waited for the deer to walk by the edge of a nearby field that was filled with deer feeders in every corner. This morning would be different. Before reaching the ladder, he stepped into the noose, tripping the wire. The tree released, rapidly unbending and rising into the sky. The noose tightened around his lower leg and dragged him a few feet before lifting him off the ground upside down. He screamed and struggled, but there was no one within earshot.

I moved from my hidden location in the brush. "You are the one who attacks women?" I questioned. I watched the fear grow on his face as he panicked, grasping at the noose unsuccessfully. I picked up his hunting rifle from the dust below him, observing its poor condition and high-caliber cartridges. I chambered a round as I cut the noose that held the man. He scrambled to his feet.

"Would you like to run? Like the deer you slaughter? Like the women you attack?"

He lowered his head and begged for his life.

"Like most men who bully, you truly are a coward, even in death," I said. "You know it is dangerous to exit your truck with your weapon loaded. Most would not chamber a round before exiting the vehicle. Accidents can happen if one is careless with a loaded weapon."

I pointed the rifle at the coward and ordered him back into his truck.

A few moments later the report of a rifle echoed across the low hills.

****

The autopsy indicated the rifle had evidently fallen from his hands as CL Reuter exited his vehicle. Ballistics revealed the bullet traveled from a low angle outside the truck and upwards. The death was ruled as accidental. There was no indication whatsoever of foul play.

Two Days Later

I sat by the fire in my snug little cavern in the small canyon one mile north of the hunting lodge. Freshly processed deer meat roasted over the fire on a spit. The fragrance filled the cavern as the smoke gently rose into the openings above me…along with my praise. I had been planning, plotting my strategy. This had been my profession in a war half a world away. The task would be made much easier in my homeland. I knew the country well.

This night I had relented from the list of names to be dealt with. This night I celebrated. I worshiped.

The news had come to me from Joseph, by way of Old Grandmother. Abby had survived and was recovering. My heart rejoiced at the news.

Most importantly, by the grace of our Creator, Sana's spirit had returned from the beautiful land.

My grandsons rested safe within her womb. My daughter, Topusana, was alive!

I worked tirelessly for hours this night. The paintings were beginning to tell their story.

Chapter 76

William Travis sat at his desk as the shadows outside his window grew long across the quaint courthouse square of Little Grove, Texas. He read again the news article concerning the death of yet another Game Warden. This account of CL Reuter Sr. losing his life in a hunting accident was plausible. He looked into the eyes of his friend Commander Bryce Houston, a retired Naval Intelligence officer, as he, too, read through the narrative.

Commander Houston placed the newspaper on the edge of William's desk and breathed deeply. "So how can I help you, Will?"

"I have been retained for the sole purpose of finding the shooter."

"Are you certain you want to do that?" Bryce asked.

Will thought for a moment. "No, I'm not. The actions of the defender of the tribe seem somewhat justifiable to me. I have been assured on completion of the task, whoever this person might be, they will not face prosecution. At least not by my clients."

"But you're concerned that others might also discover the identity and not be so grateful for his actions?" Commander Houston asked.

"Yes," William Travis replied.

"You could simply not be successful in your manhunt."

"Bryce, I honestly don't think it's much of a mystery to me who he is. I have suspected for some time now who the shooter is." Commander Houston looked surprised at the comment. "Where he is, is pretty much the only question in my mind," William said.

William Travis slid the folder across the desk to Commander Houston. "He is a former client of mine. A former Ranger who served as a sniper, three tours in Iraq. He also spent four years in the Texas state prison, for a crime he should not have been charged with."

"And that crime was?" Commander Houston asked.

"Coming to the defense of a woman held at gunpoint. He killed the perp with a single blow from what he called a war club." Commander Houston listened intently. "The crime was a setup. The man was actually the woman's boyfriend. Their plan was to scam the convenience store of the robbery, then feign innocence."

"Until your defender of the defenseless arrived?"

"Yes."

"His name?" Commander Houston asked.

"Joshua Daklugie."

"It is a small world my friend. At least within Military Intelligence," Commander Houston said, recognizing the name.

"You know of him?" William questioned.

"Yes, he was one of the best," Commander Houston said with a faraway look in his eyes. "We tried to keep him. He had other interests."

"I believe he is part of Sana's tribe," William said.

"You mean a traveler...a Dream Timer?"

"Yes."

"That would explain much to me concerning his abilities. And you're certain you want to proceed?" Commander Houston asked again.

"I'm just not sure. I asked you here for advice on both whether to proceed and help in doing so, if we decide to move forward."

"To assist in your decision making I would need to know who your client is and their reasoning."

William paused and moved to the decanters along the side wall of his office. He dropped ice into two glasses and poured a generous splash of his favorite blended whisky into both, offering a glass to his longtime friend. The men drank in silence for a moment.

"Abigail Ross," William replied. "She thinks or feels like he is still around. Or possibly living nearby. She also thinks she has met him in the past."

"You know, I'm open to much that just a few years ago my mind would have thought impossible," Commander Houston said. "Please continue."

"She described to me a man she offered a ride to several years ago, before Sana was discovered. He was obviously Native American. According to Abby he declined and then promptly disappeared."

"I'm not surprised at his ability to do that," Commander Houston said.

"She remembers very specifically the event. She says he actually called her by name." William referred to his notes and continued. "'I think I will just enjoy the walk this morning, Abby,' was his reply to her offer for a ride. He was also carrying a bow across his shoulders."

Commander Houston paused, thinking through the possibilities. "Now, I'm also very curious...I just don't see what anyone will gain. Have you spoken with Sana about this?"

"No, just Abby. She has not mentioned any of this to Sana."

"This is a big picture decision. Will, I think if the defender of the tribe ever wants to become known he will simply reveal himself, and probably to Sana or someone from the tribe.

"Further, attempting to discover his whereabouts might prove to be, let's say, harmful to my health. This is not the kind of man you want to mess with."

"I hadn't really thought of this being dangerous, but I believe you are correct," William said. The men enjoyed the quiet of the early evening and sat in silent contemplation for a few moments sipping from their glasses. William took the file with Joshua Daklugie's name across the front of it and removed its contents. He then fed each paper one by one into his shredder.

"And how will you deal with Abby?" Commander Houston asked.

William sighed deeply. "Abby is a strong, independent woman. I'm not sure, perhaps Nita might reason with her about the danger."

Two Months Later

Concealed well within the scrub oak where I often kept watch over my family, I observed through the massive front window of the Ross home. I had completed my nightly rounds. All were safe and secure. The scene before me caused my heart to swell within my chest. My grandsons slept soundly, one held by my daughter, Sana. The other held tightly by Abby.

I listened as the two spoke of the upcoming trip that William Travis and David Ross would take to California. I sensed Sana was concerned. I would need to be extra vigilant, knowing the men would be away for a few days.

Chapter 77

I was there the night the Spirit came to Old Grandmother. I had heard her singing and her prayer's coming from the lodge along the banks of the San Saba. I stood outside the lodge on the grounds of our old Home Camp. I understood once I heard the songs and the names that were lifted into the heavens.

David Ross had perished. My heart felt heavy. My soul troubled. I knew exactly what Abby would experience over the next days, and months, and years.

What would this mean for the survivors, for my little tribe, and family?

Davis Ross was a hero to all of us. A man of integrity and great influence in the modern world we were attempting to survive in. I moved away from the river and up the little canyon behind the Ross home.

****

Five days later I observed the funeral from the brush on the opposite side of the San Saba. Old Grandmother began the songs. Abby stood regally; I heard the songs as Abby sang in the Comanche tongue. She sang every phrase and melody in perfect time. Those surrounding her, Sana, Grace, Nita, and William Travis seemed to gaze at her in wonder.

Abby sang with all her heart and soul and mind, the songs of our people.

Abby Ross held her head high, her eyes closed tightly and released her burdens in worship to our Creator.

From my vantage across the river, I saw the Spirit rest upon her. The veil between the physical world we inhabit and the spiritual world that surrounds us was thin in this sacred place along the San Saba River. The place of my Home

Camp, where many of my friends and family had perished, the place where I had seen the spirit of my granddaughter rise from the burning camp, the place where the body of David Ross was laid and would return to the dust of the earth...this place was sacred and holy.

As the pastor ended the service with a final prayer, Abby Ross peered across the river, directly at my hidden location. She knew I was there. I felt, more than saw, her eyes meet mine through the mist of dry tears.

I understood in my own spirit...she was comforted by my presence.

Chapter 78

My nightly routine had continued for years now. I walked the perimeter of the little development that now included the hunting lodge, the new school, and the art studios that Grace Ross had built.

The night air was warm and comfortable. The wind was light and brought the fresh moisture laden air that flowed from the southeast this time of year. The low overcast blocked completely the light of the half-moon. I walked the few miles to the enormous security gate Davis Ross had installed. The entrance to our Homelands was now well lit and monitored by video cameras and alarms twenty-four hours a day.

Davis Ross was one of the greatest men I had ever known in my life. His passing was tragic. My heart ached for many months at the news. It was not that we were close—we had never met. I knew him due to my nights spent outside his window, in the months I had spent in isolation. His was the voice of a kindred spirit. My heart ached not so much for Davis Ross, but for Abby. I knew the loneliness she was experiencing. I too, had lost my life love.

After checking the perimeters and entrance gate, I made my way as I did each night to the Ross home below the cavern. All was quiet. After checking the home and barn and making certain the front gate was locked and secure, I moved to my place in the brush outside the huge front window. I settled in my comfortable spot concealed by the oak brush. The wind in the trees whispered; the night doves called to one another; all was well.

I listened as Abby spoke to Sana over the phone for a few minutes and then ended the call with a sincere gentle, "Good night, love."

Abby sat in her comfortable reading nook surrounded by the pleasures of her home. A warm cup of tea steamed on the little end table. A soft blanket covered her lower legs. Her school materials were neatly placed on the opposite end of the couch, within easy reach. Two novels sat near her teacup; elegant book markers placed within each book dangled gracefully along their edges, indicating her progress in the reading. I wondered what the books were about. As she ended her call with Sana, I thought her voice was always so positive and cheerful.

I was just keeping watch. I had told myself this over and over…for years now. She needed a protector. I lowered my eyes and wondered if the feelings in my heart were somehow wrong. I was only providing protection. Any whoever dared bring harm to those I loved would pay a severe…I caught myself as the word echoed in my mind.

I had watched over those I loved in secret silence for almost five years now. My daughter, my grandsons, my extended family, and Abby Ross. I realized this night Abby was included in the list of those I loved.

I lifted my eyes again, peering into the picturesque room. Abby was no longer seated on her sofa. She had moved near the window and now stood directly in front of me just a few feet away.

Abby was still an attractive woman. Her soft golden hair and graceful figure shone in the dim light of the room. I could sense the motion of her body and hear her as she breathed in and exhaled a soft sigh. I was sure she could not see me in my hidden place within the scrub oak. My heart pounded within my chest, and I felt a stirring I had not experienced in years.

"Would you like to come in and join me?" she said softly through the open window.

My heart leapt within my chest. I could not take my next breath…she knew I was here? How could that be? I did not reply. I wanted to say something. I wanted to explain. I was embarrassed. I was not some weird voyeur…I froze, my mind racing, my heart aching to say yes.

Yes, I want to come inside. Yes, I want to sit and talk. Yes, I want to hold you and comfort you. I sat in silence, unable to speak, adrenaline coursing through my veins.

The wind shifted. I detected the faint fragrance of her perfume. The evening doves called again in the stillness. I could again hear her breathing as she wrapped her arms around herself.

"Thank you for watching over me. Thank you for protecting me," she said in the sweetest, kindest, most vulnerable, gentle, and lovely voice I had ever heard.

A moment passed; she waited for my reply. Abby turned from the window, took a step, and then froze at my words.

"You're welcome, Abby. Sleep well."

Abby crossed the room, moving toward the massive front door. I stood and moved closer to the window, observing. She opened the front door wide and stood waiting. I moved around to the front of the home, my heart pounding within my chest. I climbed the front steps of Abby's porch. I could smell the fragrance of the flowers blooming in the flower boxes. My eyes took in the delicate touch of the feminine hand that had arranged the furnishings along the porch, my senses suddenly acutely aware as I moved to her open door. I paused, gazing into her soft blue eyes as she took my hand, moved it to her face, and kissed it. Her tears fell softly across my hand. That night, the darkness that had clouded my life was overcome and simply vanished.

I embraced her, emotion overcoming both of our souls as the night doves called again, cooing for the third time. I knew this meant the pair had located one another.

Only those in tune with Mother Earth know and understand that once night doves find their mate, they spend the remainder of their lives together.

Chapter 79

Sana had just swaddled baby Abigail. Closing her eyes, the vision was pure and clear, just as the water that flowed along the San Saba in winter. The Man she saw was seated on a buffalo robe. The firelight reflected off the walls of the cavern. The dim light illuminated the familiar features of his face. His muscled arms rippled as he reached for the rabbit that sizzled on a spit over the fire. The Man gave thanks for the bounty the earth had provided. He gently removed the rabbit from the spit. Rending a hind quarter from the animal, he leaned against the wall of the cavern, savoring the delicious meal. He ate slowly, methodically. It was his way. He was in no hurry. Sana could see the pure meat of the fresh roasted rabbit seemed to strengthen more than just blood, muscle, tendon, and bone. This Man possessed abilities and an inner strength beyond compare. The Man began to sharpen his arrowheads as he ate.

Sana was comforted at what she saw. The knowledge revealed to her through the vision brought much comfort. In an instant, she had seen the answers to many mysteries. The pieces fitted together neatly. The reason those who had attempted to bring harm to her tribe…had met with tragedy. She now knew they had a protector Warrior.

That very morning after the children were settled into their daily routines at the school, Sana worked her way silently toward the north across the open prairie. She knew from her vision the cavern was just north of the school. Her skills of moving silently were still complete and intact. She left no trace of a footprint or her presence. Reaching the small canyon, she moved east now along its broken course through the sparse brush. Sana spied the first little entrance but quickly determined this entrance had not been used in a very long time. Continuing down the steepening grade, the next small entrance was also unused; however, there was a distinct smell of wood smoke emanating from the little opening.

Sana paused, her heart racing. She knew the next opening would most likely be the one he was using. She took her time, traveling carefully, silently. Spotting the small opening, Sana settled within the cover of the oak brush to observe. Her position was hidden from anyone who might travel the easiest route to the cavern from the south. She waited for an hour with no sound or movement. The birds sang in the trees as they went about their morning busyness. The wind was light; the smell of spring flowers drifted through the air.

She decided he was either already in the cavern or perhaps out on a morning hunt. Sana rose from her hidden position and walked silently to the entrance, taking caution to cover over her trail. She entered the cavern and pushed the button on her small LED flashlight. The cool air of the cavern greeted her senses. The pungent smell of wood smoke brought her mind to a different place and time. She recalled the years spent in preparation for their trip into the *Dream Time*, the months she had spent living in the cavern above the Ross home. The setting reminded her of the days she had spent awaiting Tabba's awakening. She moved one hundred yards ahead. The soft light of the flashlight revealed the still-smoldering fire pit, the sleeping area, the stored food adjacent to the small spring of water. It was evident from what she observed he had lived here for many years. Her heart ached at the time she had missed with him. Why would he stay hidden for so long she wondered?

Sana added wood to the smoldering fire. Its flame caught quickly, lighting the entire room. The wall to her right was a huge slab of smooth granite. The face of the rock was at least twenty feet high and perhaps its length was near fifty feet. The rock face was covered in the most beautiful drawings she had ever seen. The artwork was detailed and stunning. She clearly recognized a magnificent mural of their former Home Camp along the San Saba. In another area of the wall was a depiction of the high mountains of New Mexico. She knew that scene from her time spent there as a child. In another area, there was a building in the foreground of the wall art and in the background the beginnings of a trail leading into the high mountains. There were two people standing at the beginning of the trail holding one another's hands. Their faces were not clear, but she knew in her heart who the two were. Her father and her mother.

Alongside this painting was a funeral fire burning against the backdrop of the heavens. The deep canyons on the outskirts of the Llano stood in the distance of the masterpiece. Sana recognized the setting where she had repeatedly made the run attempting to save the children. This was the place where her mother, Kwanita, had died. The tears burst forth in a flood of remembrance.

In yet another area of the rock there appeared to be a cross etched into a boulder above what was an expansive field of flowers. The only writing on the wall was above the scene of the delicate cross. The words written in Comanche brought an understanding to what Sana was seeing.

The Cross of One Horse.

Sana added more wood to the fire. Her tears rolled down her face. The wall was the story of The Man's life.

****

I stood outside the entrance to my little cavern. The signs were almost imperceptible, but they were there. The signs on the earth were a clear warning. I knelt, feeling the faint ridge in the dust. It was a footprint. It had been partially erased with a juniper bow, but someone had walked here this morning. It appeared whoever this might be possessed considerable skills. From what I read in the dust, it was obvious whoever had traveled here, had entered the cavern. I had been discovered. I removed my war club from my belt and entered the cavern silently.

I could immediately detect the light from the fire some one hundred yards ahead. Whoever had entered was not concealing their presence. I froze, considering how I might have been discovered. It was impossible. I left no sign. I had not been spotted; I would have been aware of the commotion that such an event would have caused. There were no enemies about. There were no activities from the state or even local officials as of late. I had received no news lately from Joseph.

Whoever had entered my home was exceptionally good at movement in the "old ways." I moved a few feet, listening intently. I heard the out of place sound. I pressed on, moving forward silently. I paused again. The sound was clearer now and distinct. I tucked my war club back into my belt as the sound of a woman sobbing reached my ears. I continued ahead until near the fire.

"*Sana,*" I called out into the semi darkness.

"*Yes, Father, I'm here.*" I heard through the apparent mist of tears. We embraced as her tears rolled across my shoulder. *"Thank you, Father, thank you for protecting us all these years."*

I had thought the previous night as I held Abby the darkness had completely departed my soul. Its scant remains floated away within the smoke of the cave fire and exited my life forever as I held my beautiful daughter, Topusana (Prairie Flower). We sat together, observing the section of the mural that contained the prairie filled with springtime flowers. It seemed I could still taste and smell the scent of the prairie in bloom before us. It was represented exactly as I remembered it in my mind, the place of my daughter's birth along the cap rock, within the prairie of flowers.

✳✳✳✳

The wedding took place alongside the San Saba River. Abby stood beside me, holding my hand. Her heart was filled with promise, as was mine. Tosahwi beamed with pride and joy as he spoke the words of life love over the two of us. The flowers danced in time with the rhythm of the earth and its seasons. The words of my grandfather came to me.

"The seasons of this life are in constant change, as are the seasons of all created things, there is, however, a time to love, and it is a season that never ends."

269

Epilogue

There is a place not far from where you live where the pavement ends. A place where there is no longer mile after mile of concrete or asphalt, where the noise of traffic no longer drowns out the songs of creation. A place where the bright lights and neon that disturb the heavenly illumination cannot conceal the grandeur of those that are called out by name each evening to display His Holiness. There is a place far from what some call progress where a man or a woman may taste and touch or drink deeply from the well of existence. A place where the created can smell the dew of morning, or the soft fire of evening, and know deep within that they are loved and cared for.

For some it is a great distance to where the pavement ends. For others who are fortunate as am I…it is but a step from the parking lot of my old high school off the pavement, and onto the ancient trail. The trail I walked along the high mountains with my grandfather when I was just a young boy. The ancient trail where I hunted the bears, caught the beautiful trout, and held the hand of my life love, Kwanita, as we descended along its way into another time.

Where the pavement ends is the place where the stories begin.

I am Daklugie, a Warrior of two nations.

I am Daklugie, Teller of One Thousand Tales.

I am Daklugie, Elder of my people. And this has been a small part of my story.

Excerpt from Book 3

These Thousand Days

Topusana

The year 2070

The first camp was designated after a walk of twenty-five miles. With excitement and eagerness, *The People* took to the task of setting up the teepees and starting the lodge fires. The smell of roasting buffalo meat wafted throughout the camp. Songs sung among the family groups drifted joyfully in the air. My heart was filled at the sights and scenes being lived out before me. My people had survived. Not only survived, but my people were thriving.

I took a deep breath and whispered a prayer for my mother Abby. Perhaps she and Daklugie would arrive soon. I walked along the makeshift path between the tepee lodges toward the council lodge. Smoke was already rising from the smoke hole. The elders were gathering near the council lodge, awaiting my arrival. I greeted many family members and friends as I moved along. *The People* were happy. That was all that mattered in this moment.

****

Early the next morning, the sun rested on the eastern horizon, the sky aglow in radiant tints of reds, oranges, and exploding pink hues. The camp was awakening. So many days we had lived in this way. This *Old Way*. The earth welcomed our presence and our activities. Today would be the first full hunting day. I wandered to the edge of the camp amidst the growing activities and preparations. I paused as I did each morning and again whispered a prayer for my mother Abby.

Tabba, along with several Warriors, departed the camp toward the north with a high wave of his lance. Even from this distance, I saw the excitement on his face. It would only be a few hours before they returned. I seated myself in the buffalo grass, closed my eyes, and soaked in the goodness of Mother Earth. Breathing in deeply, I began my worship. One hour later...I saw.

My mind could not grasp what I had seen. My body shook; my heart raced. I stood and ran toward the camp, calling out my war cry. Would we have enough time?

****

Within the sacred lodge, I shared the vision with the elders. Thousands of troops were moving toward us at this very moment. *"They will arrive from the west. That is all I have seen."*

"Send the scout Warriors now!" Tosahwi spoke. All nodded in agreement. Within minutes the scouts departed on horseback. They would travel to the west and report back before the sun set.

"William left with the first group of hunters at daylight. Send runners with the news we need him desperately." I had the ability to use the sat phone, but we knew any electronic communication would be intercepted. Again, the group was all in agreement we would communicate in the old way. A second detachment departed to the north within minutes of the order.

"And The People?" Tosahwi questioned.

"Have them prepare for war," I said. *"The Bands from the south should arrive by afternoon. However, we should send runners to the south also. They can warn them in advance."*

"What else might we do, Topusana?" the elders questioned.

"Send the women and children...all our young boys and young girls to the cavern." The order was met with a silence. My intention was clear. This had forever been our emergency plan. This order was to assure the survival of our people...in the event the worst happened. In the event we were decimated by the army from across the sea I had seen in my vision.

William, along with his father, Tabba, and the other Warriors raced their war ponies across the prairie. The men had seen the attack coming. The buffalo had warned them.

The stalk was progressing smoothly. They moved silently through the underbrush downwind from the herd. Tabba knew it was not possible the buffalo had detected them. Then the animals stampeded without warning. William rose from his hidden location as the buffalo fled. He spotted the massive formation of men moving through the sparse cover of brush. There were too many. He would need to deploy Wolf.

The first explosion was well behind the fleeing Warriors. William knew the next volley of explosives would be much closer. They separated on the hand signals from Tabbananica. Their ponies were the swiftest on Earth. But could they avoid the targeting system being deployed? William changed course again. The next explosion rang in his ears. He changed course again, his fellow Warriors doing the same. For now, the tactic worked. The emergency code on his sat phone sounded. There were only two people who had the ability to communicate with him during the annual hunt. His mother, Topusana, and his grandfather.

William drove his horse into a low arroyo. He momentarily came to a stop and looked at the display in disbelief. *"Grandfather? Is that really you?"* The explosion buffeted the air with a percussion that knocked William from his mount. The sat phone flew out of his hand. His war pony would not rise from the sandy bottom of the arroyo. The horse lay pawing the ground in a growing pool of blood…then moved no more.

William retrieved the phone and ran. With his feet digging deeply into the sand, he strained to gain traction. He saw the little depression within the bank of the arroyo. He paused, erasing his tracks as he moved; he quickly climbed into the little cave along the side of the arroyo and hid himself in the darkness. Within minutes, he could hear the soldiers advancing toward him, speaking a strange language.

Mandarin? He thought to himself. He knew he was correct in his interpretation of the language. The Chinese were advancing across his Homeland? If true, he wasn't that surprised. The United States military had focused primarily on philosophy and political correctness over the last two decades. They were in no fashion equipped militarily to win a war, much less an invasion. The possibilities raced through his mind. Had the United States been invaded and defeated in less than a day? Or was there something more sinister at play here?

The sat phone beeped softly as William quickly silenced the device. He sent the correct code successfully. Surely his mother and Grandfather received the code. *"Deploy Wolf! North and west. Red Army!"* William punched in the coordinates of his present position and noted to center the attack there. He prayed they would deploy the weapon despite him being within the field of fire.

He sent another message. *"Deploy Wolf! Immediately!"* He began to dig. Perhaps he could get deep enough to avoid the frequency band of Wolf?

About the Author

Steven G. Hightower was born on the plains of West Texas, where many of his stories take place.

Within these pages you will find many of Steven's experiences. He has sailed oceans and piloted across continents. He has sung his songs to listeners, fortunate to share his stories musically.

Life has been an incredible blessing to him. Through this amazing walk we call life, he has discovered his true gifting. He is a storyteller. He has always loved geography and history, embellishing the honest and true while giving it new life.

He is incredibly grateful to the people in his life who have simply been kind. He is trying his best to become like you.

Steven invites you to enjoy this gift...the gift of a good story, well told.

He lives in the mountains of central New Mexico, along with his wife, Ellie. They have two children and five grandchildren. They are the greatest blessings in his life.

Made in the USA
Monee, IL
31 January 2022